DOWNSIDE UP

JANE THORNLEY

Riverflow Press

I

Daniel Elson had never approved of his niece climbing the rooftops late at night, or any time, for that matter. But then, he would never have approved of his own death, either. Not that Jenna believed he'd been murdered exactly. Her mild-mannered uncle, who had lived with his sister for his entire life, hardly seemed the likely target of a premeditated attack. Still, unanswered questions demanded answers and who else but her could go out and get them?

Every muscle and tendon strained as she spidered up the side of the end unit of Marlytree Terrace. Only when she reached the topmost peak did she relax, throw a leg over, and ride the roof like a horse. Pulling the cell phone from her pocket, she pushed the speed dial button and her aunt answered on the first ring.

"Hello, Jenna. I've been waiting." Aunt Clair would be sitting where Jenna had left her—in the wheelchair by the second-floor window of the house below. Her aunt had lived by proxy for as long as Jenna could remember, and that window had always served as a porthole to a life half-lived.

"Aunt Clair," she whispered, "I'm on our roof now. Did you hear anything this time?"

"Once again, not a thing. Isn't this thrilling?"

"I'm a grown woman clambering over the rooftops at night. Somehow thrilling doesn't seem the word for it."

"Come now, dear, you find this just as exciting as you did when you were a child. Admit it."

Of course she did. Who was she fooling? Jenna gazed out across the silhouetted landscape. "Yes, it's still intoxicating, Auntie, but the fact is I'm no longer some disturbed little kid. There's a big difference between twelve years old and thirty-two."

"Nonsense. There you go again—measuring everything in years. Are you not strong, fit, and able? Now, stop telling me what you can't do and show me what you can. What do you see up there? Go on, feed me your eyeprints." The voice hummed with the excitement of their old game. That's how it had all begun: a young girl describing her "eyeprints" to her shut-in aunt. Back then, she had been a child working through grief and loss in dangerous ways, behaviors that her aunt had done everything to encourage.

And yet, it had been Aunt Clair and Uncle Dan who had helped her survive that childhood, and she owed them everything. Now wasn't the time for saying no. She had come this far, promised this one thing, and would see it through.

Why were the patterns forged in childhood so burned into the bone?

Jenna gazed past the rooftops to Kensington High Street four streets over, and began the game as she always had, taking her aunt where she could never physically go while enhancing the scene through the choicest words. "I'm queen of the castle gazing down on a tiny world. Miniature people are strolling the high street beyond the trees and they look, um—" she trawled for the exact words "—both far away and close at hand. And St. Paul's dome is glowing like some Holy Grail far in the distance."

"Yes, yes, I can see that dome in my mind's eye—the pleasure palace of the gods."

"Sir Christopher Wren probably had a more monotheistic bent, Auntie."

Her aunt giggled. "Indeed he did. He was your uncle's favorite architect, you know."

"I remember. He used to take me for walking tours to point out all the choicest bits." And even then she'd dreamed of exploring the world high above the streets. How would the world appear from Wren's dome, from Tower Bridge or Big Ben—cleaner, more noble, less crowded? Why did ground level strike her as such a grubby disappointment compared to the world above?

"And you would return home and give me every detail so vividly it was as if I'd been there."

Jenna smiled. So long ago. Tears thickened her throat.

"Do go on, dear. What else?"

"It looks as if I could brush a hand across the strolling bodies and toy with the black cabs scuttling for cover between the buildings—you know, like tip them over in my hand and spin their little wheels," Jenna whispered, her voice hoarse.

"Like those little toy cars your uncle gave you as a girl?"

Dear Uncle Dan. Jenna swallowed hard. "Exactly." He was the practical one while she and Aunt Clair had traded in the language of fantasy. Their own secret world.

"Oh, my, I can see it all so clearly. How rich."

Up here, darkness erased the rough edges of the world—the dirt, the ugliness, the sharp light of reality—and left behind the dusky magic of illusion. The child she had been had taken so much comfort on the roofs, weaving stories around that nocturnal landscape to create an alternate reality. No one could follow her, no one had even tried. For brief, treasured moments she had escaped the pain and found sanctuary.

"Do go on, dear. Feed me more. I am so very hungry for them."

"No, I'd better go." She could have videoed the whole scene, of course, but that would hardly be the same. Aunt Clair already had a steady diet of electronic images, but Jenna offered the intimacy of words.

"Yes, of course, so you must. We have a killer to catch, don't we?"

A killer to catch. Jenna shivered in the cool March breeze, the adrenaline percolating in her blood like jolts of espresso. She took a deep breath. "I'm going now. Don't panic if you don't hear from me right away."

"I'll try not to, dear."

"Don't call."

"Of course I won't call. Are you heading for his place now?" Excitement prickled in her aunt's voice.

"Yes, right now. I'll go over there quickly, take the pictures, and be back within the hour."

"But you will call as soon as you land someplace safe?"

"I will."

"Love you, dear. Bring back some evidence that the man is what we think. Your uncle will be watching."

Jenna plunged her phone deep into her pocket. The thought of her uncle's ghost hovering over her shoulder didn't help. He'd probably be gently admonishing her.

She turned to gaze at the twisting chimney pillars of the Victorian terrace houses ahead. Clay chimney pots rose like a march of mutated sentries silhouetted against the sky, each row standing at attention over the twelve linked units. If only they were really soldiers defending her against evil the way she had believed years ago, because tonight the reality of this nocturnal landscape seemed anything but friendly.

But she had work to do. She patted the flashlight secured to her belt and made sure the phone was deep enough in her pocket not to slip out.

It was relatively easy once she was aloft. All she need do was shimmy along the long interconnected roof and climb up and over the chimney walls. There might be extensions and roof conservatories along the way, but the basic structure had remained the same for over a century.

She inhaled the scent of hyacinths wafting from the gardens below. Something vivid and alive tingled in her blood. Heady zaps of stimuli electrified her veins with surprising intensity.

Over the roof peaks of the row houses ahead, the windows, skylights, and rooftop conservatories glowed in the dark like human terrariums. Those skylights hadn't been there two decades ago, but throughout the years these old houses had been bought by prosperous owners who paid designers to renovate in swaths of glass and light. Skylights and patios, conservatories and garden houses, infused a modern mood to the Victorian sobriety. Half the houses were still works in progress.

Those inhabitants might think their slice of sky private and sacro-sanct but no roof window was ever private, at least not from her, not that night. To Jenna Elson, they glowed like interior realms. As much as she tried, she could not resist glancing down or in, even though it meant invading someone's privacy. When she roamed the roofs at night, those glimpses became portholes into other worlds, each peopled by humans captured in the amber of her observation. Like reality TV, the glass peeled away a layer from another life, a life that only seemed simple on the surface.

At her aunt's insistence she'd made four nocturnal climbs in the last two weeks, just enough to gain a passing knowledge of some of the occupants along the twelve-unit row houses that comprised numbers 40 to 51 Marlytree Terrace—the elderly lady with the cats at number 43, the newlyweds with the twin babies crying in the night at 44, the banker and his wife with the lush garden at number 45, and the actor, Nicholas Hewitt, with his newly renovated double end units at 50/51.

She didn't really know them and yet she did. She'd glimpsed the exhausted young mother pacing the floor with a crying babe in each arm while her husband slept on; snatched a look at the banker's wife and her lover as their heads came together over candlelight in the rooftop conservatory; and witnessed the achingly lonely life of poor widowed Mrs. Chester watching television late into the night surrounded by her cats.

She had imagined getting close enough to check in on Nicholas Hewitt, too, but had so far resisted. It's not like she had reason to go to the end of the row, and maybe it was better that she continued to imagine his beautiful face in her dreams alone.

Besides, the artist Brian Dunn's rooftop conservatory was the target tonight at number 48. During the first excursions, Jenna had seen canvases propped against the glass—an assortment of modernistic nudes painted in electric colors. On the second trip, she'd glimpsed the artist himself, a scrawny man dabbing at his canvas. A young girl had stood trembling and naked on the artist's dais while the painter slashed the canvas with flesh-colored paint. The sight burned a vivid eyeprint into Jenna's mind too deep to erase and would join the other eyeprints —the term her aunt had coined for her memories—now permanently lodged in her cranium.

Uncle Dan had been so averse to sexual display that he'd turn offending magazines face-in when standing in line at the newsagents. And yet, apparently he had visited Brian Dunn on the night he died and, according to Aunt Clair, not for the first time. But when the police questioned Dunn, he had denied knowing Daniel Elson other than to exchange neighborly nods over the rosebushes. Why lie?

Swinging a leg over, Jenna edged along the one long peak that joined the row houses like a backbone interrupted only by banks of chimneys standing at attention on three-foot-high walls. Aerials, satellite dishes, and the like spouted up from the roofs like growths, but she knew them all by now, navigating them with ease. Weather, skill, and happenstance made for successful roofing, that and a good flashlight. It was dark amid the shadows, despite the ambient light from the city sky.

The artist's conservatory studio sat on a third-floor balcony in a curve of glass. Tonight it was enveloped in darkness. Good. Now perhaps she'd get close enough to see something, evidence of some kind. She had no idea what to look for—just anything that could link the artist to her uncle. That wouldn't prove that her uncle had been killed by this man, but it might indicate Dunn had been lying. Despite her love of fantasy, these days Jenna tried to fix on facts.

Jenna gazed over the roof to the next level. The climbing route was blissfully straightforward—down a trellis to the balcony—dead simple. It seemed that Brian Dunn loved to garden and cluttered the exterior of his glass studio with pots large and small, grouping the plants around a hardy climber that suckled along a trellis and on up the wall.

She tested the structure and found it securely fixed. Getting snarled in honeysuckle seemed the only hazard. She swung over and gripped the slats, up to her elbows in plant. Like swimming in kelp, she thought as she climbed down. Jumping the last two feet, she landed on the flagstones.

Creeping along the balcony towards the conservatory, Jenna flicked on her flashlight to illuminate the canvases closest to the glass. The platform in the middle of the studio where the models posed was clearly visible but everything else lay jumbled in shadow. She slipped closer. She'd never been at the correct angle to really see the paintings, though samples of Dunn's work were readily available on his website. Critics had described his unorthodox nudes as "a visual portrayal of man's frustration over modern womanhood." A misogynist by any other name.

Propped on an easel sat a large jigsaw nude nearly three feet across. A smorgasbord of female body parts spread across the canvas, livid in red and pink. For a moment, she just stared, picking out the occasional famous face among the appendages. Her gaze slipped to the next. Worse. Here, the artist had sliced thick red paint across the slim, delicately painted flesh of a reclining woman. The subject lay flat on her back, her legs and arms splayed wide in a gesture of sexual giving. Open. Vulnerable. Violated by the slashing paint that cut a deep V across the tender flesh.

Sick bastard.

She shivered as a dry leaf scuttled across the flagstones. This stuff would have worked her poor uncle's sensibilities into a pitch. Like his sister, he'd never married. Who knew what he really thought about sex?

With trembling fingers, she plucked out her phone and took aim through the glass to photograph what she'd already captured by eye and mind. The camera provided documentation only. After clicking two shots each of the paintings, she beamed the light deeper into the interior, looking for signs of something—anything—while panning the phone video recorder back and forth. A stack of canvases sat propped against a back wall, one large unfinished piece with several small canvases tucked behind. Her eye registered what her brain would study later.

If she could only get inside and search systematically, but that wasn't going to happen. Her personal statute of limitations took her up to the glass but no closer. This was only a fact-finding mission, a game. Why would Brian Dunn murder a retired banker, a sweet man who would never hurt a fly—literally? Her uncle's death had to be an accident. And so what if Uncle Dan had visited Dunn?

She turned and retraced her steps, slipping past the glass enclosure heading for the trellis while trying to tuck the flashlight back into her belt, but her clammy fingers lost their grip and the flashlight clattered to the stone in a flash of silver. Before she could catch it, it rolled between the balustrade slats, bounced onto a dormer below, and fell straight over the edge. Shit! She froze as the metal slammed onto stone, listened as the thing rolled for a few seconds before coming to a stop. Damn, damn, damn, and double damn.

There looked to be a flagstone patio on the ground-level garden three stories below but she saw no sign of the flashlight. It must have rolled off into the shrubbery. Damn cretinous thing. Directly beneath her, the dormer roof would provide a suitable landing spot from which she could grasp the drainpipe on the right side—currently out of reach thanks to the balcony bump-out—and shimmy down to the garden. She hated shimmying down anything. Still, she needed to get that flashlight somehow.

Swinging over the edge, she grasped the concrete balustrade and hung there until her feet touched the dormer roof, at which point she released her grip and landed on the dormer on all fours.

She paused, waiting and listening. No sound, no sign of alarm below. Fine. Eyeing the drainpipe about two feet to her left, she estimated the distance, how far she'd have to spring, and where to brace her feet and place her hands once she reached it. No time for overthinking or miscalculations. Climbing was all flash-decisions and calculated risks. She sprang, gripped the metal pipe, and in seconds was easing herself down, relieved to find the brackets fastened the pipe firmly to the brick.

It took only a minute for her to reach the garden—a narrow slice of greenery reaching deep towards the service lane. Decorated here and there by banked flowerpots and a little wrought-iron table and chairs, the garden was pleasant enough enclosed behind the back wall. She glimpsed briefly towards the darkened conservatory behind her before searching for the flashlight.

The breeze fingered the trees and the scent of hyacinths dispersed their pungent perfume from pots nearby. Dunn had edged the tall brick walls separating his house from his neighbors' with a thick boxwood hedge. That had to be where the flashlight scampered. Falling to her hands and knees, Jenna reached under the hedge fumble-feeling for the runaway. Only by luck did she catch the flicker of movement in her peripheral vision. Someone had entered the conservatory!

She sprang to her feet as a flood of light washed the patio, and was halfway up the drainpipe when footsteps scuffed across the flagstones. By the time she reached the dormer, she was trembling and drenched in sweat. She perched still, willing herself to become one with the roof, as the man below paced.

His footsteps shuffled back and forth, the acrid burn of his cigarette wafting upwards. Surely he couldn't have seen her, or he'd say something, or do something. She was afraid to breathe. Finally, after a few minutes, he went back inside. The door clicked shut, leaving her to lean against the window in relief.

Too close, far too close. She had to get back up to the top and away. To hell with the flashlight. She sprang for the balcony, her hands stretched overhead, grasped the rails, and hitched one leg up, followed by the other. Scrambling by the studio, she leaped for the trellis and was back on the peaks in seconds, wasting no time in putting as much space between her and Dunn's house as possible. Only when she was three houses away did she relax long enough to straddle the peak and steady her heart.

Leaning back, she allowed the contours of the roof to meet her spine and to gaze up at the sky through half-closed lids. This would be her tiny moment, just her and the sky. Above, nothing but stars trying to puncture the ambience of a million buildings while a misty moon hung unfocused in the urban sky. Sanctuary. This had to be the headiest drug of all. She relaxed.

High above, a plane began its descent into Heathrow Airport, the throb of its mechanical heart competing with the thumping of her own. She opened her eyes to watch the red and green running lights flicker across the sky before closing them again and taking a deep breath. It was then that she caught the faint sound of a mellifluous voice sweetening the air. She keened her ears. Someone talking, no, *reciting*. Deep, rich, husky, the words slipped across the roof peaks.

"FIE ON'T! AH FIE! 'TIS AN UNWEEDED GARDEN,
"That grows to seed; things rank and gross in nature
"Possess it merely. That it should come to this!"

THE VOICE OF HAMLET HOVERED ON THE ROOFTOPS DOWN THE ROW above the connected units of 50 and 51, home of Nicholas Hewitt. Versatile thespian, talented, Shakespearean-trained, unbelievably beautiful with high cheekbones and dark curly hair, the man had the kind of articulation that made love to language with every roll of the tongue. She'd seen him in the movies, imagined him as her lover on cold nights when nothing real could ever suffice, but tonight his disembodied voice held power enough.

She turned her head, listening. His words affected her like an antidote to nasty old men, deaths in the family, and messy secrets. His voice stroked the surface of her skin with living heat and, even from her perch, she burned.

If only she could creep closer and listen, maybe steal a glimpse into his world through that huge new skylight. But no, not that. She had no good reason to go along the full range of the terrace roofs when the easiest route down was back the way she'd come.

Moments later, she retraced her route soundlessly along the peaks towards her aunt's end unit at number 40. It would be easier still to scuttle across to Mrs. Chester's yard, drop onto the shed into her weedy garden, slip through the broken fence, and dash into the service lane that threaded behind all the row houses. Easier, but not preferable. Her uncle had died back there.

Jenna slipped down the trellis and dropped to the ground at the brick wall of 40 Marlytree Terrace, her aunt's end unit. The leaves of the plane trees rustled overhead and a dog barked from somewhere beyond the gardens while voices filtered through from the street. Marlytree Square had sunk into a soft nocturnal lassitude, neither fully asleep, nor completely alert.

Being at the end wall put her at a dilemma. She could sprint to her aunt's street-front door and risk being seen, or bolt around the corner into the alley and to her aunt's garden gate. Pushing through the shrubs, she paused at the entrance to the alley, a service lane. Gatepost lamps and a single streetlamp illuminated that dark river of refuse bins and garage doors.

Uncle Dan had died at approximately 11:15 p.m. three weeks earlier at the opposite end, behind Nicholas Hewitt's house. In the daytime, pedestrians and service vehicles kept the lane bustling, but at night the alley took on a different cast.

She had yet to witness the spot where her uncle had died. He had struck his head on a stone gatepost, according to the police, but he must have walked past the same spot countless times. The alley was a favorite pedestrian shortcut to the streets beyond. Why on one night out of thousands had he tripped over his dog's lead, as the police suggested? It didn't make sense. Mac wasn't one of those silly animals that wound himself around people's feet. But why couldn't she bring herself to look at the spot? She was a journalist, for heaven's sake. Her reluctance was ridiculous.

She bounded a few yards down the lane as far as her aunt's gate. Though only a short distance, her heart still beat hard until she flung the gate open and entered the sanctuary of home turf. With her back against the inside gate, she paused to catch her breath.

Ahead, the narrow yard sat awash in the conservatory lights. Upturned pots, rakes leaning against the shed door. Mounds of soil formed an obstacle course of landscape work in progress. She breathed the loamy scent of freshly turned soil.

Her ringing cell phone jerked her nerves. She pulled out the phone, saw the caller ID, and pressed Talk. "Aunt Clair, you said you wouldn't call."

"And you said you'd let me know as soon as you landed. It's been too long. I was worried."

"I'm in the garden now." Though her aunt was no longer framed in the upstairs dormer, Jenna knew she'd probably seen her enter the yard moments earlier. "I'm coming right in."

She picked her way around the pond dig, careful not to trip over the tools, and sprang for the conservatory door. MacTavish, the West Highland terrier, stood wagging his tail just inside the glass. Mac wiggled in glee as she scooped him into her arms and headed through the long hall that linked conservatory to kitchen, down to where the dining room and parlor opened up just before the front door and the staircase.

"Did you miss me, Fuzz-face?" she cooed into the dog's ears. If only Mac could talk. He had been with Uncle Dan the night he died, refusing to leave his master's side until a policeman brought him home the next morning, the poor little animal trembling in the officer's arms. What had he seen?

Jenna hugged the dog closer, fighting back tears. She'd cried enough to salt a beach already. Her uncle had been like a father to her, a father far more present than her real father had ever been. Strange how fresh grief gouged open old wounds.

Unlike the conservatory with its glass and indoor greenery, the house's interior remained much as it had for the last century, dark and traditional. Uncle Dan did not abide squandering money on fancy home improvements like new flooring, open-concept living, and certainly not on skylights.

Still, the house enveloped Jenna with the comfort of well-worn jeans or a shabby stay-at-home sweater. The taupe walls and parquet flooring, the parlor with its bow window and marble fireplace and all its slip-covered furniture, had soaked in the memories of her childhood. She'd spent many years in this house, and even more summer holidays, until strolling its halls felt like excavating the sediment of her life. Her mother's death, her father's remarriage, and all the tangled hurt of childhood in between seemed soaked into the layers of paint and wallpaper. Her birth home in Toronto had never felt like home the way this one had.

"Jenna?"

"Coming." She bounded up the stairs past the electric wheelchair lift and down the hall to her aunt's back den. Aunt Clair was already at the doorway, her electric wheelchair humming as she cruised into the hall. "Well?"

Jenna held up her phone. "I managed to get closer this time, but I didn't see much. I was just finishing taking the photos when I dropped the damn flashlight."

"You dropped the torch?" Aunt Clair stared at her with eyes the color of old Wedgwood china. Her halo of wiry gray hair framing a round, unlined face reminded Jenna of some aging cherub queen perched on a wheeled throne. "Oh, dear, what did you do?"

"I tried to retrieve the thing, of course. I shimmied down the drainpipe—the drainpipe, Aunt Clair, you know how I hate drainpipes —until I reached the garden. I was rummaging around under the hedges when he stepped out into the garden."

"And then what?"

"I bolted back up the drainpipe, of course, probably ripped the thing off its brackets in places, not that I slowed down to check.

Anyway, I managed to get up top without him seeing me, I think. I hope."

"Oh, my. This is not good at all."

"It rolled deep under the boxwood. I doubt anyone will find it for a while. I'll just leave it."

"Dunn's gardener comes every Thursday, and I understand he's quite a thorough chap. Best you try to retrieve it soon, dear."

"It's just a flashlight with nothing that can link back to me."

"Not so. It bears the inscription of your uncle's Barclay Bank, being one of those trinkets the bank bestowed upon its employees, along with pens, calendars, and the like. Didn't you notice the inscription?"

"I just grabbed it and ran."

"Your Uncle Dan never threw anything out. We wouldn't want Mr. Dunn knowing that we're on to him, would we?"

"We're not actually on to him," Jenna said gently. Sometimes the lines between her aunt's sense of reality and fiction seemed like parallel universes that would too often intersect.

"Nonsense, of course we are. Let's look at what you've captured on your phone. Come along." Her aunt did a ninety-degree turn and zoomed back into her den, Jenna following.

Her aunt's den opened up around her like a cockpit glowing with monitors and pilot lights. Aunt Clair had more technology than most offices—two laptops, two desktop PC computers, and one thirty-six-inch-screen Apple, various auxiliary monitors, a couple of storage drives, plus two iPads, including a new tablet-sized one that had just arrived the day before.

A box of some new gizmo sat unopened in the corner, waiting for the weekly visit of Harry, the young man she hired to teach her the newest techno tricks and run her network. Since polio had devastated her legs as a child, Clair Elson extended her reach first with books and now with a steady feed of technology, often with the two running in her head simultaneously. Uncle Dan had only shaken his head, commented on the expense, and hurried back to the sanctity of his books.

"Pass me the phone, Jenna dear." Her aunt held out her hand.

Jenna dropped the smartphone into her palm, watching in fascination as her aunt picked up her own phone to signal the Wi-Fi to load the contents onto one of the big-screen monitors.

"You use your phone as a remote?"

"Of course, Jenna. You really should keep up with devices more. I could schedule some sessions with Harry, if you'd like."

"I'm good, thanks."

"Anyway, I've been keeping an eye on our Mr. Dunn—indeed I have. He's not to be trusted. All those young girls going to his house at all hours of the night, taking off their clothes. It's just disgusting."

"How do you know that?"

"I keep an ear to the ground."

Jenna lowered herself into one of the room's two oak rail-back chairs. "Well, you know artists have been painting nudes for centuries."

"I do know, but not like this."

"No, not like this," Jenna admitted, "but that doesn't mean Dunn killed Uncle Dan, even if we do find proof that he's lying about knowing him."

Aunt Clair swung to face her. "Dan took Mac out for his walk at 9:45 on two consecutive nights. Not his usual time, mind you. Your uncle was a creature of habit and Mac had his walk three times a day: once at 8:30 a.m., once at 1:30, and just before *Masterpiece Theatre* at 8:30. Never at 9:45. What kind of time is 9:45? Your uncle always did things in evens. He couldn't abide irregularity. I remember the time exactly because that show was the only one we always watched together, and it was unlike him to change a habit. On that last walk, I saw him carrying a package under his arm as he crossed the conservatory for the back door. When I asked what it was, he pretended not to hear. He did so like to pretend not to hear me sometimes."

"Wasn't he going deaf?"

"Selective deafness, more like it, something I understand to be a particularly male affliction. No hearing aid can fix that one." Aunt Clair paused to press a hand to her mouth, tears suddenly welling in her blue eyes. "Oh, we did argue sometimes. I'm sure he found me very trying."

"He loved you very much. You were his dear little sister, and he'd do anything for you."

Aunt Clair stifled a sob. "He would. He *did*, but I did try his patience sometimes. Still—" she brightened "—one must be oneself, isn't that so?"

Jenna nodded. The two siblings had always interacted like a long-married couple. Uncle Dan was compulsive in so many ways—the perfectly aligned picture frame, the chair legs tucked in orderly row around the dining room table, the craving to deadhead his beloved roses the moment they began to fade. Aunt Clair had her own quirks, but predictability wasn't one of them. They had differed in countless ways, and yet had lived together companionably for over fifty years, a counterbalance of opposites.

It was the only image Jenna had of a happy home. Her mother and father had fought constantly, when George Elson was home long enough to interact, that is.

Jenna jolted from her reverie and pointed at the monitor filling with images from the night's excursion. Aunt Clair turned to investigate. "Oh, my."

Jenna shook her head. "The pictures don't do them justice. My eyeprints scream violation in every respect. I fought the urge to squeeze my legs together."

Aunt Clair peered at the photos, one by one, jerking the mouse around to zoom in on select shots. "Terrible, terrible," she muttered. "The man is seriously disturbed. He'd make a perfect killer."

"You don't know that. It could be like a horror movie where the creators show something ghastly like zombies devouring a town, but hardly go around chomping on corpses in their private lives."

"Are you defending him, then?" her aunt asked without turning.

"Not defending him, no. I don't like those paintings any more than you do, but that's not the same as accusing him of murder."

"If this doesn't represent his hidden desires, why is he painting such hideous filth?"

"Who knows? I could make a guess, but some people are remarkably adept at partitioning their art from their lives. Dunn may seem like the most distasteful human being on earth, but that doesn't mean he's a killer. And, for all we know, Uncle Dan did exactly as the police said: tripped over his dog while taking a walk down a poorly lit lane and hit his head against a gatepost."

Aunt Clair swung around, fixing her with those bright blue eyes. "Since when did you become so rigid in your thinking? As a writer and an explorer, your mission is to consider all possibilities."

"My job is to discover the truth, not perpetuate assumptions."

"Whose version of the truth? The truth is nothing but a moving target."

She had her there. "Look, I'm a journalist, not a novelist. Fiction is my entertainment, not my business."

"You could have been a novelist. You are so gifted," Aunt Clair said, her hands waving in the air.

Back to that again. "How about I keep on being a gifted *journalist*? Let's focus on the matter at hand. Look, I have an eyeprint and I want to show you the photo. I tried to get a good shot of it."

Aunt Clair turned back to the screen, moving the mouse around, sporadically clicking on images. While her aunt clicked, Jenna studied, pulling back her mind's eye to assess each picture as a whole, as well as to zero in on the sections her aunt expanded. "Wait." She touched her aunt's shoulder. "Go back."

"Back where?"

"Three clicks' worth—there."

Her aunt brought up one of the first shots Jenna had taken: a long sweep of the studio with the canvases leaning against one another propped against a table. Hovering the cursor over the image, her aunt shook her head. "I don't see anything," her aunt said.

Jenna leaned forward and pointed to a small canvas tucked behind a large nude. "Zoom in on that section."

Aunt Clair did so. "What?"

Jenna swallowed. "Why does that one have a West Highland terrier looking out at us?" She glanced down at MacTavish, who looked up and wagged his tail. "My God," she whispered. "That's one of Uncle Dan's paintings."

❧ 3 ❧

The next morning, Jenna sat across from her aunt at the kitchen table while Sara, the woman who cooked and cleaned for the Elsons, washed the dishes, despite the newly installed dishwasher. Jenna kept breaking off pieces of cold toast from the rack and feeding Mac under the table.

"Your uncle would ever approve of that," Aunt Clair said without looking up.

"He wouldn't, would he?" Jenna remarked with a smile. Her aunt missed nothing. "But the poor little guy needs his solace, too." She scratched Mac's ears. "Anyway, maybe Uncle Dan was taking painting lessons from Dunn?" Jenna suggested, though the thought struck her as ludicrous—her uncle's dog-and-sunset dabblings had nothing in common with Dunn's expert but lurid nudes.

"Oh, I doubt that," Aunt Clair said. "Nevertheless, your uncle appears to have visited Mr. Dunn on many occasions, though it seems he did not want me to know."

"Why do you say that?"

"Because of the painting, dear. Why not tell me he was giving Dunn one of his Mac paintings?"

"Because that would have opened a proverbial can of worms—more like a nuclear reactor actually."

"Whatever do you mean?"

"Aunt Clair, you would never have approved of that friendship, if it even was a friendship, and would have kept after Uncle Dan to end it."

"Nonsense," Aunt Clair said, straightening. "I would merely have suggested that he bring his friend around so I could meet him, something your uncle and I had agreed to do decades ago. Our lives were intertwined, after all. It was fitting that we each know the other's friends."

Only neither of them had any friends, a point that Jenna had never realized before that very moment. Through all the years she'd lived here, outside visitors had been few. Uncle Dan must have had collegial friends at the bank, of course, but he never spoke of them, and Aunt Clair, agoraphobic as well as wheelchair-bound, never made any of her own, that Jenna knew of. "Well, at least you had one another."

"Yes, we did indeed, but your uncle was getting more secretive in his advancing years."

"Auntie, Uncle Dan was only three years older than you."

"But he did seem so much older."

Sara slid up to the table with a pot of fresh tea, her face guarded. She was an odd one—very tight-lipped but with a face that hinted of a mouthful of unspoken opinions clenched between her teeth. She'd worked for Aunt Clair and Uncle Dan for at least a decade, but Jenna could never get a fix on her.

Aunt Clair looked at her sharply. "Sara, would you mind checking to see if the post has arrived?"

"It doesn't come until quarter to the hour, Miss Elson."

"Nevertheless, do check for me, please. It's been known to come early."

Sara untied her apron without a word and strode from the room. The moment she was out of earshot, Aunt Clair turned to Jenna. "You must go back up. You have no choice." She dropped two spoonfuls of sugar into her tea and stirred vigorously.

Jenna focused on pouring milk into her cup. She had to call the Toronto office at 10:30, London time. That was priority one. Annette, her editor and friend, expected her editorial by tomorrow, at the latest. That would be her first editorial as the incoming editor of *Wanderlust International*, and it was almost complete. The photographs had already been submitted and the piece written, but not polished. That would be tonight's task.

"There's always a choice, Auntie, and going back roofing strikes me as a bad one." It was already 9:30 and she'd been working at her laptop for nearly two hours already before breaking for breakfast.

"But you've always loved being aloft."

Jenna laughed. "When I was twelve. I'm not that kid anymore."

"You are always yourself at the core, nothing can change that. Fool yourself, if you must, but you can't fool me."

Jenna held up her hands. "Okay, okay, I admit roofing is an illicit thrill, but as an adult with a responsible career, I can't continue, obviously." Her aunt's constant wheedling had made it so difficult. Over the years, Jenna's visits to her aunt and uncle had become less frequent. She could count her visits this last decade on one hand—two Christmases, one stopover, one birthday, and once when Aunt Clair fell down the stairs.

"Oh, now now, really. Since when did you see the world in black and white? Besides, you're no peeper. You're *investigating*. That's quite different."

Jenna inhaled deeply. "Actually, there are new skylights up there, and sometimes when I'm passing overhead, I look down and see things, things people would rather I didn't see, private matters."

Aunt Clair leaned forward. "I remember when you'd hide in the bushes and peer through the windows at the neighbors before reporting back to me with the details."

"You encouraged me, as always."

"Nobody knew, and you loved it. Where's the harm? Anyway, what did you see last night?"

And here she was at it again. "I'm sure I saw Mrs. Oswald with a man not her husband."

"The banker's wife? She's stepping out on that handsome man she married?"

"It looks that way. Did you ever wonder what it would be like to be married?" Jenna realized she had never asked that before but her question today served as more of a distraction.

"Yes and no. I think it would be nice to have a partner with whom to share life's great adventure, someone to love."

"But you loved Uncle Dan and he loved you."

"Of course, dear, but we didn't choose one another, did we? Our bonds were different. I often wonder why you have yet to find yourself a partner when, indeed, you have so much to offer—beauty, talent, brains, imagination."

"Ah, Auntie," Jenna sighed, picking up the teapot. "You're deflecting again. You know my lifestyle doesn't accommodate a man. I have tried that route but found it infinitely unsatisfying. Anyway, I have my work."

"We'll leave that alone for now but quickly before Sara returns: did you see anything else interesting?"

"Afraid not, but I did hear a fabulous male voice reciting Shakespeare."

"Nicholas Hewitt? He lives down at the end of the row, doesn't he?"

"He does. It was amazing actually, to hear that voice way up on the roof like that—like having my own private recital."

"Oh, I can imagine it would be, and he's quite the attractive fellow, too."

Attractive enough for her to borrow his persona for her latest pillow love. Before him, she'd had another, and another before that, sculpting each one in her mind's eye to be her perfect man: funny, kind, endlessly devoted to her alone, loyal, brave, intelligent, and literally a dream lover. Just thinking of them now brought on the heat. No real man could ever compare.

"Will you go back tonight to fetch that torch?"

"I'd better stop while I'm ahead."

"But you're not ahead, darling. We need more evidence, and right now, we need that torch. Besides, since when do you shy away from risk? You were always the risk-taker, dashing off to expeditions in Africa and beyond. It was Antarctica last, wasn't it? Can there be a lonelier place?"

Jenna focused on the tablecloth, a new printed linen design that perfectly matched her aunt's blue china. "'Antarctica is austerely beautiful, like a winter queen. Some mornings the sun cracks the frozen sky in a thin gold band and hovers there for hours, as if holding its breath.' I'm quoting from my current article. Do you like it?"

"I love it, dear, but don't change the subject. And you say I am good at deflecting." Aunt Clair reached across the table to grasp Jenna's hand. "We need to find your uncle's killer and we must do it together."

Sara came in at that moment and slammed the cupboard door before continuing with her dishwashing. "No mail, as I said. Too early."

"Thank you for humoring an old woman." Aunt Clair winked at Jenna. "Would you mind making fresh toast, Sara?"

"You've barely eaten the last batch."

"Yes, but Jenna's Canadian now and likes hers warm."

Jenna looked up at Sara's unsmiling face. "I'm fine with what's here."

"I'll make some fresh," Sara said, turning away.

Aunt Clair studied Jenna, her cherub-like face intense. "Well, Jenna, on another matter, I worry about you."

"Worry about me why?" Jenna raised her eyes. "I'm a successful journalist about to become the editor of a prestigious magazine, and no one in our family has ever had to worry about money, needless to say. What's to worry about?"

"Check, check, check," her aunt said, counting on one hand. "Sounds like a grocery list to me. Don't you agree, Sara?"

"Leave me out of it, if you please," the housekeeper said without turning.

Aunt Clair closed her eyes and said under her breath, "Impossible," before carrying on more loudly. "I shall get right to the point, Jenna: you should move back to London and live with me."

Jenna caught her breath. "I can't do that, Aunt Clair. I thought you understood."

"Understood what, that you've been away too long living in one of those glass-and-concrete high-rises in some soulless city? You always loved London. This is your real home and I am all that's left of your family."

Jenna carefully set down her cup and considered gnawing on a piece of cold toast by way of distraction. "And I love you with all my heart, but my life is in Toronto now, as is my job—everything—but I promise I'll come visit you as often as possible."

"Which won't be near enough now that I'm alone. You know your uncle would have wanted it."

"And that, Auntie dear, is called emotional blackmail," Jenna said, keeping her tone light. "I'm going to do everything it takes to make sure you're comfortable and all the details taken care of before I leave. Let's not talk about this now."

Sara slid a plate of warm toast before her and Jenna picked up a slice and began buttering it.

"Sara, please go down to the cellar and fetch one of those nice jam preserves Mrs. Chester sent over last year, there's a dear. I'm sure Jenna would like it with her toast."

"I'm fine with marmalade," Jenna insisted.

"Nonsense. Hilda Chester is the best jam and jelly maker in the city of London, I'm sure of it. Your uncle and I made a point of holding our own little taste trial among seven prime brands and hers came out on top. I even printed her out a little certificate and Dan presented it to her. She was quite chuffed."

Jenna waited until Sara's had swung open the cellar door and dashed down the basement stairs. "Aunt Clair, you'll drive Sara away dispatching her on all these makeshift jobs."

"Nonsense," her aunt whispered, leaning forward. "I'm looking for a new housekeeper, anyway. She was Dan's choice, not mine. He preferred the taciturn type so he could read his newspaper without yet another woman chewing off his ear. I was distraction enough apparently. In any case," Aunt Clair hurried on, "let's focus on the matter at hand, and we'll get back to the other later. Brian Dunn has one of your uncle's paintings in his studio and now your uncle's torch under lies his hedge. You must go back."

Jenna swallowed, her first bite of toast going down hard. "I don't see the flashlight as such a big deal, and what do you want me to do about the painting, anyway? I can't just break in and steal it back. How would that help besides making me a felon? Whatever evidence I find wouldn't even be admissible in court. Leave it to the police."

"They aren't taking this seriously, you know that. I told them Dunn was lying, but they paid me no never mind, acting like I was some batty old woman who makes up stories. Now we have proof."

"Technically, this isn't proof. And breaking into his studio won't gain a thing," Jenna whispered.

Aunt Clair gazed at her steadily, her own toast unattended.

"You're not eating," Jenna pointed out, checking the wall clock— 10:15. Aunt Clair was both a night owl and a late-riser while Jenna preferred to start the day at the break of dawn.

"I've quite lost my appetite. I'm thinking of your dear uncle, of how he sat right where you're sitting, reading the paper. He'd keep saying: 'The truth is stranger than fiction. Facts never tell the tale.' He was right about that. Such an old fussbudget ..." Her voice trailed off as her eyes filled with tears.

"He was ... a dear old fussbudget." Jenna said. "I miss him so much."

"How will I go on, Jenna? How can I bear his absence day after day, forevermore?"

Jenna dropped her toast to the plate and squeezed her aunt's hand. "You know you can and must."

"I think of every little spat we had, feeling guilty all the while. We didn't always agree, you know, but we were family and, except for you, all the other had. After you returned to Toronto, we resolved to buck up and get along with our lives as best we could. Had you been our own daughter, you would still have left someday, wouldn't you? That is the way of the world. The young leave, and the old ones stay behind. We understood that. Dan would be so very pleased to know you have returned to keep me company."

Jenna gave her aunt's hand one big squeeze before pulling it away. "I only came to help you adjust to the loss—for both of us to adjust— and then I'm returning home to my life."

"Home isn't home unless you share it with people you love. I'd give you half the house. We could renovate, make this little home as magnificent as those in the magazines or down the street. Wouldn't that be fun?"

"Please let's not talk about this now."

"It's not as if you have a husband and children. We are so much alike, you and I. I'm alone now, and so don't want to be by myself. You're young, you don't understand how terrifying it can be to see all the years stretch ahead, and know you'll be taking them all alone."

Jenna took a deep breath, trying to loosen the knots in her neck. "But you could hire a live-in companion. That has to be better than me, considering that I might be traveling at least half the year."

Aunt Clair stared unblinking. "You can't seriously believe that is in any way preferable? Even knowing you would return in a week or a month is better than facing day after day without a loved one in sight. Wouldn't you find it a comfort to know that someone who loves you awaits at home?"

Not like this. God, she felt so guilty. Jenna gazed around at the tiny kitchen. Why hadn't she remembered it as being so small? The lino floor, the tired blue walls, even the speckled countertops, all squeezed in around her like a labored breath. As a child, these same walls had enveloped her in security, chasing away the demons of a shredded life, but even then she'd felt caged. Walls strangled her still, but did that justify why she couldn't give back a little of what she'd taken?

"Here's the crab-apple preserves," Sara said, returning from the cellar. "That place is a mess down there. I tidy when I can but it seems to get dirty regardless. I'll just finish drying up and be off. I put soup in the fridge for you and there's still meals frozen up top."

"Fine, thank you," Aunt Clair said, releasing Jenna's hand but not breaking eye contact.

And then the doorbell rang and Mac erupted into furious barking as a deep voice called out: "Miss Elson, hallooo!"

"Oh, it's Harry come to install my new computer," Aunt Clair said, her face brightening. "In the kitchen, dear," she called out. Then, turning to Mac, she scolded: "You be quiet now. He always reacts that way to male visitors," she told Jenna. "Hush, I said!"

In bounded a tall, well-built young man in high-top sneakers, his head a mass of red curls, and his face split by a bold grin. "Hi ya," he greeted. "Morning, Sara. You're looking fetching today. New apron?"

Sara only shook her head and strode past him.

"Never mind her, Harry. Sara's such a grump," Aunt Clair said. "Here's my niece, of whom I've told you so much about—Jenna, the writer. Jenna, Harry is my network dude. He's quite given me a new lease on life since your uncle passed. He used to come monthly back then but now I have him drop over more often. Mac, I said hush!"

Jenna smiled up at the young man as he shook her hand. "Great to finally meet you, Harry."

"My name's not actually Harry, but Henry," he said with a grin. "Your aunt keeps calling me Harry."

"Because you look so like Prince Harry, don't you think, dear?" Aunt Clair said, turning to Jenna.

There definitely was a resemblance—the hair color, the build, the boyish grin. Jenna only smiled, got to her feet, and picked up Mac. "Hush, Fuzz-face. I'll let you two get to work and take this little guy with me. I have to make a call to my editor, anyway." She checked the wall clock. "After that, I'll take Mac for his walk and squeeze in my run. Can I get you anything from the store, Aunt Clair?"

"Yes, please. Could you go to the greengrocer's and pick me out some bread, fresh milk, and maybe a box of that tea I like? Also, Mac needs another tin of his chicken dinner, oh, and Harry likes his digestive biscuits."

"You don't have to do that," Harry-Henry protested. "I'm only here for a bit."

"Nonsense. You must have your biscuits with your tea."

The young man grinned and shrugged. "Sure, thanks."

Jenna nodded. "No problem."

"Go on, use the house phone, Jenna," her aunt said. "I don't object to the long-distance charges the way your uncle did."

"That's okay. I have her on speed-dial on my cell." Jenna reached for her phone and stepped into the conservatory, her favorite place in the house, and shut the door. Today the potted plants pressed against the glass as if starving for fresh air and sunlight. Sympatico.

She sat Mac on the floor and opened the door to the backyard for him as she listened to the phone ringing through thousands of miles away. One, two, three rings, and finally Annette picked up. "Annette Robishaw speaking."

"Annette, so glad to hear your voice. For a minute, I thought you might have ducked out early."

The woman on the other end laughed low and husky. "Jenna? My last day as editor of *Wanderlust International* is officially at the end of the week and I'm not wandering anywhere until then, despite certain individuals attempting to shove me out the door."

"You're still editor until I'm officially appointed, anyway," Jenna said.

"Until your appointment is officially announced, you mean. Nevertheless, the upwardly mobile see retirement as a rotten tread on the ladder of success, something to be kicked away so the fresh one can take its place. You should witness the jockeying—fun and games. I wish I could declare you as our new editor and stop this foolishness, but we must follow procedure. It's not a great time to be away from the fort. How's your auntie?"

Jenna shot a glance through the glass door to Aunt Clair and Harry. "Working through her grief in her own way."

"I hate to push, but how's your editorial coming?"

"'You hate to push'—now that's a laugh," Jenna said, "but it will be in your hands tonight, I promise. I just need everything to be perfect so I'm taking one more run-through. The deadline isn't for two days, anyway. Look, you know I'm not one of those waiting to get you out of the way, don't you?"

"Hell, yes. Do you think I've forgotten how hard it's been to steer you in this direction for all these years? You're the most un-upwardly mobile person I've ever known."

"Roof-climbing aside."

Annette laughed. "God, woman, don't tell me you've succumbed to your aunt's pleas?"

"I have, and what's worse is that I love every tingling minute of it."

"Isn't that trespassing or something?"

"Probably that plus a bunch of somethings, but, Annette, it felt so intoxicating up there."

"Watch yourself. The new editor of *Wanderlust International* can't be seen as some kind of peeping Thomasina."

"I know it. Anyway, I'm done now, but it was fun while it lasted. It brought home all kinds of childhood memories. Is my appointment still secure?"

Mac was sniffing around a pile of dirt, his little white paws browning up by the second.

"Of course. How could it be any other way? Nobody else has your combination of experience and acumen. I've made no secret of my preference, either, though it's technically against the HR rules. Hell, I'm leaving, so who cares? As for Hellen, I told her that she needed more experience before taking over the responsibilities of this position."

"Bet she loved that."

"You can imagine her reaction. So, when are you coming home?"

Jenna glanced back towards the kitchen where she could still see her aunt and Harry head-to-head through the glass. What did those two have cooking up that engaged them so thoroughly? "Hard to say. I just don't have everything stabilized yet. I need to answer a few more questions for Aunt Clair and myself."

rarefied gourmet stuff, while wondering how she could ever leave her aunt without wrenching herself in two. Yet, if she stayed, she'd be torn apart, anyway, only by a much slower death. Death by confinement. Death by emotional suffocation. Death by love?

She paused over a stack of oranges, considering. It was true: love required sacrifice. It took courage to accept that responsibility and she clearly wasn't up to the challenge. The death of her mother when she was a child, followed by her father's abandonment, had left her damaged in ways that Uncle Dan and Aunt Clair had eased but never cured.

The line was light. She queued behind a tall man wearing a broad-brimmed hat with a beige trench coat that looked like it was tailored for someone two sizes smaller. Though his back was to her, she could just see the long fingers holding his wallet, the broad shoulders.

She looked away, focusing on the elderly woman shuffling into line behind her. The woman, bent over with rheumatism, was trying to manage an overstuffed shopping basket filled with brown-spotted bananas and multiple boxes of cookies.

"Would you like me to hold that for you?" Jenna offered.

The woman peered into her face and nodded. "Would you, love? There's a dear. I let myself get carried away with the biscuit sale."

Jenna smiled as she wedged the woman's basket under her one arm. "Those biscuits are worth being carried away by," she said.

"You're American, aren't you?" she asked. "My nephew lives in Boston."

"I'm Canadian, but close enough when you're on this side of the Atlantic," Jenna said. God knew, when she was traipsing all over the world, anybody who hailed from North America seemed like a neighbor.

While the lady chatted, the man ahead reached the counter and asked for cigarettes. He appeared to be in his mid-fifties with shaggy blond hair that belied his sturdy build. There was something amiss with that hair, too. It looked like the whole coif was listing to the left as if he had plonked a cocker spaniel on his scalp. "Make it a double pack, no filter, thanks."

That voice. Oh, my God. Could it be? Jenna stared. He emanated a nervous energy like a man fuelled by too much caffeine, bouncing on the balls of his feet while he waited. He kept glancing towards the window. Then he turned around, scanned the store, caught sight of her, turned away, then swung back again.

Him. It was Nicholas Hewitt trying not to look like Nicholas Hewitt, though the drab trench, wig, and dark glasses did little to contain the man. He held her gaze only a moment before swinging back to count change for his purchase. He knew she recognized him. It was as if he begged her not to give him away, and she wouldn't; of course she wouldn't.

"I know all about Americans as a result of Tom living there," the woman was saying at her elbow.

"Do you?" Jenna mumbled. Her heart was racing. What was wrong with her? She didn't swoon over actors. Even when she was younger, she never plastered posters of rock or film stars all over her walls. For her, it had always been about places, not people. But her heart kept galloping. *My God, what's wrong with me?* Blame his eyes, that voice, the way he read Shakespeare, something. The fact that she hadn't been with a man since that brief fling with Des two years ago didn't help. The fact that Nicholas Hewitt now had star billing in her dream matinee made it ten times worse. She'd never been this close to the reality of an infatuation.

"The Americans are far more lenient with things like that," the lady was saying.

"They are?" What was she talking about?

Moments later, she watched Nicholas plunge his hands into his pockets and stride out the door, both relieved to see him go and pained by his absence.

Breathing deeply, she fought to steady her heart. *Get a grip.*

She forced herself to listen to the lady and smile, paid for her stuff, and scrambled out the door. Nicholas Hewitt had disappeared by then. Good. No, *damn.*

She untied Mac, baffled by her trembling fingers, the way her heart danced in her chest. The whole thing was beyond ridiculous. So what if he was a good-looking guy with a dusky baritone? Was she spinning away into some kind of youthful regression? It's true that the whole dating scene had eluded her until she was well into university, but it wasn't like she was some kind of vestal virgin. She'd had and been had by men. In the end she figured that, emotionally as well as physically, relationships weren't worth the effort. Her imagination tended to her needs well enough.

But for reasons she couldn't fathom, she still felt as though she had fallen into the orbit of some magic planet only to be jettisoned out into the cold vacuum of empty space.

5

On her return trip, Jenna almost hurried past the alley the way she'd been doing every day. Instead, she paused, staring into the shady lane winding behind the backyards of the two parallel streets.

Though only at the opposite end of the lane from her aunt's, it seemed a marathon distance away. In broad daylight with a garbage truck rumbling along collecting the rubbish, the alley couldn't look more innocuous—only a service lane lined either side with tall gates and garage doors, after all. How many times had she strolled this route —a hundred, a thousand times before? She knew every garage door, every garden gate. Now it was as if each object had been doused in shock and sorrow.

Mac whined at her feet. She looked down. "I know, boy, we've been taking the long route home every day but let's get this over with."

Together they stepped into the lane threading its way between the backs of the two sets of row houses. Tangles of budding branches overhung the garden walls. A car was backing out of a driveway ahead, a dark blue Aston Martin that did a three-point turn before easing along behind the garbage truck ahead of it, the lane being one-way.

An ordinary day in an ordinary London lane, and yet the closer they came to the stone gatepost where Uncle Dan had died, the more the air seemed to thicken. She fought that crazy sense that the atmosphere itself had taken on the consistency of water, as if her limbs had to push their way forward along a riverbed. Sometimes imagination was no friend.

As they passed Nicholas Hewitt's double unit on the Marlytree side, she could hear workmen pounding on his roof, though she couldn't see them from her present vantage. She walked quickly by until she reached a section where the gatepost flanked the driveway of a house that fronted Dresden Lane, the street running parallel to Marlytree. The owner had painted the garage door a dark hunter green, installed old carriage lamps on top of the stone posts, and coaxed glossy holly to all but obscure the fieldstone wall.

Jenna caught her breath. Why would he stumble here, of all places?

At various locations along the lane, motion sensors had been installed, though the closest one was across the lane and two houses up, and a few owners had cameras embedded in their garage doors. Nobody had seen anything, and the cameras had only picked up whatever was directly in front of them.

Jenna took a step closer, forcing herself to stare at the gray stones, cringing as if half expecting to see signs of blood. But there wouldn't be, of course. Not now. Had there ever been? The accident was weeks ago. Everything would have been cleaned and tidied, all visible signs of death eradicated.

Except for her and Aunt Clair, that is. For them, Uncle Dan's death still throbbed with painful immediacy. Had he been conscious before the blackness swallowed him? Had he cried out with terror? The neighbors had heard a dog barking on and on—Mac, of course. She looked down. The little terrier whimpered and backed away. What did this little dog know that he couldn't say?

"Okay, we've done enough for one day. Let's go home."

It wasn't like her to be affected this way, to avoid a spot just because of a death. She'd seen enough of death in nature—violent, without conscience, driven only by the will to survive—and she made herself study it, accept it, understand it as a part of the natural cycle of things.

But the death of a loved one was different. While her mother's death had ripped her world apart, her father's had little impact, not just because she had been an adult, but because he was already dead to her. No, Uncle Dan had been her true father and now he was gone.

Jenna was still shaken when, several houses along, she approached Dunn's walled yard. It had been his Aston Martin she'd seen backing up, she realized, but now both the car and the rubbish truck had gone. Taking a deep breath, she picked up the pace and nearly jogged to the end, Mac's little legs scrambling to keep up.

When they reached her aunt's yard, she paused. A motorcycle sat on its kickstand near the gate, beside a trailer that appeared jerry-rigged as a kind of tool conveyance. Sounds of digging battered the earth behind the wooden fence. The damn garden dig. Mac growled. She tugged at his lead and together they sprang for the street, rounded the corner, and marched up to the front door and into the house.

Mac's nails were clickedy-clicking on the tiles as he darted towards the back of the house, barking all the way. She heard him growl and then whimper as her aunt scolded him. Kicking off her shoes, she padded towards the kitchen. "Aunt Clair?" she called.

"Out here, dear."

The terrier had dashed straight through the kitchen into the conservatory. Jenna placed her satchel on the kitchen chair beside a stack of gardening catalogs, and followed him out. He was sitting on the floor beside her aunt's wheelchair before the open door. A sun-laced breeze wafted in from the garden along with a pungent earthy smell.

Aunt Clair called out to someone. "I rather prefer it that shape. Yes, that's excellent. Maybe a few more inches to the right. There. Yes, I think that will do wonderfully."

Jenna stepped up behind the wheelchair, gazing out at a tall young man dressed in coveralls and biker boots standing knee-deep in muck with a shovel in hand. Around the widening trench lay a tangled mass of roots, some wrapped in burlap. For a moment, she could hardly speak. "Uncle Dan's roses?"

Her aunt looked up at her. "Oh, there you are, dear. Yes, Jake is working on your uncle's memorial koi pond. I thought it would look splendid if it wound about under the little bridge Jake will build for me. There I shall drive my chair and imagine myself in exotic climes. In place of the rosebushes, we shall plant acanthus and elephant ears, maybe some ferns and umbrella trees—anything to impart the tropical ambience. Plants that will not abide the cold will be overwintered in the new garden shed, as in the old garage that hasn't been used as such since your uncle sold his car. Maybe we could make it into an orangery? Wouldn't that be fun? Jake has planned everything. What do you think?"

She thought her heart would shatter in two, that's what. "But Uncle Dan loved those roses," she whispered.

"So he did, the dear man. He was so set in his ways, wasn't he? I'd ask for something more exotic, and he'd bring home a potted palm. However, I found roses rather pedestrian myself, even suffocating. Why only roses? I'd ask. Roses are so ordinary. Everyone has roses. Why not a nice crop of delphiniums or even an English cottage collection, if we must be traditional? But he wouldn't hear of it. The garden was his domain, you see. Now, I cannot allow it to be frozen in memory and me with it. We must move forward, and new projects help. I must make the garden mine. You do understand, don't you?" She reached around to grasp Jenna's hand.

Jenna nodded, her throat swelling. She really did understand—or she tried. Moving forward was the best medicine for grief, and she was relieved that her aunt was moving on, even if it was at an alarming speed. Yet, seeing this garden gouged like an open wound hurt so deeply it may as well be her heart out there exposed. Those roses. All those years watching her uncle carefully tending their fragrant faces, instructing the child she'd been on how to nurture a living thing. "Careful with the thorns, Jenna. Even those we love can draw blood ..."

"I'm just going upstairs to work, Aunt Clair."

"Wait, dear. I'd like you to meet Jake first. Jake's in the know with all the other gardeners on this street, and he told me a most disturbing piece of news. Jake," she called out the door. "Come meet my niece, why don't you?"

Jenna watched as the young man tossed the shovel to the ground, flashed a grin, and climbed out of the pit. He couldn't be older than twenty-five, lean and impressively muscled, with an array of body tats snaking over his exposed skin. A bandanna wrapped around his head, pirate-style. The rakish Johnny Depp look suited him. Girls probably swooned. Jenna fought the urge to kick him in the kneecaps.

He dipped a bow in old-fashioned courtesy. "Morning, Ms. Elson. I'd shake your hand but it's a mite grimy at the moment." East London accent, lopsided smile, charm in buckets.

Jenna's gaze landed on the skull inked on his bicep. What was it about millennials and skulls?

"Hi, Jake. Call me Jenna."

"Hey, Jenna. It's a bit of a tip back here right now but it's going to be a knockout when I'm done."

"I'm sure it will be." She already felt a little bruised.

"Jake, tell Jenna what you told me," her aunt prompted.

He glanced from Aunt Clair to Jenna and back again. "About the fountain?"

Oh, God, there was going to be a fountain, too?

"No, not about the fountain, about Mr. Dunn's gardening plans."

The young man paused and rubbed his forehead, leaving a two-fingered streak above his left brow. "Mr. Dunn? You mean about him hiring the lads to do a major landscape job?"

"To modernize the garden, yes."

To the kid's credit, he seemed puzzled. "Yes, well, Mr. Dunn is having a bunch of the lads from the Artfully Scaped Landscaping service build this new Zen garden for him—you know, with pathways and a two-level deck, all very posh."

"Of course it would be in this neighborhood, wouldn't it?" Aunt Clair said. "And when is this massive dig to launch, Jake?"

"Right away."

"Right away as in ...?" Aunt Clair prompted.

Jake gazed at her quizzically. "Right away as in tomorrow?"

"Tomorrow exactly. That soon. Thank you, Jake. You've been very helpful. Carry on, and in the meantime, I shall peruse those catalogs you so kindly brought." She turned to Jenna. "Just close the door for me now, there's a dear, and let's go back in for a bit of a chat."

As Jenna leaned forward and eased the glass door shut, her aunt reversed the wheelchair and zoomed towards the kitchen. "It's growing a bit too breezy," she called over her shoulder.

Jenna hadn't reached the kitchen before her aunt spun around to face her, hands gripping the armrests. "You must realize how imperative it is for you to retrieve that torch before the project begins tomorrow. How terribly inconvenient it would be should we be called to answer questions as to why that torch ended up under that horrid man's hedge. What if you were accused of trespassing or worse?"

"So, I should trespass in order to avoid being accused of trespassing?"

"Don't be obstinate, dear. You must see how this could jeopardize our search for your uncle's killer. We absolutely must not leave a trail or all will be ruined."

"I doubt that a flashlight constitutes a trail."

"Well, suppose Dunn discovers our suspicions and traces you back here? Supposing he breaks into the house to strangle us in our beds, or even worse—if there is such a thing as worse than strangulation—he chooses to make our deaths look accidental? He did that very well with Dan, he did, and may yet try a similar technique with us. I am chairbound and very vulnerable, while you are young and out and about every day. So many places to launch a trap or ambush. He might—"

"Stop!" Jenna lifted her palms. "Aunt Clair, please. Look, I'll go back tonight and grab that flashlight, if it will make you feel better, but this has to be the last time."

"The second to last time."

"Pardon?"

"One more time to retrieve the torch and one more time to hunt for evidence—two more times."

"Auntie!" Jenna threw up her hands. "Why do you keep doing this to me?"

"Doing what, dear?"

"Prodding me to do things against my better judgment."

"Oh, come now, Jenna. I don't make you do anything you don't really want to do, regardless of your better judgment. Who says that what we're doing is wrong, anyway? Some dreary old rule? Since when do you abide by rules? You've always loved to climb. You feed on the adrenaline, as do I, allowing me to ride your back, so to speak. We are kindred spirits. More importantly, your uncle has died at the hands of that detestable man and only we can bring him to justice!"

Jenna shook her head. Aunt Clair was both right and yet all wrong at the same time. And Jenna always fell for her wheedling even when she recognized it. "I'll go tonight at least. After that, I promise nothing. In the meantime, I doubt Dunn is going to bound over the fence and knock us off if he should find a flashlight under the hedge."

Aunt Clair grinned. "Thank you, dear. I will rest ever so much better if you take care of this one little detail for me, and shall tingle in anticipation imagining tonight's excursion. We'll talk about other roofing treks later."

Jenna squelched the pulse of excitement. She couldn't afford that, damn it.

"Now, let's sit down over a nice brew while you help me pick out the plants for my tropical escape garden," Aunt Clair said, her face alight.

"No thanks. I still have my editorial to proof. Maybe later."

"When will you leave for your mission tonight?" Aunt Clair called out behind her.

It was a mission now, was it? Right then, she needed to get away, escape to her room, *think*. If she could, she'd shuttle back to Toronto and hide out in the life she'd made for herself far up in her skyscrapers, but it was still too soon. "I don't know. Maybe 11:00 or 11:30. I'll set my alarm when I take a nap."

"Very well, dear."

৩৯৩

THE SECOND FLOOR HOUSED A LIBRARY, HER UNCLE'S PAINTING room, a spare bathroom, and a guest bedroom, while the top floor had been divided into two wings—her uncle's half on the front overlooking the street, and her aunt's at the back. Both domains had spacious en-suite bedrooms and a private den. Jenna's girlhood room was wedged between them like jam in a sandwich.

Fitting enough, she thought as she headed for her uncle's den. As a kid, she'd always felt suspended between their two strong personalities. Uncle Dan, usually measured, thoughtful and quiet, counterbalanced his more extroverted sister, whose quest for novelty often tested his patience. How sad and ironic that the one bound to a wheelchair was the sibling who most yearned to wander, while the one happy to stay home could have gone anywhere but hadn't the interest.

Uncle Dan's book-walled sitting room remained cozy, manly, and as traditional as the man himself, and Jenna had commandeered it as her study. She loved the olive-green walls, the antique furniture and plumply padded wing chairs. So grounding, like being planted in a forest.

Her laptop sat propped incongruously on his eighteenth-century roll-top desk. He hadn't owned a computer himself, preferring to leave technology to his staff at the bank and, later, to his sister. As vice-president he had become used to being surrounded by helpful, efficient women. After he retired, he considered the cell phone his sister insisted he carry to be all the personal technology he needed.

Jenna perched on his chair and switched on her computer. In seconds she was deep into her article, polishing the words until they sparkled. This, of all posts, had to be perfect. Her writing voice hit the balance of confident and authoritative, while still being warmly accessible, a tone she'd mastered over the years. Though she mostly avoided close relationships with humanity, she cared about people passionately. Her multiple substantial charitable donations proved that much, didn't it? She sat staring at the screen. Of course it did. She'd given away a million dollars last year alone. That had to mean something. She frowned.

Shaking off her thoughts, she refocused on her work. Assigning the photos to the words was still the best part. She likened it to dancing on a table after slogging all day in the trenches. The words could tune the readers' minds into her perspectives of humanity's relationship with the wilderness, then the photos themselves told their own story with absolute impact. Let the reader think of the Antarctic as someplace otherworldly and unbelievably faraway, and then let those photos— brilliant and absolute—transport them beyond their tiny existence.

Hours later, after meticulous line editing, she hit the send button and imagined her editorial zipping away like a silver rocket aimed right towards her soon-to-be prestigious editorial seat. Staring unfocused at the blinking cursor, she thought of how much she craved that job, and yet longed for anonymity at the same time. She wanted the position for all the wrong reasons yet still she persisted. It was all about succumbing to society's benchmark of getting ahead.

She could have been happy hiding behind her articles forever, a staff travel writer constantly on the move, but when Annette announced her retirement, the thought of having the wrong editor take her place was all too much. Hellen could ruin everything she and Annette had struggled so hard to create. So Jenna was being upwardly mobile in ways she knew didn't suit her.

She returned to her room to lie down on her narrow childhood bed. Nothing here had changed since she'd left for university eons ago. The same William Morris Strawberry Thief wallpaper tangled the room in its rich vining colors. Blue-green everywhere. She'd always felt like Sleeping Beauty here, as if those furling leaves wove wards of protection against the outside world. The wallpaper was Aunt Clair's choice, the blue velvet love seat in the corner Uncle Dan's. She relinquished her own taste to pacify them both. Sometimes it had been tough keeping the two of them happy.

Soon she dropped into a deep dreamless sleep. When she awoke, nightfall poured darkness through the room, leaving only the street-lights washing pale luminescence through the dormer window. The furniture rose and fell in the shadows like a distorted landscape. Jumping up, she flicked on the light, forcing the room back into reality.

Her smartphone alarm buzzed away on the bedside table. Deactivating it with a tap, she stared at the numbers—10:45. A little over an hour to accomplish her task. She wanted to be back and tucked into this very bed by 12:00, at the latest. Midnight was her pumpkin time. One can't be up at 6:00 but go to bed after 12:00.

In seconds she was climbing into her black yoga pants, black turtleneck, scraping her curls behind her ears, and slipping her feet into black sneakers. Easing open the door to the hall, she almost tripped over Mac.

"What are you doing here, Fuzz-face?"

The dog jumped up, wagging his tail and whimpering.

"Oh, right, you need to pee." She glanced to the end of the hall where her aunt's lights blazed. She'd probably be deep into some television show now, still a long way from bedtime, and oblivious to the little dog's needs. Uncle Dan always took care of Mac. "What if we had a doggy-door installed, would that solve the problem?" She rubbed his ears. "Come on, I'll let you out in the garden, or what's left of it. No time for a walk tonight."

With Mac scampering ahead, she bounded downstairs.

The Tiffany lamp shone on a multicolored pool on the kitchen table as she passed. In the conservatory, a night-light cast a soothing green glow over the leafy shapes. Colored lights in the darkness were her metaphors for life.

Unlocking the door, she eased it open. "Make it quick." She stepped out onto the flagstones as Mac bounded across the wounded yard, just a little low blur against the shadows. "Don't go too far," she cautioned, but he had already disappeared.

She couldn't afford more complications that night. "Mac, come back!"

But the dog didn't come dashing towards her the way he usually did.

She stepped down to the first step. "Mac!" Damn, damn, damn. On this of all nights, Mac decides to play bad dog? She dove into the yard, navigating around the pond pit. Mist shrouded the occasional street-lamp over the back fence and she could smell the dampness. Still no sign of the dog. Then halfway to the rear gate, she could hear him growling. "Mac?"

In seconds she had bounded towards the fence, past the potting shed, leaping over the buckets, the bags of leaves, the tangle of tools lying haphazardly in the mud, the dying rosebushes. The back gate hung wide open and Mac stood in the middle of the lane, ears flat against his head, growling.

6

Jenna scooped the terrier and stared down that river of darkness. God, how she hated that alley. Nothing moved down there—at least, nothing she could see. And yet she felt watched. Something clinked far down at the other end—a flowerpot falling over?

Mac growled, his little body trembling. "Cool it, boy. Probably a cat or something." As if she believed that. She dashed back into the yard and swung the gate shut, bolting it behind her. Jake had better get his act together.

Back in the house, she locked the conservatory door, wiped off Mac's paws, and headed upstairs to her aunt's room, Mac scrambling ahead.

Aunt Clair, perched before her big flat-screen TV, turned when Jenna entered. "There you are! I was just about to rouse you for the night's mission."

"I let Mac out for a pee. Jake left the garden gate open."

"What, no, really?" Aunt Clair paused the TV and swiveled her chair around to face Jenna. "But that can't be. He's such a careful lad."

"Not careful enough apparently. He was the only one back there."

"I'll talk to him tomorrow. Now, on to the task ahead. I see you are dressed and ready."

"I am. Do you like the look?"

"Very ninja."

"I was thinking more Zen cat burglar."

"That works, too. Will you take me with you?"

"Yes, but don't call. I'll call you when I get aboveground, okay?"

Aunt Clair clasped her hands. "Agreed! Will you go straight there or take a detour so I can see the city from way up there?"

"I won't promise anything but I'll try." Jenna imagined the roofs-capes rising and falling against the night sky and tried to suppress her anticipation.

"Very well, dear. I'll be waiting."

Jenna gave her aunt a quick kiss and made for the door. "Keep Mac with you, okay?"

"Of course. Which way will you go? Mrs. Chester's is the safest— only two doors down."

But Jenna was already downstairs and didn't want to name her route in case she changed her mind. Mrs. Chester's might be the quickest path up but her shed was in such rotten condition that Jenna avoided it. Better to take her uncle's trellis again. The structure, abloom with climbing roses, stretched up beside their end unit's bow window, taking her up to the dormer on the second story and then to the roof via the third-story bump-out where Aunt Clair often parked for her street views.

The trellis was high and strong like Jack's beanstalk, and knowing that her uncle had had it built made it seem like a ladder straight to him. Which was crazy. She didn't believe her uncle's soul hovered up there in the heavens somewhere.

On the other hand, she didn't believe he had just gone, either.

In seconds she had slipped outside to the street. Marlytree Square hung quiet in the late evening, the cloud cover reflecting the lights while the city hummed beyond. The Georgian row houses glowed on the other side of the park like eyes in the darkness. She used to imagine them watching her, not unfriendly exactly, but definitely judgmental. Good girls didn't peer into people's windows or climb roofs. Good girls obeyed the rules, played everyone else's game.

A figure passed across the upstairs window on the top floor of the house directly across the park. Someone readying for bed, somebody normal who didn't climb roofs at night or hunt for flashlights under hedges. Why did she care so much about being normal, anyway? Normalcy was pedestrian.

Jenna bounded to the edge of her aunt's corner lot. Here, the rose-bordered wrought-iron fence shielded her from the street while her uncle's trellis formed a little ladder to the sky. When had he built that and why so high? All the minute details of his life were now lost to her, and nothing would ever bring them back. She was halfway up the side of the building, the thorns scratching through her spandex, when a fresh pang of loss stabbed deeper than the thorns.

All the opportunities she could have come home to see him—both of them—but didn't. She had always believed she had time, time to make the next birthday, the next Christmas, but they had all slipped away. Squandered moments, all of them.

All she had to do was spring to safety and the sanctuary of the upper realms would be hers. The trellis stopped two feet below the second-story dormer but she had no difficulty in grabbing the eaves and hoisting herself aloft, and from there upwards to the third-story balcony, which wasn't a balcony so much as a decorative barrier. The chances of being seen were greatest here but, luckily, Londoners rarely looked up, and she had the benefit of blending in with the shadows. Seconds later, she was on the terrace's long conjoined peak, the backbone of Marlytree Terrace.

She sat astride the peak, breathing in the damp air and gazing out on the city. The roofs and trees rolled into the distance while the traffic on the main road coiled like a magic snake through the darkness. It was as if she was part of the world, yet several degrees removed —above it but not in it. Up here it was all fantasy, her private sanctuary, an alternative dimension where she could escape the world's misery—her misery—and just be ... elsewhere. Jenna and the Beanstalk, half giant, looking down and over.

She smiled at the thought. If her counselors could see her now, they'd think they'd failed miserably. And maybe they had. Pulling off one glove, she lifted her hand as if to brush the trees with her palm, imagining the twiggy branches snagging her fingers. Silly, but oddly comforting, like coming home to some part of yourself long abandoned. *I am home, world.*

Twisting around, she gazed down at the lane winding through the shadows and her gut clenched. She had to get over to Dunn's and fetch that damned flashlight. Besides, she couldn't phone Aunt Clair until she was deep into the roof range and away from the street.

She jumped to her feet, balancing on the slate tiles on either side of the peak with her sneakered feet, her thighs clenching while she shuffled along towards the first stand of chimneys. From there, she hoisted herself up the three-foot wall, squeezed between the chimney pots, and dropped down the other side.

Number 41 Marlytree, their closest neighbors, were a retired couple who kept resolutely to themselves and had only moved in a few months ago, besides—the Whartons? The Waltons? No skylights there, nor at number 42, either, where the widower Mr. Rambolt lived. Jenna wedged herself between the chimney pots where she felt safest and totally shielded from the street and called Aunt Clair.

Aunt Clair picked up immediately. "What do you see, dear?"

"I'm deep in the peaks now above Mr. Rambolt's, sitting amid his chimney soldiers."

"Stuffy Mr. Rambolt. Your uncle didn't like him much. He must be a thousand years old by now."

Jenna smiled. "I have no idea," she whispered, "but look, I'm going to head over to Dunn's now and I won't have time to call again. Can you hold tight until I return?"

"Well, I shall have to, won't I? Can you give me an eyeprint before you go, dear?"

"There isn't much to see now. I'm leaning against a sentry, staying out of view. Nothing inspiring at the moment. I'd better get going."

"If you must, dear. I'll be waiting."

Jenna clicked off, set the phone on mute, and plunged it deep into her stretchy pocket. After minutes of stealthy scampering, she finally reached Mrs. Chester's. She was about to pass by as always but paused at the edge of the roof, looking down at the cracked and grimy skylight on the ground level.

The skylight had been constructed by the late Mr. Chester years ago and ran four feet over the extended living-room kitchen, which had once been a leaky conservatory. Now Mrs. Chester had claimed it as her prime living area and, where once had been a family table, now a battered couch sat propped in front of a television. Though the TV was out of view, Jenna saw the blue-green light flickering about the room as Mrs. Chester sat with her feet up, one marmalade tabby in her lap, another curled up behind her. A crack ran a jagged lightning bolt across the glass.

Jenna pulled back and continued her journey. Next came the Hiltons with the twins, and here the sound of the babies crying almost covered the argument below. Jenna skirted their roof quickly, avoiding looking down into their tiny kitchen skylight on the ground level. How awful it must be to be saddled with two small babies plus a large querulous man. And people claimed marriage a good thing? More like a prison with dubious benefits. Next came the banker and his wife, their three new skylights gracing each level in a stepped modernistic structure topped by a glassed-in balcony at the rear top. Everything was darkened and still that night—good. Out on a date or off living separate lives? Probably the latter.

She crossed numbers 46 and 47, another double unit undergoing a massive renovation which involved tearing down walls and gutting the interior. The new owners had yet to move in, leaving that expanse of roof dark and dead. She planned to cross that black landscape quickly, but a sound made her pause. She peeled her senses into the darkness. It was a peculiar sound, not the random noises of an abandoned house but a regular, deliberate sound powered by intention and intelligence. Right below her hands and feet, deep into a dark building, someone was ... hammering at this time of night?

Jenna studied the roof. No skylight previewed this interior but there was an old trapdoor beside the chimney stand that had once provided workers of old access to the roof. Someone must have modernized this hatch at some point since the original wood had been replaced by metal. Every house of this vintage had once had something similar, though most, like her aunt's, had been barricaded long ago.

She crept over and lifted the hatch, the rusty hinges screeching as the lid rose. The pounding abruptly stopped. Jenna paused, sensing the darkness below, sensing someone listening back. Oh, shit. She swiftly eased the lid back down. This was crazy. So what if the owners decided to burn the midnight oil to complete their renos? It wasn't her business, and she had enough to do that night. Stifling her curiosity, she carried on, reminding herself that everything made her uneasy these days. She needed to stay focused.

At last she reached Dunn's and her pace settled into a soundless prowl of shadow through shadow. She could quiet herself down to nothing sometimes, imagining herself as some bodiless entity floating above the surface—another childhood fantasy: floating, streaming, flying far above it all.

Tonight Dunn's rooftop studio remained in the dark again, but this time, it was all about the garden. She swung over the edge and landed on the dormer where a light glowed behind the curtains. Pausing only long enough to check for signs of life inside and assuring herself the room was empty, she sprang for the drain. She had shimmied down two feet or so when she heard voices coming through an open window, or maybe a door, below—a man and a woman. She braced one foot against the wall and gripped the drain, tense and listening. A woman was crying softly, and was that Dunn's voice comforting her? Shit. Or was that old bastard urging some sweet young thing out of her clothes?

They had to be deep inside the house somewhere. Maybe the patio door was open. All she had to do was slip down to the garden, reach under the boxwood, hopefully find that damn flashlight, all without making a sound. And if she should happen to overhear what they were talking about, so be it.

In seconds she had reached the patio. Light and shadow shifted across the flagstones as she scanned the landscape, trying to see past the mutated silhouettes of upended equipment, bags of soil, shovels, and spades.

Interior light stroked the stones from an open glass door. Slipping closer, she peered in through a darkened conservatory to a kitchen where two people stood with their backs turned in a kind of kitchen/sitting room. One, obviously Dunn, had his arm wrapped around a woman—cropped gray hair, dark blue sweater, pencil skirt, black tights. She was weeping and, Jenna realized, so was he.

"Come, come, Fran. Let us pull ourselves together now. Nothing will undo what is done, in any event. We must carry on; *you* must carry on." Silence followed until Dunn added, "Let's step outside for a little air."

The woman choked a laugh. "Air? For you to smoke, more like it. Must you kill yourself? Oh, very well." She blew her nose and turned, leaving Jenna with a flash impression of a silver-haired woman, red-faced, swollen-eyed, before she dove behind a pile of bagged potting soil and pressed herself flat against the pavers.

Forcing her breath to steady, she listened to footsteps shuffling on the flagstones, hoping desperately that she didn't leave a footprint or anything to betray her presence.

Dunn coughed and exhaled.

"That's killing you," the woman remarked.

"Perhaps. Even so, it won't help terribly to stop now. The damage is done."

"Must you talk that way?" the woman said.

"Now, Fran, let us not pretend with one another. We know the inevitable. In any case, I do hope to see this garden completed so that you will inherit it fully imagined."

"Oh, just stop. I don't want to live in this house without you in it, and I have two places, as it is. I can't bear another loss, in any case, so you'd better get well and cease being so maudlin. If you took better care of yourself, we wouldn't be having this conversation. Anyway, I'm shivering out here. I will wait for you inside."

Shuffling footsteps, the sound of a screen sliding open followed by Dunn's shallow ragged breaths. Jenna lay facedown, eyes closed, wondering what the hell she was doing hugging the ground like a slug. This was such a bad idea.

At last she heard what sounded like a shoe grinding a cigarette into the pavers followed by retreating footsteps and the door sliding shut.

She let her shoulders sag only for an instant before springing to her feet and bolting for the drainpipe.

But she came to an abrupt halt two inches away. If she didn't bring that flashlight back, Aunt Clair would keep harping on about it. Damn. One more attempt. Creeping back to the hedge, she dropped onto her hands and knees, stuck her arm under the hedge, and fumble-felt the muddy earth for anything chrome. Nothing. She inched along in the muck, one arm still stuck under the hedge, and froze. Voices again, this time coming from the other side of Dunn's stone wall, in the alley.

"Don't push me," a woman cried.

"I'm not pushing, I'm steering," a man responded in a deep smoky baritone that was unmistakably Nicholas Hewitt's.

"I don't want to go to Bri's. I want to stay with you," the woman cried.

"Keep your bloody voice down, woman, and you're absolutely not staying with me. Brian will pour you into a cab and you can sail home after Fran douses you with coffee."

The woman sobbed. "Why are you doing this? You're such a bastard!"

A latch clicked, a gate scraped open. "Watch it. Stop, Zanna, you'll break your neck in those heels."

"What do you care? You ... just want to get rid of me."

Footsteps, the sound of something shattering against a wall. Jenna, pressed as far back into the hedge as she could go, picked out the shape of a woman hurling a pot followed by clots of mud. Nicholas was dodging the missiles and cursing.

"What is going on out here?" Dunn asked, stepping onto the patio. "Zanna, is that you? What are you doing, dear girl? Stop at once."

"Oh, Bri, he's such a bastard," the woman sobbed. "Such a fucking bastard!"

"Come, come. Look at you, covered in dirt. Step inside at once and we shall clean you up. I'll take over from here, Nick, old boy."

"Good, thanks again, Dunn," Nicholas said. "See if you can talk some sense into her."

Zanna's answer was to hurl a rock at Nicholas, who dove out of the gate, slamming it shut behind him.

More sobbing followed with Dunn murmuring comfort as the screen slid open. Jenna heard Zanna crying as her voice retreated inside. "I hate him, Fran!" before the door slammed shut.

Jenna squeezed her eyes closed and swore under her breath. Enough of this. The flashlight could stay wherever the hell it was until the sky froze over.

7

"Dunn was too busy consoling the women to pay much attention to anything awry in his yard." Jenna stood in the conservatory peeling off her muddy clothes while Aunt Clair sat in the kitchen doorway. Sheltered by the fence, Jenna felt perfectly safe from prying eyes, an irony which didn't escape her.

"Too busy consoling women, whatever do you mean, Jenna?" Aunt Clair said, gripping her armrests.

Jenna filled her aunt in on the night's events while tossing the soiled clothes into the corner and wrapping herself up in her uncle's old gardening shirt. "He had a woman with him—older, short pixie-style gray hair, very trim, about five foot three—I thought it might be his wife."

"Dunn is definitely not the marrying kind, of that I am quite certain," Aunt Clair said. "But who was this woman and why was she weeping?"

"I have no idea, and I was too busy pressing myself against the pavers to get much detail. They were very familiar with one another, I can tell you that much, and she was crying while Dunn comforted her."

"Comforting her, not causing the distress?"

"No, definitely comforting, not causing. This wasn't about his art, this was personal. They knew one another well and she was implying that he was ill—made references to 'the damage was done' and all that. She doesn't like him smoking, said it was killing him. Then, right after they returned to the house and I crawled out to get back to work, along came Nicholas Hewitt arguing with a woman named Zanna."

Aunt Clair pressed her hands together. "Fighting, you say? How terribly delicious, like an episode of *Coronation Street*. What did this Zanna look like?"

"I didn't really get to see her accept for a shape briefly crossing my peephole between the sacks. Very shapely, in a tight dress—tight everything—really high heels, which I heard Hewitt reference rather than actually saw. That's it. She was hysterical, drunk probably."

"What happened next?"

"Hewitt seemed to be foisting this drunken Zanna onto Dunn for him to manage. I sensed that Zanna and Nicholas may have been an item once, but that he wanted to end the affair and Zanna was devastated. Things obviously got messy and Nicholas could no longer handle her so he resolved to deliver her to his neighbor."

"He just passed her onto Dunn like, what, a troublesome child?"

"I know, right? Dunn appears to be a consoler of damsels in distress, as well as a painter of our sex totally distressed. Does any of this make sense?" She stepped towards the kitchen and Aunt Clair zoomed the chair backwards. "Clearly, everybody knows one another well down there—Zanna knows Fran, Hewitt knows Dunn, and all the combinations between."

"I put the kettle on," Aunt Clair said.

"Perfect, thanks. So, I'm hiding out behind bags of soil and finally the drama goes indoors and out of sight."

"Oh, but wouldn't you just love to eavesdrop to see how it all plays out?"

"Like who is Fran and how did this Zanna come to be such good friends with both Hewitt and Dunn?"

"Sounds so incestuous but, all that aside, could they be any link with your uncle? Nicholas and Zanna were using the lane, were they not?"

Jenna plucked the kettle from the counter and poured the boiling water into the teapot her aunt had readied. "Everybody uses that lane, Aunt Clair. I'm guessing Nicholas steered her out through his backyard —he has a sizable stone wall and equally impenetrable wooden gate— down the lane to Dunn's. They're all like one big unhappy family down there, and probably know one another from the art and theater circles. How does Uncle Dan relate to any of them? Could you get anyone less trendy?"

"No, my dear Dan was not one for the fast set. Your uncle knew Dunn, of that we are certain. He would never discuss him with me, however. He would just close in the way he did sometimes and say he was heading upstairs to read."

Jenna stared down at the teapot. There was still that Mac painting. A connection was there, if only she could find it. "That still doesn't mean that Dunn had anything to do with Uncle Dan's death."

She heard her aunt sigh and turned to look, seeing the tears in the older woman's eyes. If she lived to be a hundred, a vision of those blue eyes welling would be forever eyeprinted into her memory. "Yes, we all have our secrets, dear," her aunt said, "and I know your uncle had his, but I am afraid, so afraid. I fear that dark forces are afoot, something that killed my brother could be after us, too. It's this street, that lane. Too many secrets. You've glimpsed them. You feel them, too."

Jenna thought back to her night's roof crossing, of the things she'd heard or sensed. "We both have to be careful not to let our imaginations run away with us, as Uncle Dan warned, remember?"

"I remember." Her aunt sniffed, plucking a tissue from her pocket. "He was always the sensible one, your uncle. When I think of all the measures he took to protect me and yet, when he needed me most, where was I?"

"Stop it," Jenna said. "You are not responsible for his death. Don't think like that. No one could have known he'd hit his head, or whatever happened. And I'm sure there isn't some dark force coming after us." Except death itself, but that came to everyone eventually. That alley just unsettled her, that's all—the darkness, the shadowy chain of secrets linking house after house. There was a reason she always felt safer away from the ground.

"Did you bring back the torch, Jenna?" Her aunt sniffed.

Jenna picked up the teapot and began pouring the brew into the two Delft cups. "I couldn't find it. If I can't find it, presumably neither will anyone else. Forget about it. I'm not going back."

"I shan't be able to forget about it. Just knowing it's out there like a ticking bomb will be keeping me awake at night. It could bring Dunn straight back here."

"It's just a flashlight, Aunt Clair, not a nuclear explosive, and Dunn seems increasingly an unlikely suspect. Drink your tea."

8

Jenna couldn't sleep. For most of her adult life she had tried to walk the legal line—keep her impulses in check, be the good little adult her counselors advised her to become. Yet, all that had ever done was leave some part of her empty and craving. Her aunt was right: she constantly warred against herself and it was exhausting.

And now this. She needed answers, she craved detail. Everything she'd seen, sensed, or heard in these past few weeks chewed away at her like ravenous rats. What was Dunn's relationship with those women, with Nicholas Hewitt, with Uncle Dan? She longed to tune into their world, study them, plumb their connections, their feelings, their beliefs. God help her, but she loved to spy, and always had. As long as she didn't get too close.

Flipping to her side, she stared into the darkened wall, trying to switch off the brain-feed. Fresh eyeprints and those accompanying sounds—the short gray-haired woman, the dismal crack across Mrs. Chester's skylight, the wailing Zanna, the sobbing Fran—kept her wired. And Nicholas Hewitt, him especially.

She flopped onto her back. Deep inside her imagination's boudoir, Nicholas Hewitt had been her perfect man until now. Noble and kind, he was the type of man upon whom all women could depend, though his heart belonged to only one—her, or at least a fantasy version of her, who was no less an epitome of perfection. She always constructed romantic daydreams in cardboard. It was easier that way but now she'd have to source out another.

Squeezing her eyes shut, she started counting skylights in a perverse attempt to lull herself to sleep. Even here, she kept trying to peer into those picture windows instead of gazing past. What was wrong with her?

Sleep must have claimed her eventually because, hours later, she found sunlight streaming through her window. Something woke her. The sound of hacking in the garden somewhere. Jake again. Uncle Dan had a small cherry tree next to the fence. Was that due for execution today?

Mac needed his walk. She'd go for a run in the park, check in with Annette. Slowly, she dragged herself out of bed, showered quickly, and threw on her clothes, stepping into the hall just as Aunt Clair was about to zip past her door.

"Ah, there you are, Jenna dear. I was thinking to rouse you, though I did want you to sleep longer seeing as you were clearly growing over-tired. How are you feeling today?"

"Fine, thanks, Auntie. Where's Mac?" She missed the little terrier's enthusiastic morning greetings.

"Sara tied him out in the yard. She has fixed oatmeal for breakfast, just the way you and dear Dan loved it, with the brown sugar and cream, but before you go down, come see what I've done."

Jenna followed her, having no idea what to expect. Stepping into her aunt's room always took her aback, though she should be used to it by now. She rubbed her eyes in a show of disbelief. "Am I imagining things, or do you have even more technology than the last time I was here? You're like the Wizard of Oz."

"Oh, I do love thinking of myself as a wizard. So much better connotations than a witch." She cackled for effect. "There. In any case, I'm always trying new things, dear. I must learn as much as I can while I still have a brain to do so and the will to try. Technology serves as my legs, plane tickets, everything—a wizard indeed. Harry has been such a help, really opened up my world. Before he showed me how to use all these glorious tools, I felt so trapped. He's given me wings. With the Web, one can go anywhere, can't one?"

Jenna nodded. "Yes." Suddenly remembering something, she turned to her aunt. "Uncle Dan didn't approve, did he? I recall him telling me on the phone once that you'd bought a new something or other, and that he thought you were getting carried away."

"No, he did not approve of a room filled with 'blinking, whizzing things.' That's what he said, can you imagine? As if they blinked and whizzed all the time. He did not approve of me spending my allowance on technology, more like it—there's the crux of it."

"Your allowance? But you inherited a quarter of Father's fortune, just as he did. Three million pounds had gone to each of you, and though I disagreed with Father on most things, on his will, at least, we were in sync." She had received the other half, which she thought fair and she'd invested it very well, thanks to Uncle Dan's advice.

Aunt Clair turned the chair around to face Jenna. "Yes, I did, but it was decided that the monies should be kept for me in a kind of trust managed by your uncle, who was convinced I'd squander it all away. *Trust* is such an ironic word, considering there was a distinct lack of it towards me. Both my brothers believed I should be tended like a small child with monies doled out in tidy, bite-sized chunks. Your uncle always said that since I had everything I needed, why not let the funds accumulate interest? Your uncle was a maestro at money-making. He invested everything and netted quite a fortune in the end, as you know."

"I know. He did the same with my share and it's amassed nicely."

"But you have control over yours, correct?"

"Yes, as I assumed you did."

"Not so. In any case, both brothers were so good with pennies without ever realizing that true wealth comes from enjoying what you have."

"Father managed to enjoy plenty with his mistresses."

"Now, Jenna dear, don't go there again. Men are much weaker creatures than ourselves. We must forgive them their failings."

"A man who abandons his grieving daughter after his wife's death so he can take off with a younger version won't be getting forgiveness from me."

Aunt Clair shook her head. "Still so much rancor after all this time."

"Yes, and the psychologists Father sent me never managed to work the anger out of me."

"That's because you have to do the real work, not some doctor. Did you think they could just extract it like an abscessed tooth?"

Jenna grinned. "Now, there's a thought. Is there a doctor for that?"

"In any case, whatever criticism we levy at your father, George left us all rich. For that we should be grateful."

Yes, she could never fault her father in the fiscal department. What he couldn't provide in love, he doubled in lucre. Maybe that's the only way he knew how to show he cared, if he cared. Pathetic. In any case, she had attended the reading of her uncle's will and was relieved to know Aunt Clair had been left soundly rich. If that hadn't been the case, she had been prepared to divest part of her inheritance accordingly. But she'd had no idea about the allowance part.

"Enough of that. Come see what I have prepared." Aunt Clair zipped across the room to a long wooden trestle table that ran the whole length of her den. Between the printers, monitors, and hard drives, a large diagram lay anchored by paperweights. "I did up a schematic of the roofs—very rough, of course—on that new plotter Harry taught me to use. It does diagrams and such, but look, it renders the basic layout of the streets rather well, don't you think? I had to fudge the roofs with that shape-making app, however. They probably don't look quite so triangular, or do they?" She gazed up at Jenna.

"From the street the row looks like one long ridge with chimney walls between the segments."

"Our chimney sentries."

"Our chimney sentries," Jenna agreed. "But from the back it's far more complex and quirky—really fascinating actually. Everybody's renovated their units according to their unique ideas and interests. I never tire of gazing down into those worlds."

"How I wish I had a drone to gain a more accurate perspective, but that would hardly be acceptable in London, would it? Wait and I shall just check."

Jenna laughed. "Are you really going to Google that now?"

Aunt Clair stopped abruptly and swung around to face Jenna. "Perhaps later, then. But you're my drone in the meantime, aren't you, dear?"

"I'd rather not think of myself as a living robot, if you don't mind. I mean, where are you going to find spare parts?"

"Oh, you tease." Her aunt chuckled. "I always wanted to go where you go, do what you do, see the world from a different perspective. Imagining myself up there with you helps."

As if Jenna didn't know that, hadn't known it all her life. "But why this diagram?"

"For an added visual, of course. I thought it could imagine myself with you more fully. I am hoping you will relent and make another trip to glean more information, if not locate that troublesome torch. I know you must be as thrilled by the eyeprints and eavesdroppings you brought home last night as am I. It is like some television episode to which we have been exposed now wrenched from our gaze before we know the outcome. It is unbearable. You must go back up, Jenna."

Jenna shook her head. "Since I've returned I'm like some recovering alcoholic being dangled one drink after another."

"Oh." Aunt Clair gazed up at Jenna and shook her head, her eyes wide. "What a disturbing analogy. You are no addict, and this is just a harmless bit of investigation."

"It isn't and you know it. We're both indulging in the same behavior that drove Uncle Dan crazy and almost got me sent to reform school."

"Dan would never have allowed that to happen, nor would have your father in the end, you know that. He and that constable he brought with him that night were only saber rattling."

And yet those sabers managed wounded still. It had been one more betrayal heaped on more of the same. "Father probably paid him for those long diatribes he breathed in my direction."

"Which were nothing but fumes of puffery."

"Inconsequential dragon-farts."

"All heat but no substance," Aunt Clair said with a nod. "You must forget all that, my dear, and move on."

"I have moved on, but I *was* sent to London so that the constant care of my uncle and aunt would somehow rid me of all these wayward tendencies." Jenna sighed and gazed towards the window. "We know how well that worked. It's just such a shock to find them still so alive inside me."

Aunt Clair sighed. "You cannot simply banish your true nature without dire consequences. Yes, I contributed to your escapist passion, but it kept you alive in all the ways that mattered. And George finally realized that you'd just keep breaking out of all those boarding schools he insisted on sending you to after your mother's death. I always told him that imprisoning a broken heart would never keep it caged, and you kept proving me right time after time. You were incorrigible. How I loved your spirit, totally undaunted, always climbing up and away. In the end, I was so relieved when he finally agreed to dispatch you to us. No one could have loved you more, Jenna."

Jenna gazed down at her aunt's cherubic face. "And yet why am I still trying to escape?"

"Maybe you have yet to come to terms with your wounds?"

"But it's easier just to forget them rather than to dwell." Jenna wiped away a tear. Again? This constant slobbering was getting annoying.

"I fear the things we avoid always come back to bite us in the end."

"Yeah, don't they?" Suddenly Jenna gave in to the overwhelming urge to fall to her knees and place her head in her aunt's lap, as she once did as a child. She *was* regressing. Once there, she focused on the tiny flecks in her aunt's housedress while her aunt stroked her hair. "You know, since my childhood days, I have been trying to get beyond my past. For instance, I'm about to take a prestigious job of a big publishing enterprise. I figure that's progress."

"Really? You think that sitting all day in an office somewhere is progress just because you're the boss of something? If I could do what you do, I wouldn't be stuck at a desk."

Jenna wiped her eyes on her aunt's cotton skirt. "You're just trying to get me aloft again."

"Guilty as charged, but my message is true, regardless. Embrace who you are. You're hurting no one but yourself by fighting your nature."

Jenna looked up at her aunt and reached for her hand. "You never give up, do you?"

"I never give up on you, no, never."

"You're manipulating me into more roofing."

Aunt Clair smiled sadly and squeezed Jenna's hand. "Maybe I am but what of it? You are intent on leaving me, no matter what I do, so this will be the last time."

"Make this the very last time you goad me—promise." They always kept their promises to one another.

"I promise. At least get that blasted torch and then I shall rest easier—not perfectly, mind you, but easier—and find out more about this Dunn. For all we know, he may be readying to kill again."

Jenna climbed to her feet. "I doubt that. And how will this map help again?" It was just a means to change the subject.

"It serves as a reference only. See here, dear." Her aunt swung her chair around and pointed to a thick felt-tip line that cut a red path out the garden gate, a short way down the lane and through Mrs. Chester's yard to her potting shed and from there up the roof to Brian Dunn's and back. "I had rather wanted to make the renderings more realistic but haven't the skill, though you've described them in great detail. I've asked Harry to help with the structural nuances. I've worked out your route, you see? I merely used the marker in the interests of time. And see that blue X there?"

"Where Uncle Dan died." If possible, the symbol looked even more ominous than the real thing.

Aunt Clair shook her head. "Sadly, yes."

"I make a moving mental plan when I go. There are usually details like handholds and foot braces that can only be found in the moment. It's hard to explain."

Aunt Clair gazed up at her. "But isn't this just a little useful?"

Jenna leaned forward. "Plans change so quickly when you're on the move. Maybe the landscape alters slightly, something you notice only when you're already off the ground. And there's so much construction going on this street it's like half the houses are in a constant state of flux, as are its inhabitants."

"A good metaphor for life, don't you think?"

Jenna smiled. "I've often thought so."

"That's why I thought Mrs. Chester's the safest route. She's not going anywhere, that I know of."

"But her place is falling apart. Wish I could figure out how to send her some money without her knowing."

"That's very generous of you, Jenna. Let me think on that. I'm sure I can help. In the meantime, hers is still the quickest way up, surely?"

Jenna studied the map more carefully, her gaze tracing on the red line. "I'd rather avoid Mrs. Chester's yard."

"But no one can see you from the alley or the street, and I'm certain Mrs. Chester won't notice should a troop of elephants tramp through her yard. She goes to bed at nine o'clock and she removes her hearing aid long before then."

"I have another way. The last two times I climbed the trellis to the balcony on our corner wall I exited through our garden, then rounded the corner to the side of the house, and was up the trellis to the roof in a matter of minutes. I know it's risky being exposed to traffic like that, but it's not for long. I'll hide in the shrubs until the coast is clear and then spring for it."

Aunt Clair paled.

"What is it?"

"Jake suggested I cut a trellis down because he claimed it was damaging the brickwork. He felled it just this morning. Oh, Jenna, had I known, I would never have let him touch it!"

"The trellis is gone, too? But, Aunt Clair, Uncle Dan had that built for his rambling roses."

"I'm sorry, dear. I've never seen it. I didn't realize it meant that much to you. Jake has such a lovely plan for the front yard, too. Would you like to see it?"

"No!" Jenna pressed a hand to her temple, struggling for calm.

"Now you're upset. Forgive me."

Jenna squeezed her aunt's shoulder. "It's okay, Aunt Clair. I'll get over it. It's just that seeing all these changes around here hurts. It feels like a piece of Uncle Dan is being uprooted and cast aside."

Aunt Clair began to cry. "I know, I know. I am sorry, but they say that the best way to move ahead is to refashion your environment for one's new life. That's all I'm trying to do, Jenna. It helps, it does. Seeing all these plans makes me think that there can be a future without him, that perhaps I can be happy again. That's all I want, Jenna. Won't you stay here with me and help?"

Jenna bent down and gave her aunt a big hug. "I can't, Auntie. I know this is hard but it will get easier, and if renovation helps you to move ahead, then you must do it," she whispered into the woman's shoulder, her eyes burning with tears. "I love you. It'll be okay."

"I love you, too, dear." The older woman sniffed.

They cried quietly before Jenna pulled herself back together. "Well, I'll go have some breakfast and take Mac out for his walk."

"All right, dear."

She left her aunt weeping quietly and headed downstairs. She was such a heartless bitch. Why couldn't she stay here and take care of her aunt? Why did that, of all things, seem so insurmountable? *Because you've never made real sacrifices for love*, she heard one counselor, Dr. Randal, say in her head. No, she hadn't. She admitted it to herself again and again, but it didn't change a thing. She still needed to return home, there was no question about that.

In the kitchen downstairs, Sara seemed unusually pleasant as she served the oatmeal. In fact, with Aunt Clair out of earshot, the woman was primed to talk.

"The basement is a mess. Have you ever been down there?"

"No, I haven't." And she meant never. Basements were the last place she wanted to go. Even as a child, she imagined that they harbored evil things like bogeymen and demon spawn.

"Well, you should take a look and ask your aunt to stop permitting the workmen to store tools down there. I almost tripped getting the preserves yesterday."

"Have you mentioned this to her?" Jenna asked while scooping up a bit of brown sugar.

"I may as well talk into the wind, for all the good it does me."

Listening to Sara discuss her aunt when she wasn't in the room wasn't right. "This oatmeal is delicious. Thanks for making this for me, Sara. I forgot how yummy oatmeal is," she said as she scraped her bowl clean.

"It was your uncle's favorite. I would have given you a second helping had that hoodlum out there not devoured the rest."

"Hoodlum?" Jenna cast a quick look towards the yard but the gardener wasn't in view.

"Did you see those tattoos? If he's not up to no good, I don't know what is."

"Skulls are a fashion statement these days," Jenna pointed out. "You can even get undies covered in them."

"Ridiculous. Your uncle didn't approve of those two—no, he did not. He let that one mow the lawn one day when he had the flu, but said he'd rather grow a meadow than let him have another go, and that Harry—" Sara leaned closer to Jenna "—mind you don't let your aunt fall for that phony-baloney charm. He's a snake in a puppy's clothing, that one."

"It's not like he's going to pilfer the silverware or bite you on the way out the door, Sara. He's only giving Aunt Clair technology lessons, which she enjoys so much. It takes her mind off things, that's all. Everybody handles loss in their own way. She's working through her grief," Jenna said, sipping her tea.

"Working through her money, more like it."

"She's trying to make a new life for herself. Where do Jake and Harry-Henry live, anyway?" Jenna asked, changing the subject.

"I have no idea. I heard Harry say he lived off Kings Road and the other one in Camden. Do you want me to freshen your tea?"

"I'm fine, thank you." Jenna returned her gaze to the wounded yard. Though Jake wasn't in sight, the steady thunk-thunk of shovel hitting earth continued. Mac sat at attention beyond the glass door.

"I can't stand the sound of all that digging and hacking," Sara muttered, as if sensing her thoughts.

"I'm sure it's going to look gorgeous once finished."

"It looked gorgeous before, if you ask me. In any case, I will just tidy up and be gone. I've prepared lasagna for supper tonight."

"Another one of Uncle Dan's favorites," Jenna remarked.

The woman paused and gazed back at Jenna. "As you say, we work through our grief in our own way."

After she left, Jenna fastened the lead onto Mac's squirming little body and dashed out the front door, grateful to feel the sun on her face. She wondered whether the new garden truly would entice her aunt to leave the house and enter the yard. She'd always longed for her aunt to feel the sun kissing her face and sense new growth pushing up from the earth. How could she stand being prisoner for all these years?

The sight of Jake attacking the sod in the front yard brought her to a halt. She watched as he axed the earth in long strong strokes. Sweat drenched his tee-shirt as he focused on his task with a fierce determination while his checked shirt snagged on the fence flapped idly in the breeze.

"Was it really necessary to cut down that trellis?" she called.

The young man shot around, the loam-ladened shovel suspended midair. "What? Pardon, Ms. Elson?"

"It's Jenna." She stepped forward. "You told my aunt that the trellis should be cut down for some reason, but it was perfectly sound, and those roses were so robust and glorious. Uncle Dan loved them." Shit, she couldn't let herself cry again.

Staking the shovel into the dirt, Jake straightened and wiped his forehead. Oh, yes, he was well-built, all right. "Come, I'll show you. Mind your step."

He led her around a series of freshly dug holes and the dying remains of the vining roses to the side of the house. There, a ladder leaned beside a ragged outline where the trellis had once attached to the brick. At the base, bits of brick and crumbling mortar had been raked into heaps along with splintered wood and shredded plant, the red petals caught in the debris like drying blood.

"See how the shrub was destroying the brick?" He pointed up to the discolored mortar. "It was growing up past the trellis, and those vines are the worst. Grows thick trunks that dig little suckers into the mortar. Can pry the bricks apart and ruin your house, if you're not careful. I advised your aunt to cut it down for the good of the structure. Sorry it upset you. I suggested a little arched arbor to give height and maybe grow a cluster of hollyhocks and clematis."

Jenna was about to remark on the English cottage garden concept running contrary to her aunt's current exotic bent, but decided against it. The more she studied the brick, the more she realized that her own weight had probably contributed to the damage. In fact, she was the true culprit, not the roses. Best just leave it. "Right, well, I'll miss it, that's all." She turned to go.

"Wait, is there anything more I can do to help?" he asked.

She turned around. "What do you mean?"

"Besides gardening. Take out the trash, paint the inside, fix the boiler, that kind of thing. The gardening will last to the end of the summer but I'll be free after that."

"I'm sure if my aunt thinks of anything, she'll let you know." With that, she tugged Mac's lead and dashed to the sidewalk, hanging a right towards the bottom end of Marlytree. The last thing she wanted was to chat with him. Besides, she had to suss out another route before nightfall.

She breezed along the street, attempting to appear like any dog walker with no particular agenda. Whenever Mac paused to sniff, her gaze wandered up to the houses. Picking out climbing routes had almost become an unconscious act these days. She assessed every roof according to routes up and down, mentally testing hand- and footholds, studying railings and sills for stability.

As a child she'd done something similar, only then she added hiding places. Escape and sanctuary had become her predominant focus. At the boarding school, she'd shimmy out the window and slide along the ledge to the first dormer and then reach the roof that way. That Gothic Revivalist architecture was perfect for escape artists. That is, until they started nailing her bedroom window shut.

But Marlytree Terrace was where she really grew up. Most of the older residents had gone now, Mrs. Chester and Mr. Rambolt being the only ones remaining from those days.

Nobody knew the woman walking her uncle's dog today had once been a public nuisance, even prompting one neighbor to call the police. And she would never forget that stern constable her father delivered, or the way he glared down at her, his face frozen in some seizure of disapproval. "Only one place for bad little girls like her," he had said as if she weren't standing right in front of him. "That's reform school."

Like that had deterred her any. All she wanted to do after that was climb higher and farther, leaving her Uncle Dan scrambling for ways to keep her grounded, in the truest meaning of the word.

All the angst she caused her uncle. She should have been smarter than that, known that she was just acting out. Eventually she grew up —learned to play well (better) with others, obey rules and regulations —but the longing for the sanctuary of remote places never quite left her. So she escaped to international destinations as a career choice.

She reached the end of Marlytree where the street ended on Pembroke Lane making up the bottom line of the square. Here Nicholas Hewitt's house claimed its dominion. From the sidewalk, the peak of his glass skylight could be just seen glittering behind the chimney soldiers. But it wasn't the roof that interested her today so much as how to get up there. Since she refused to use the alley, the end units were the best way to get vertical. Unlike her aunt's gardener, Nicholas Hewitt's had no compunction about using climbing vines.

A tall stone wall edged the Hewitt property along the Pembroke side and carried around to the alley to enclose his garden. The wall looked easy enough to scale with its scrumble of holly, but better still, she could see multiple arteries of hardy ivy clambering over the brick around his bow window and the dormer above.

Without being too obvious, she encouraged Mac to sniff around the wall while she tried peering towards the eaves. She saw her highway to the stars in an instant: this ivy crawled up his wall with unlicensed abandon. It was a British thing, she decided. Uncle Dan loved them, Nicholas Hewitt obviously loved them, too, and now, by default, so did she. Jenna Elson: defender of the climbers. How fitting.

9

"But it had been such a lovely afternoon," Jenna remarked as she stared out the conservatory window, already dressed for the night's excursion. At last the boys had gone so she could finally talk to her aunt freely. "Now look at it."

She turned. Aunt Clair was peering down at her tablet screen. "They are predicting rain, quite a lot of it. It's sweeping in from the North Sea with high winds expected. Oh, no, you mustn't go roofing tonight, Jenna."

"I'll leave early. I have everything mapped out in my mind, and I'll just get back before the deluge." Besides, bad weather never troubled her. Weather was just weather. She'd slept outside on the sides of mountains while thunderstorms raged. "When I get back, I'm hereby grounding myself."

"Which sounds like punishment."

"It's called reality. It's the world in which I work."

"It's called prison, but I promised not to prod you further. It is your life, your decision. But, Jenna, you were never meant to live in the world of meetings and deadlines. Your uncle told me stories of what those boardrooms were like. I can't picture you constantly negotiating. Isn't that a prison of another kind?"

"It's about to become my job," Jenna said.

"You're a writer, that's your job. You can write anywhere, anytime. You were never meant to be shackled, Jenna. Picturing you inside one of those dreadful office buildings ... oh, my, I keep thinking that one day you'll escape some tedious meeting where everybody drones on and on, break a window, and spring for the roof."

Jenna snorted. "And drop forty-four floors to the concrete below. I work in a skyscraper, remember."

"My point exactly. Mind my words, Jenna: you won't be happy just because you've been endorsed by some fancy title. You don't need that kind of validation."

"Let's stop taking about it," Jenna said, growing annoyed. Her aunt had never encouraged her to get ahead. Why was that?

"Very well, then. So, will you take me with you tonight, this one last time?"

Jenna shook her head. "This will be a quick up and back to Dunn's."

"But you say this will be your last episode," Aunt Clair said, her voice verging on a whine.

"I'm going to get that flashlight and, hopefully, more information, period. No detours, no lingering, no *peeping*."

"But you'll take your phone?"

"Yes, of course, but I won't be calling you, and don't, whatever you do, call me. Promise."

Aunt Clair gazed at Jenna for a moment before sighing. "Very well, I promise. You need to do this your way, but if you get held up for any reason, you must at least let me know there's been a delay so I won't worry."

"Of course." Totally impractical but she had to agree.

Two hours later, Jenna slipped out the front door. Marlytree Terrace hung softened by mist as if all street life had seeped into the night. Lights still shone in many of the windows all around the square while others sat in the dark waiting for their owners to return. It was that time of day when supper either drove people indoors to their houses or into pubs and restaurants, leaving the streets mostly deserted.

And here came bad little Jenna off on another excursion, her last, she reminded herself as she crossed the street and strolled the full length of the communal park's wrought-iron fence.

A man with a briefcase hurried past, eyes to the pavement. She kept her gaze averted, too. The urbanite's privacy screen suited her, that night especially. Without Mac, she felt conspicuous. When she reached the corner of Pembroke, she crossed the street to Nicholas Hewitt's brick wall, noting the absence of light in his windows. Now all she had to do was bolt over his wall into his yard and then crawl up the side of his house without being seen.

Pressing into the shadows, she squeezed her eyes shut and forced her pounding heart to steady. What had seemed so easy in the light of day now struck her as insurmountable. But this was her last big challenge before forcing herself to land for good, so she'd bloody well do it right.

Scaling the wall with its thicket of holly seemed easy enough, but what about the rest? Hewitt probably had an excellent alarm system installed—motion detectors, security camera, the whole deal. She'd had it all figured out a few hours ago but now everything struck her as incredibly stupid.

She continued breathing deeply, calming her mind with facts: motion detectors would likely be on the inside of buildings or outside around doors and ground-level windows.

She focused on one thick river of ivy streaming right up to the eaves. It looked steady and well-supported by the branching tributaries. That would be her route. If she climbed quickly enough, her weight would be evenly distributed.

Footsteps suddenly approached from the other end of the street. Springing for the holly, she gripped its trunk while simultaneously levering her feet against the wall. In seconds she was springing over the top and landing on all fours on the grass on the other side, a six-foot drop. A motion light blasted, but by the time she'd flattened herself against the house, it had switched off.

One, two, three ... she counted the seconds waiting for an alarm, pacing the moments with the beat of her heart. All clear. She was vaguely aware of the daffodils glowing softly in the streetlights. Swinging around, she began hauling herself upwards through the ivy, relishing the effort, the way the blood sang in her veins.

Climbing was half strategy, half gut-searing guesswork partnered with instinct and reflex. Mostly you didn't know where the next hand-hold would come, when your foot might slip and leave you hanging. Mistakes could be deadly, and yet she loved it—God she loved it. This urban thrill was so tantalizing. This was real; this was electricity pouring through her body in a surge of adrenaline, urging her higher and higher.

Her last climb had to be a good one.

Almost to the top now but she couldn't afford to relax. The faster a foot left one brace and landed on the next, the safer—there was power in momentum—and she was still visible from the street. If anyone chanced to look over Hewitt's wall to the side of his house, they just might catch the movement of a black-on-black inching through the shadows. Everyone had cell phones. The police could be called in seconds.

And then she heard the footsteps directly below as if she'd summoned them with her thoughts. She froze, holding her breath.

She expected the clickety-click of the high heels to walk briskly by but these stopped just beyond Hewitt's wrought-iron gate. Jenna couldn't see their owner but her curses rang clearly enough. And jingling sounds, as if the woman was riffling through her purse. Something clattered to the sidewalk and was quickly retrieved.

Perspiration dampened Jenna's back and her muscles ached as she waited, her gloves gripping the ivy's trunk. She felt the plant shifting beneath her. Seconds burned into minutes. If she didn't move soon, the whole thing might rip away from the brick.

What was the woman doing down there? At last she heard, "Got you," followed by what sounded like metal on metal. Now she was rattling the gate. "You changed the lock? Are you bloody kidding me? Open up, you bastard!"

Oh, God, it was Zanna! Jenna hung there sweating while the branch beneath her left foot loosened. At last those heels below scurried away, punctuating the concrete like exclamation points between the curses. Jenna began climbing again. Gripping the edge of the bow window's sill, she hoisted herself up to the ornamental balcony, the house being the mirror image of her aunt's. Over and up the edge of balcony to the eaves and she was aloft at last.

For a moment, she just lay facedown on the roofspine, her arms dancing on either side of the peak. Slowly, she lifted her head and gazed across the roof of Nicholas Hewitt's double unit. It had a surprising number of extensions from this angle—terraces and God knew what else.

She had to climb over his two chimney stands to reach Dunn's and had no idea what lay between, other than that enormous skylight. Some things can't be seen properly from the ground. This roof was different.

And the clouds were thickening overhead. One glance skyward confirmed the worst: a roiling black mass hurled in from over the Thames.

Shifting to a crouch, she took a deep breath, and sprung towards the first chimney wall. She was familiar with this, every wall being exactly the same, variations of chimney pots not withstanding—six chimneys per house. She knew how to lightly swing up and over, landing with practiced stealth on the other side, how to balance her weight evenly between two feet as she scuttled along the roof spine.

No one would hear her unless they had their ear up against the topmost ceiling. She could be fast; she *would* be fast. If all went well, she'd make up for lost time and be over at Dunn's in ten minutes, fifteen at the most.

Landing on the second roof, she turned to face the skylight as the first drops began hitting her face. All she could see between herself and that glass confection were tarpaulins, piles of slate, and wood balanced on a network of scaffolding. Shit—the renovations! For the first time, she didn't know how to proceed. She couldn't see clearly and had no choice but to guess her footing in the half-light, allowing instinct to guide her along a scaffold like a tightrope walker.

It began raining harder. She drew a deep breath as sheets of water hurled down from the open skies. An upstart torrent streamed under her feet as she balanced, one foot before the other, inching towards the skylight.

And when the skylight suddenly burst into light ahead, startling her so much that one foot slipped and down she fell, whamming into a pile of lumber. She scrabbled for a handhold as she slid, only just managing to grab the top of the dormer as she toppled over the edge, the scaffold crashing down around her head. It was all she could do to protect her skull and maintain her grip at the same time.

Shaken, she clung there for a few seconds before grappling for a foothold and pulling herself back up. There she sat shivering, wedged against the dormer window. But she had to move. Turning, she grabbed the roof edge and hoisted herself to the main roof, coughing as water sluiced into her mouth. Blinking furiously, she peered over at mounds of black tarp as she crawled her way through the scaffold wreckage.

Everywhere there were tools and materials under plastic tents as the rain hurled against every surface. It was impossible to see. Desperate for cover, she crawled under the nearest tarpaulin and huddled there with a stack of tiles.

Someone had to have heard that crash. And then a belch of thunder ripped overhead and she knew any noise could be excused away as part of the storm. She didn't know whether to laugh or cry.

Drenched to the bone and stupid beyond measure, that was her. A flashlight wasn't worth this. But it wasn't about the flashlight and she knew it: she'd made the decision to go roofing tonight. She wanted to, she craved it. Who was she kidding? Imagine the editor of *Wanderlust International* caught huddling on a London roof? She waited and waited, cursing herself until, at last, the downpour eased.

She lifted the tarp and stared out. The glowing glass structure rose before her like a cruise ship sailing through the night sea, all interlocking slices of glass amid sheets of clear plastic. Her breath caught. Hewitt was home.

She pulled back, heart pounding. And she was way over her time budget. Soon Aunt Clair would panic and then what? She had to move. Crawling out from under the tarp, she hesitated at the edge of the skylight. Somehow she must navigate around the glass structure and reach the next peak without being seen.

With excruciating care, she inched along the edge of the skylight, the first half only a wall of stretched plastic. She may as well be on the deck of the *Titanic* tiptoeing around a crystal iceberg. Shit, not the *Titanic*, she amended, not something about to sink, for God's sake. Eyes straight ahead, she kicked bits of debris from her path. She could damn well do this.

Halfway along, she chanced to look over and down. Big mistake. Through a pane of rain-speckled glass lay Hewitt's world. A long tiled room. Books lining the walls. A suit of armor that may have hailed from his *Sir Lancelot and Guinevere* film standing at attention beside a leather couch and two companion chairs. Potted palms spreading their canopies amid the furnishings like exotic sprouts. He'd created a library conservatory in this long halogen-pooled hall, decorating it equally with bits of whimsy and British tradition.

She couldn't move. It was all so warm and inviting down there while she balanced in a cold and brutal world, so absolutely excluded, a woman on the outside looking in. She hesitated, sucking up every detail, as if this vision alone would help her plunge back into the night.

When the actor strolled into view holding a book in one hand and a wineglass in the other, Jenna forgot to breathe. He was reading aloud. His voice, projecting liquid vowels and crisp consonants through the plastic barrier, seemed to reverberate through her blood. She couldn't focus on the words, all that mattered was that voice.

And then a thundering knock reverberated through the house. Jenna tensed, watching as Hewitt disappeared, his footsteps clopping towards the back of the house. Carefully, she lowered herself down until she had stretched lengthwise beside the window—madness but she didn't care.

"Hello?" she heard Nicholas's voice boom.

A woman replied. "I've been wandering around the outside of this bloody house for ages. I had to go through that stupid effing alley! Did you disconnect your effing doorbell or something?" *Zanna*.

"I did. The ringing was driving me crazy," Nicholas said. "Go away,

Suzanna. I told you I've had enough. No, don't do that. I'm serious. This has got to end."

Suzanna? Sobbing followed by a desperate wailing. "You're just like all the rest!" she cried. "I thought you were different. I thought you loved me!"

"I never told you that, not for one bloody minute! We agreed to have a mutually entertaining fling, no more. I made no pretense about our relationship. You've twisted and poisoned everything once again. Go to Dunn's. Stop that!"

"He's in the bloody hospital! I sent a message, which you probably deleted!"

"Is he going to be all right? Look, I'll call you a cab."

"I don't want a fucking cab! I want you."

"I'm not up for grabs, Suzanna. How many times do I have to tell you?"

Something crashed against the tiles. Jenna risked leaning further over to see what had fallen, but by then, Nicholas had Suzanna by the wrists and she was kicking out at him.

"You're bloody going to leave me alone. I've had it!" He was dragging her down the hall, her legs flailing all over the place, kicking at furniture, things crashing to the floor. The door opened and slammed shut out of view. Fists began pounding the door with ferocity.

Footsteps returned. Jenna backed away, then eased forward again to stare down transfixed as the actor sank into the leather divan directly below her perch. He sat with his head buried in his hands, the long fingers digging into the curly hair, his broad shoulders hunched over his knees. She pitied him, she pitied Zanna. Another two humans unable to find happiness together. Unanchored, fractured.

God, she had to leave. Now. But she couldn't. She didn't. It was too risky. He was right below.

He just sat and sat, while she just waited and waited, while the fists pounded and pounded until they suddenly stopped. The pattering rain drenched the silence as another sky-spigot loosened. Her cell phone rang in her breast pocket. Shit. She forgot to put it on vibrate. Fumbling for the phone, Jenna hoisted herself to her feet. God, she had to shut that thing up!

But she lost her balance, twisting around in time to see a stack of bricks hurling down on her as she tipped sideways.

Her phone jettisoned from her hand, tumbling onto the glass along with bricks and tiles, and her going down with it all.

She watched the skylight rise to meet her as if in slow motion, heard the plastic barrier rip, glass shatter, and saw Hewitt's shocked face as she plummeted towards him.

❧ 10 ❧

Overhead, a jagged patch of night sky. Rain spattering her face. Pain battering her skull. A phone ringing from somewhere ...

It hurt to move but she had to. Couldn't stay here, had to get going. She forced herself to roll onto her side. A toppled bookshelf and a floor lamp lay strewn across a mess of broken tiles and shattered glass. Memory seeped in like ink to water, constantly moving, clarifying nothing.

She'd fallen, she remembered that much, but where or why? Attempting to stand walloped her with such venom that down she went again.

And that phone ringing ... was her phone. It stopped once, went to messages, and launched again.

Pushing through the agony, she propped herself onto her knees, and stared down a long corridor. Images fractured her brain. Armor sprawled in segmented pieces across the floor, the decapitated helmet lying on its side. Red splattered everything, including the edge of her silver-cased cell phone visible under a crust of broken glass. She reached out and plucked it up with still-gloved fingers. "H-hello?"

"Get out of there right now."

"What?"

"Jenna, you must leave immediately, do you hear me?"

"Aunt Clair?" Jenna struggled to think. "I fell?"

"That's why you must leave immediately, do you hear me? Now!"

Something groaned behind her. Jenna slowly turned. A man lay sprawled on his back.

"You're hurt. Get out of there at once."

Jenna stared.

"Answer me!"

"Oh, God, no." Jenna dropped the phone. Crawling forward, she pulled away the breastplate that lay against his chest. It landed with a clatter beside a heraldic shield and a pair of gauntlets. An axe lay not more than five feet away beside a clear footprint and a pool of red. *Blood.* There was so much blood!

What the hell? Jenna stared from the axe to the blood to the footprint and back to Nicholas Hewitt—click, click, her brain capturing each image in excruciating detail. She picked up the phone. "Call an ambulance to Hewitt's house. There's been an accident or something. Do it now."

"No, wait, I—"

"Now, Aunt Clair!" Jenna dropped the phone again. With one hand pressed over her mouth, she fixed on Nicholas Hewitt. Blood drooled from his right temple. The bloodied set pieces scattered in ways that made no sense. She looked up towards the ruined skylight but the pain crashed into her skull with sickening venom. Forget that.

She crawled through the broken glass and leaned over the man. His eyes were closed but his breathing steady. Not dead, thank God. There was that gash on his temple but no other injuries that she could see, certainly nothing to account for all that blood. Unless it was hers. No, that didn't add up, either. God, she felt so sick.

Then he blinked and stared up into her face.

"Lay still. I'll get help." Jenna lurched to her feet and staggered down the hall. She'd call an ambulance, do something, but her legs buckled and she toppled against a wall. She needed a phone. Wait, she had a phone. Turning, she limped back. Stumbling, she thought she caught movement out of the corner of her eye, just a blacker smudge moving in the shadows of an adjoining room.

"Hello? Anyone there?" No answer. She was shivering uncontrollably. Lurching back to the mess, she snatched up the cell.

"Aunt Clair?"

"Don't hang up on me," her aunt's voice demanded.

"Call an ambulance. And the police," Jenna ordered. "There's blood on the floor, everywhere. Too much. My head feels ... cracked open. I can't remember ... the emergency number here." She shivered uncontrollably. "It's not 911 ... what?"

"You're hurt. You must leave immediately!"

Suddenly Jenna's legs gave out and her knees crashed down on a pile of broken glass. "Nicholas is hurt ... I'm hurt. Call ... the ambulance. Call them now. I fell on him. I hurt him ... badly."

"We'll talk. The police are on their way. You have to leave before they get there."

"I can't leave him like this!"

Nicholas groaned and rolled to his side, eyes closed.

Aunt's voice kept demanding. "What can you do for him? Nothing! You can't be caught inside that house, do you hear me? Come home immediately! Head for the alley!"

Jenna bent over amid wave after wave of dizziness. She was going to vomit, faint. Brain pummeling her skull, she lurched to her feet, shoved the phone into her pocket, and stumbled down the hall towards the back of the house. French doors led into what she hoped would be the kitchen, and the kitchen lead to the conservatory and garden beyond. Stainless-steel surfaces and granite countertops blurred past as she pushed through to the conservatory door.

Outside, she retched violently into the bushes. Stumbling away, the world heaved around her, a bucking deck of a storm-battered ship. Her skull was morphing into a brutal creature that pounded thoughts from her mind while racking her body with agony.

She staggered into the service lane, a tunnel of darkness thickened by rain. She had to get home. Rain stormed inside and out. Everything tipped and heaved. Footsteps pounded the earth behind her. She tried picking up her pace but her limbs dragged her to the earth.

"Leave me alone!" she screamed. And then a sudden flash of pain followed by blackness.

11

"Jenna, can you hear me?"

Someone squeezed her hand. A voice sounded a thousand miles away.

"Jenna?"

She forced her eyes open.

"Oh, Jenna, I've been so worried." Aunt Clair.

"Where ... am I?"

"In your bed. You've suffered a head injury. The doctor says you were very lucky."

"Everything ... is so ... dark."

"The curtains are drawn, dear. The doctor says to shield you from light." Her aunt sniffed. "I thought I'd lost you. I thought he'd killed you, too."

"Who?" Jenna whispered.

"Why, Dunn, of course."

Jenna struggled for a coherent thought. Eyeprints pushed their way to the surface but couldn't quite reach her brain. "I fell," she said, blinking up into the shadowy room.

"You did."

"But I don't remember ... much."

"No, of course not. It's the concussion. The doctor said you'd likely have some amnesia."

She realized the curtains were drawn, soaking the room in a green light. It's as if she'd awoken at the bottom of the ocean and needed to paddle her limbs against the weight of the water just to sit up.

"No, no, you must rest, dear. Lie back down. There, there. Here, take a sip of this." Her aunt passed her a glass with a straw, which Jenna sipped.

"How long ... have I been like this?" she asked after she'd had her fill.

"Two days. You were feverish for part of the time."

"Two days?" Jenna pushed herself to sitting, alarms jangling while discordant eyeprints crashed against her skull. She struggled to see them clearly. "That long?" And then the first clear image hit: a man's face looking up at her in shock. "Oh, my God, I fell on top of Nicholas Hewitt!"

"Now, calm down. You've had a nasty fall. Lie back."

"I fell on top of Nicholas Hewitt!"

"Perhaps, but you managed to get home before you collapsed. Nobody caught you."

"What? What about Nicholas?" The torrent of lurid images banged around inside head, hellishly brutal. "There was blood everywhere. I— I saw him lying there. I thought I'd killed him. So much blood."

"You are not remembering things clearly. Brain injuries are like that. I was just reading all about them on the Net. Jenna, do lie back down and try to rest."

"It wasn't a dream."

"Not a dream, perhaps, but things must certainly be distorted."

"I crashed into somebody's roof, for God's sake! I fell on top of someone and hurt them!"

"Dr. Munjamba said there must be no agitation, no sudden movements. Now lie back down at once."

Jenna did as she was bid, but only because she simply could not stay upright a moment longer. Easing herself back against the pillows, she waited for the brain-throb to lessen. "Did you call the police and the ambulance?"

"Nicholas Hewitt has been attended to, yes. Police and ambulances have been all over Marlytree since. He suffered no life-threatening injuries, as I understand."

"I remember bricks falling on me—or I think they were bricks—and me crashing through his new skylight. There was all kinds of plastic and loose material up there. Everything ... under construction. And then I toppled—by the force of the bricks, I guess."

Only something about that didn't seem quite right, either. The image of Nicholas Hewitt's startled face as she flew down to meet him was the clearest eyeprint of all. "He—he looked up. I landed on top of him, face-first, I'm sure of it." She paused, grappling with the images plastering her brain. Why had she blacked out after landing on him? Would tumbling bricks cause this gash at the back of her head? "Did you say something about a doctor?"

"Yes, of course. Dr. Munjamba. He's my physician, one of the rare ones to still make house calls. Lovely man."

"What did this Dr. Munjamba say about my ... head?"

"Whatever do you mean? He claimed it was serious and was most concerned."

"No hospital?"

"He did want you to go, of course, but we couldn't have that, could we? Not unless it was absolutely necessary."

"Why wasn't it necessary?" Jenna could barely see her aunt's features in the brackish light.

"Because you could be arrested, of course. What would we tell the police as to why you were on that roof?"

Jenna closed her eyes, trying to think. "Hewitt might press ... charges—should press charges. I must pay ..."

"Jenna, you really must rest."

"What did you tell him?" Jenna asked.

"Tell whom?"

"Nicholas Hewitt!"

"Why, nothing. I certainly have not spoken to him directly. Why ever would I? As for Dr. Munjamba, I told him that you'd tripped into the pond dig while letting Mac out for his wee. It made perfect sense, given the state of the yard."

Jenna struggled to process that. "And he believed you?"

"I can be quite convincing. I did add a few details, such as how Jake had placed an old window over the pit for safety's sake, which you crashed through. That accounted for the cuts on your face, you see. Jake was most helpful in finding an old window we could smash to make things look convincing. I wonder where Sara is with your soup?"

"You're kidding me? What about forensics?"

"It rained, Jenna," her aunt said patiently. "Presumably evidence would be down the proverbial drain by now."

"But what did you tell the police?"

"I didn't speak to the police. They're the last people I want to have dealings with after the manner in which they treated me after Dan's murder. Now, do rest, dear. I'll just check on the status of your lunch."

"But, Aunt Clair," Jenna said, trying to prop herself on her elbows. "You should have spoken to the police—or better still, I have to speak with them. Something's not right with what I saw—the eyeprints don't add up. He saw my face. He might be trying to identify me. There was all that blood."

"Calm down, Jenna. This won't do at all. Your brain is befuddled. One must expect a touch of delirium. Now rest. I'll be right back."

"But I do remember what I saw, or parts of it," she called after her aunt as the wheelchair zipped out of the room, but Aunt Clair didn't stop. "It's just all jumbled up ... in there. Besides, how could I ... injure the back of my skull when I landed face-first?"

Jenna fell back against the pillows with a groan. It hurt to speak. It hurt to think.

Sara arrived moments later with chicken soup. "You suffered a nasty fall, I hear," she said as she propped up the pillows behind Jenna's back. "You fell into that pond dig?"

Jenna sensed the woman's disbelief. "Is that what happened?"

"Apparently."

"I don't remember much," Jenna mumbled.

"Your aunt called me saying there'd been an accident in the yard. By the time I arrived the next morning, the doctor was here. Now, you sip your soup and try to rest."

Aunt Clair entered the room moments later. "I have two prescriptions for you, dear. The doctor says you are to take the first one every three hours and the second pill three times a day with meals. That one is an antibiotic, I believe. Here, take them with your soup."

Jenna did as she was told. Whatever the pills were, one certainly helped her sleep. That along with her head injury caused the hours to bleed one into another.

Harry dropped by twice—once to bring her an old CD player so she could listen to music, and once to see if he could get her something at the shop.

"Where's my iPad, my phone?" she asked. "I have my own playlist on those."

"Out of your reach for a moment. Doc says you should avoid electronic stimuli so I just dug up some of your aunt's old CD's."

"Seriously? Then bring me some newspapers," she told him. "I'm desperate just to find out what's going on."

"Hey, can you even read yet? I mean, your head must hurt like hell. I don't think you're supposed to do much but lie there."

Like she wanted to hear that again. She tried to see him in the murk, but other than the silhouette of his large frame against the hall light, he remained in shadow. Something about that shadow pinged a fleeting eyeprint but she couldn't grasp it. She shivered. Her imagination again. "My head may hurt but I'm also bored."

"Yeah, I get that. Must be tough, but look, you can listen to music and chill."

"Thanks for bringing that. Who brought me upstairs from the yard?"

"Um, that was Jake, I think. She called me first but I must have been out with my mates and didn't hear the ring. He says he found you facedown in the mud."

"What do you think happened?"

"I have no idea. I'm just trying to stay out of it, you know? Well, look, if you don't need anything, I'll just be off. I have a paper due."

"Paper as in school?"

"Uni. I'm taking economics at London University and, I tell you, it's tough. So, if you don't want anything ..."

After that, day seeped into night, night into day. Her curtains remained shut and all electronics, even phones, remained banished, though now she had music to ease her isolation—lots of Queen, passionate symphonies, and the Beatles. Otherwise, nothing. Reading was out of the question, since Jenna's eyes blurred over the print. She couldn't bear the light, in any case.

Eventually she gave up, spending her time sleeping or rubbing Mac's ears and listening to music. Freddie Mercury's words entangled with her brain. During one wakeful hour, she tried forcing her mind to recall the eyeprints in sync instead of leaving them in a scattered mess in her brain.

Why couldn't she determine the source of this panic racing inside her? It had to be the fall and the sight of all that blood, though maybe, just maybe, that part was all hallucination. She needed to keep her mangled brain busy, that had to be the key.

She'd straighten her eyeprints, that would help. It was like plucking photos from a tumbled pile and tacking each one to a wall in the order in which they occurred. In this case, the wall was her mind, those pictures her memories, each appearing sharper and more vivid than usual, yet horribly distorted and out of sync. They were disjointed puzzle pieces, some so bizarre she couldn't factor if they belonged on her wall or should be stored elsewhere, maybe in a category labeled "Possible Concussion Spawn." Oh, hell, it hurt so much to think but she had to plow on.

That axe smeared in blood had to be the stuff of nightmares. Somehow her brain must have morphed the sight of Hewitt's armor standing at attention before the fall with some bad movie version of a medieval battle scene, complete with props like gauntlets, segmented armor, and that bloodied battle-axe. Nicholas himself was playing the felled knight, of course. Trust her imagination to unscramble that one. He was, after all, not only the star but the most vivid eyeprint of all. As much as she had tried to wrestle her imagination in line for all these years, it still acted out during times of trauma. A head injury certainly qualified. She needed to get a grip, literally.

But one eyeprint rose in her mind in perfect clarity: Hewitt lying on his back, his beautiful face in repose, blood trickling from his temple, and when he opened his green eyes ... that memory, at least, must be real. She'd fallen on top of him, so those details made sense. Everything else, from the bloodied footprint to the armor, must be a hallucination. Certainly her fall could not account for the blood-smeared memories?

And that argument with Suzanna. That much she heard prefall. That was real. She needed to talk to Nicholas Hewitt to clear up the details, only she was in no condition to do anything unassisted, and no one would help. Phones lay out of reach, lights remained low, and Aunt Clair seemed agitated, yet valiantly trying to pretend otherwise. Jenna lay trapped in a nightmare.

Sara brought tea and food up regularly and Jenna dutifully took the antibiotics until the second day when the pills were delivered along with some odd red liquid in a little cup.

Jenna tasted it tentatively. "Yuck, what's this? It tastes like fermented bugs."

"I don't know about that, but your aunt thought it might settle your stomach."

"You mean settle the wooziness?"

"I guess."

Just looking at it reminded Jenna of blood and she had to force herself to swallow the stuff. By the second day, she left the sedative on the plate but still drank the liquid.

"You're not taking both your pills?" Sara asked.

"I want my brain back. Yesterday I was out of it when the doctor came. I couldn't focus on a thing he said."

"Suit yourself," Sara said. "Your aunt wants me to insist but I'm not shoving anything down your throat. I made you a batch of biscuits. They're cooling on the counter now. I'll be back up with a couple with your tea."

"That's sweet. Thank you," Jenna said as she lowered herself back to the pillow.

Meanwhile, the house remained active—footsteps amid the manly voices of Harry and Jake, Aunt Clair calling to one of them or to Sara, Mac barking when he wasn't sneaking into her room to keep her company. The doorbell rang several times, sending him into a yapping fit. Once she heard a man and two women entering the house, despite Aunt Clair's objections.

Her aunt's tone fell into the cadence of agitation and denial. Mac was shut into the downstairs library yapping in outrage as some confab went on without him. Maybe Mac could detect the tone if not the words, the way she could—Aunt Clair agitated, querulous. When her aunt finally entered Jenna's room later, she claimed the visitors were the Jehovah's Witness, which Jenna thought odd. The Jehovahs never entered the house if her aunt had anything to do with it, though Uncle Dan had been known to engage them in the occasional debate. Aunt Clair was hiding something. That was worry enough.

"Sara, what's going on?" she asked her point-blank when she came to collect the lunch dishes and medicine cups on the fourth day.

"I've been told to keep my mouth shut, and so I shall. Ask your aunt."

"She's hiding something," Jenna said.

"What else is new? Would you like some fresh tea, help to go to the toilet?"

"No, thank you."

"Very well. I'll be back up later to check on you. Your aunt is downstairs being examined by the doctor."

"Is she okay?"

"Just all in a tizzy, as usual."

The moment she'd left, Jenna swung her legs over the edge of the bed and placed her bare feet on the floor. Mac kindly licked her toes while she prepared herself for the first unassisted walk. Until then, bathroom trips were conducted either with Sara's help or with the aid of one of Aunt Clair's old wheelchairs, a cumbersome thing she couldn't maneuver without running into walls. Now the chair steadied her as she trembled to her feet but the dizziness was much worse than it had been. Still, she could do this, *must* do this.

Using furniture for support, she took hesitant steps to the window and pulled the curtains apart. Shards of light stabbed her eyes. She stepped back, blinking furiously before trying again. It took several minutes before she could focus on the street below. A police car cruised slowly past, a cluster of what she guessed might be reporters loped down the sidewalk—nothing new for Marlytree with a famous actor in residence, and yet the activity seemed heightened. She needed her phone, her iPad, and computer. They were not in her room, which meant Aunt Clair probably had them in her den.

In the hall, she listened as activity hummed through the house in a percussion of tapping, clicking, and footsteps, beneath the steady stream of her aunt's *Carmina Burana*.

The dizziness intense, Jenna padded silently down the hall, one hand bracing herself on the wall. When she reached Aunt Clair's study, she pushed open the door and froze. There, with his back turned to her, sat Harry in her aunt's chair furiously working on one of the computers while wearing earphones. So, he was doing his homework here, too, was he?

Jenna didn't want to talk with him, or anybody else at that moment. Spying her laptop, iPad, and phone sitting in a pile on a table near the door, she scooped up the lot, and scrambled back to her room without the whiz-kid even noticing. Exhausted after her excursion, she fell into bed, shoving her technology under the covers. Every single item needed to be recharged, a problem she'd solve later. She lay on the edge of her bed. Had she seen a crack on her phone screen? Plucking it out from under the covers, she stared. Yes, a jagged crack divided the glass in two. Shit. She'd worry about that later. For now, she had to rest.

Later, Dr. Munjamba arrived with Aunt Clair in tow. Jenna sat up, relieved to be able to focus on his face this time.

"Good afternoon, Ms. Elson. I must say, you are looking so much better." The doctor, who Jenna knew to be Kenyan, educated in England, spoke a better version of the Queen's English than most Londoners.

"Dr. Munjamba, I have so many questions to ask you," Jenna said. "I feel much better and I need to use my iPad and computer. Staying isolated like this is driving me nuts. I promise I'll turn them off the moment my head begins pounding."

"Good, good. And of course you may have your technology back. I do not recall suggesting otherwise." The doctor gazed down at Aunt Clair as if asking for an explanation.

"Jenna," her aunt said, her cheeks pink, "perhaps it is best to permit the doctor to do his work without barraging him with unnecessary questions."

The doctor, a middle-aged man with white hair in stark contrast to his chocolate skin, continued to peer down at the elder Elson from over the top of his horn-rimmed glasses. "I don't mind questions in the least. In fact, I am most happy to answer them, and perhaps pose a few of my own."

"That won't be necessary," Aunt Clair said, looking up. Today, with her wiry hair hair sticking straight up from her head and her hands gripping the armrests of her chair, she looked like a charioteer riding into battle.

"I don't mind," Jenna said, studying her aunt in the lamplight.

"Nevertheless, I think it best for me to stay," Aunt Clair began. "My niece isn't well. I should be here in case she grows too tired. I—"

"Miss Elson, if you don't mind, I would prefer to examine your niece in private."

"Pardon me? Oh, that's not necessary, surely?"

"Indeed, it is standard practice."

"And it's what I prefer," Jenna added, staring pointedly at her aunt. "Wait outside, please, Aunt Clair."

Aunt Clair, perched in her chair unmoving, shook her head. "No, no, no."

Dr. Munjamba cleaned his glasses with a handkerchief he plucked from his pocket. "I really must insist, especially in light of the recent events."

"What recent events?" Jenna asked. Oh, God, what recent events— the break-in at Hewitt's house? She tried to remember if Sara had mentioned anything about a break-in but her brain wouldn't function.

"I don't want her upset, Doctor. We agreed on that," Aunt Clair said.

"It's time, Miss Elson. Now just wait outside and mind what I said about your blood pressure."

"My blood pressure is the least of my worries," said Aunt Clair, but she zoomed from the room.

The doctor shut the door and returned to Jenna's bedside.

"What recent events?" Jenna repeated.

"May I examine your skull?"

"Of course." Jenna bent over to allow the doctor to remove her bandage.

"The wound is healing well and you may bathe now, but be careful with the stitches. Regardless, you really need to have an MRI and X-ray to assure there's no fractures."

"Make me an appointment and I'll be there. What recent events?"

"Had your wound not healed sufficiently, I would have insisted you go to the hospital immediately. In truth, I should have from the beginning, but your aunt is most persuasive."

Jenna's gaze fixed on a leaf pattern twining across the printed bedspread. "I know it. How did she make you go against your better judgment?"

The doctor didn't comment as he cleaned the wound and changed the dressing. "How did you come by this blow to the head?" he asked finally.

"I have no idea." Jenna winced as he dabbed the wound with antiseptic.

"You fell into the trench face-first, I understand."

Trench, was it? "I fell face-first, yes." She didn't recall anything about a trench but anything was possible.

"And yet you have a gash at the back of your scalp that appears to have come from a heavy blunt object."

"How heavy?"

"I would say from a deliberate blow—perhaps a shovel."

Jenna stared down at the acanthus leaf curling green against the winter-white background of her bedspread. Her mouth went dry. "I have no memory of anyone hitting me on the head."

"What do you recall?" the doctor asked.

"I blacked out."

"I suggest that, at your earliest convenience, you contact the police. There have been disturbing events in this neighborhood in which the authorities are extremely interested. Your unexplained injury may be related. Though not a forensic physician by any means, in my opinion wounds such as this are usually the result of a blunt force object."

She tensed. "In other words, somebody slugged me?"

"Possibly. Were you aware of anyone else in the garden?"

She couldn't even recall being in the garden. "No." She tried reining in her galloping heart, forcing her mind to focus, but all that just provoked her head to throb even more. "May I begin walking around now?"

"Yes, just be cautious and use common sense. If you grow fatigued, rest."

Aunt Clair zipped into the room the moment the doctor left, her eyes narrowed, her face still flushed. "Well, what did he tell you?"

"That I'd been struck on the back of the head deliberately."

Aunt Clair crumpled. "He tried to kill you, too! Oh, Jenna, I've been so terrified."

"Are you referring to Brian Dunn again?"

"Of course. He must have found you after he killed—"

Jenna leaned forward. "Killed who? What aren't you telling me?"

"Oh, my!" Aunt Clair clutched the armrests. "I didn't want you to know. I didn't want to upset you. It's all been so horrible. Jenna, I was frantic. Brian Dunn has killed again and tried to slaughter you, too! There's been another murder, Jenna, right there in the alley the same night as your fall."

✣ 12 ✣

SUZANNA LAKE FOUND MURDERED IN LONDON ALLEY.
NICHOLAS HEWITT RELEASED AFTER TAKEN INTO
CUSTODY.

JENNA DROPPED THE IPAD TO HER LAP. IT WAS DATED THREE DAYS
ago, already old news. "Suzanna Lake ... *Zanna?*"

"Yes. Horrible, isn't it? Calm down, dear. Here, let me fetch you a
sedative. It will help, I'm sure."

"No, thanks. I've got to wean myself off those things. Tell me more
about Zanna's death. And she was an actress, too?"

"Suzanna Lake was quite famous once. She starred in that film
about the serial killer who did nasty things to his victims."

"Neon Blue?"

"Yes, that was it. Anyway, now she's his latest victim. You see why I
had to keep it from you. You were in no condition to hear such
distressing news. Naturally the police suspect Hewitt, as if he were the
only man mucking around with that trollop. There were others, but

more importantly, Brian Dunn. He frequently used her as a model while she lay there as naked as the day she was born. We have proof."

But Jenna wasn't listening. She pressed a finger between her temples. "Wait. Nicholas was arguing with Suzanna that night. I heard them when I was on the roof, heard her shouting at him, I'm sure I did. He pushed her out the door just before I fell. I'm a witness."

"Nonsense. You were unconscious when this murder happened. What kind of witness is that?"

"I need a phone. I'll use the house phone." Her phone was completely dead.

"Jenna, you absolutely cannot call the police."

"I crashed right into a murder scene!"

"That hardly makes you a witness. You were unconscious."

"I was there! My head is filled with evidence."

"Your eyeprints are scrambled, you said so yourself, and if you call the police, you'll become a murder suspect. You'll be involved, right in the thick of it."

"I'm already in the thick of it, and why would I be a suspect? I have no motive for killing Suzanna Lake. And if I don't tell them what I saw, Nicholas Hewitt may be arrested for a murder he may not have committed, or maybe the true killer will get away. And maybe somebody tried to kill me, too!" Only she couldn't quite untangle what she saw, or may have seen. She dug her index finger into the bridge of her nose as if that would clear her thoughts. It didn't. "Get me the phone, please, Aunt Clair. The one in the hall will do nicely." If worse came to worst, she could haul her battered butt to the street and hail a passerby, anything to get to a phone.

But her aunt would not give up. "If you bring in the useless police, matters will only become more complicated."

"They can't get any more complicated. Pass me the phone." Jenna held out her hand while throwing back the covers and making to stand.

"All right, all right. Sit back down." Her aunt sighed and scooted into the hall to return with the phone, dropping it into Jenna's palm. "What will you say?"

"The truth."

"You don't know the truth, dear. You're not thinking clearly and this will upset you terribly."

"I'll just say what I saw. Or try to."

The call went through to a desk officer. "Hello, my name is Jenna Elson and I have information regarding the night Suzanna Lake was killed. I've been unable to report until now."

The doorbell rang less than thirty minutes later. It appeared the police were already in the neighborhood. Sara was instructed to send them upstairs.

A tall man and a younger uniformed woman appeared at Jenna's doorway holding their identifications badges. "Mrs. Elson? I am Chief Inspector MacKinnon and this is Constable O'Reilly."

"Hi, and it's *Ms.* Elson," Jenna corrected, propping herself to sitting. "I presume you've already met my aunt. Come in."

"Good afternoon, Miss Elson," the man greeted her aunt, and then said to Jenna, "I understand you have information pertaining to the recent murder."

"I think so. I mean, yes, I do. Come in and take a seat. Aunt Clair, would you mind waiting in your den?" The room was just getting far too crowded, for a start.

"I certainly do mind. This is most inconvenient," Aunt Clair protested on her way out the door. "I spoke to you both two days ago and have nothing further to add, in any case. Don't agitate my niece. Her condition is very delicate." And with that she zipped down the hall.

Jenna met Chief Inspector MacKinnon's steady gaze. "You have suffered an accident, I understand."

"A concussion. I was whacked on the head on the same night Suzanna Lake was killed. I only just found out about it today. I've been in bad shape. As soon as I heard, I called. Take a seat, if you can find one."

The officers stepped in, quickly closing the door behind them. Chief Inspector MacKinnon took the room's only chair while the corporal perched awkwardly in the old wheelchair.

"And where did this happen?" the inspector asked.

"I don't know. A lot of what I see in my mind makes no sense. I'm trying to sort it out."

"Please explain as much as you are able. Where exactly were you at the time?"

Jenna gazed at the inspector. He bore the long face of a man who'd observed too much sorrow in his younger years to be moved by anything in middle age. He sat loose and rangy in a serious blue suit, gazing at Jenna with eyes the color of a muddy puddle. Besides being tall, maybe close to six foot three, he had large farmer hands suitable for milking cows or chopping wood. The uniformed Corporal O'Reilly, on the other hand, was young, porcelain-skinned, and petite. "I was on the roof of Nicholas Hewitt's house," she said.

Chief Inspector MacKinnon didn't flinch. "Indeed. And why was that?"

Jenna swallowed. "My aunt is convinced that Brian Dunn killed my uncle and I was humoring her by crawling over roofs gathering evidence. I know it was foolish, but old habits die hard and I admit to enjoying the game."

"Old habits?"

She filled him in on her childhood tendencies. "I thought that if I resurrected this old game of 'be my eyes,' it would help us both through our grief after the loss of my uncle. The night I had my accident was supposed to be my last time."

"Indeed. Begin at the beginning, Ms. Elson."

❧ 13 ❧

Jenna focused on the worn leather club chair where the crocheted doilies clung to the armrests like desiccated jellyfish. Uncle Dan used to sit there sometimes and just talk with her. Shaking off the memory, she began, filling the police in on the events as she half-remembered them. When she was just about to describe her fall, the inspector stopped her.

"You were physically on the roof of Hewitt's house and you heard Susanna Lake arguing with Nicholas Hewitt?"

"Yes ..." She knew that part would interest them. "Right, between units 50 and 51 where he's constructing a new skylight. Half of it was covered in plastic and there was all this scaffolding around. He has a voice that carries—both of them do, or did, I mean. I didn't realize she was an actress, too."

"And you heard that conversation?"

"I did." Jenna told them the specifics exactly as she recalled them. "I'd also heard Suzanna arguing with him the night before. He called her 'Zanna.'"

"On another one of these excursions?"

"Yes."

"And where were you on that occasion?"

She told him. "But both times Mr. Hewitt escorted Suzanna away. I mean, there was no violence, nothing like that."

He drilled her further on every excruciating detail before allowing her to continue. Unfortunately, she had little she could add about the actual fall since everything remained such a blur, so he moved along to the scene itself.

"What about the armor?" he asked.

"Well, there was this suit of armor all in pieces, like I said. I had heard Suzanna grabbing and kicking at things as Hewitt escorted her out the front door earlier but the suit of armor wasn't one of them—it was back against the wall when I last saw it—and I didn't land on the armor so why was it in pieces?" She buried her head in her hands, pressing back the throbbing. "None of it makes sense."

"Please continue. What did you do next?"

"I answered my phone." *She answered the phone.* It couldn't have been broken, then. Hell.

"Continue, please," McKinnon prompted.

"Ah, so my aunt was frantic. I told her to call the police, an ambulance, but I was feeling so battered by then I could hardly stand."

"Just a moment: you say your aunt called?"

Jenna stared down at her lap. Her aunt *had* called. "Yes ... she called again and kept calling."

"What did she say?"

She looked at him. "I don't remember. She probably told me to come home, that she was worried or something. I ... told her to call an ambulance, the police ... I don't remember the rest."

"Then what did you do?"

"I headed out the kitchen door ... I needed to vomit. I was so out of it. I don't remember anything after that. It's all a tangle. I collapsed, I guess, but I have this blow on the back of the head." And then for some reason she didn't grasp, she started to cry. "I woke up a few days ago. I'm trying to remember things clearly but I can't."

The door flew open and Aunt Clair wheeled into the room. "Chief Inspector, it's time you left. You can see that my niece is not well. Please leave immediately!"

Jenna lacked the energy to protest. Exhausted, she leaned back and closed her eyes.

But Aunt Clair continued. "Brian Dunn killed my brother, Chief Inspector, as I've told you so many times before, and Jenna was off getting proof, since you wouldn't. We found it, too. And now he's struck again. How many must die before you bring him in?"

Chief Inspector McKinnon unfolded himself from the chair. "Miss Elson, this is a police matter and I advise you to desist from encouraging anyone from getting involved. You can be certain that we will find the perpetrator." He turned to Jenna. "And, Ms. Elson, once you are recovered sufficiently, I would like you to come to the station. In the meantime, should you remember anything further, please contact me immediately. Here's my contact information." He slipped a card onto the bedside table. "I'll leave Corporal O'Reilly to finish up here." And with that, he left the room.

"Finish up?" Aunt Clair said, turning to the young officer. "We *are* finished."

"One more thing," Corporal O'Reilly said. "We'd like all the clothes you were wearing the night of your fall, Ms. Elson—gloves, shoes, underwear, everything."

Jenna opened her eyes. "Of course. They are … evidence. Aunt Clair?" She hadn't seen the gloves or any of those items since the accident.

"They have been disposed of," her aunt said, lifting her chin at the officer. "Why ever not? They were quite muddy and ripped, weren't they? I burned everything in the library grate."

"You're not serious?" Jenna stared at her.

"Of course I'm serious. Why would we ever want to keep dirty clothing about? Quite appalling."

"Why not have them washed?" Corporal O'Reilly asked, addressing the elder Elson.

"You did not see them, Officer. They were simply not salvageable, so I made a decision to burn them."

The officer studied Aunt Clair. "Did you dispose of them yourself, Miss Elson, or did one of your staff do it?"

"One of my staff?" Aunt Clair waved away the notion. "Really,

Corporal, do I look as though I have a household of minions available to answer to my every call? I took care of the matter myself. I may be chair-bound, but certainly not helpless. Are you quite done now? My niece needs her rest. I'd appreciate it if you'd leave at once."

"So, just to be clear," the corporal continued, "you thought the clothes were unsalvageable so you burned them, as opposed to throwing them in the trash, for instance?"

"Yes, I burned them!" Aunt Clair said. "They were a mess, I said, and totally unsuitable for any purpose at all."

"Except as possible evidence," O'Reilly remarked, giving her a long thoughtful look.

Once the corporal had gone, Aunt Clair rolled up to Jenna's bed and squeezed her hand. "Don't worry, dear. I will make sure that monster doesn't sneak in here and kill us in our beds. I have taken measures, indeed I have. Now you rest."

Jenna had no energy left except to whisper, "What have you done?"

"What do you mean by that, Jenna? I did everything I could to protect you, as always. You came home covered in blood. What was I to think? I didn't know about Suzanna's death at that point but I knew you'd fallen on Hewitt."

"How?"

"Because you told me, that's how. For one terrible moment I was afraid you may have killed him."

"Seriously?"

"Not deliberately, of course not, but I thought you might have accidentally killed Hewitt when you fell on top of him. I panicked. What if the police arrested you? I had to burn the evidence. I had to, Jenna. Surely you understand that?"

"The only thing I understand," Jenna said wearily, "is that now we both look as guilty as hell."

❧

JENNA SLEPT THE REST OF THE DAY, AND WHEN SHE FINALLY WOKE UP hours later, the house was dark, Mac sat curled up beside her, and there were voices coming from downstairs. Propping herself on her elbows, she stared at the half-open door.

"Who's down there, Mac?" she asked. In response, he licked her hand. She longed for a private conversation with her aunt. Pushing herself up to sitting, she picked up her phone again, staring at it in confusion. When did the screen crack? Hadn't she spoken to her aunt on that phone the night she fell? Her head hurt thinking about it. In any case, the thing was unusable.

She put it aside and picked up her freshly charged iPad and scrolled through her messages, alarmed to find multiple texts from Annette. She hadn't contacted her or the office in days. They must think she'd dropped off the face of the earth. In a way, she had. But it was too late to call, so she shot off an email explaining how she'd suffered an accident, and that her return home had to be put off yet again. Setting the tablet aside, she stared at the floor. The situation was growing intolerable.

Moments later, she shuffled into the bathroom. She'd have a shower, dress, force herself into some measure of normalcy. She needed her life back.

Nearly forty-five minutes later, she was clutching the railing on her way downstairs, Mac dashing ahead. When she reached the entrance to the kitchen, she hesitated. Aunt Clair was leaning over the table with Harry sitting forward, patting her hand, their heads mere inches apart. She was nodding, he was smiling.

Jenna stood for a moment hoping she might overhear something interesting but it appeared the moment was over. "So, am I interrupting anything?"

Harry jumped from his chair, sliding another out for Jenna. "Jenna, you're up! Are you feeling well enough?"

"Feeling well enough to walk downstairs," she said.

"Jenna, what a surprise," her aunt said. "I was just discussing all this trouble with Harry."

"Really? What trouble exactly?" Jenna asked, lowering herself down into the chair Harry offered. How much did this kid know, anyway?

"Would you like some mac and cheese?" Harry asked. "Mrs. Hudson made up a batch before she left and it's delish. Here." He jumped up to the oven and busied himself in scooping up a helping onto a plate warming nearby.

How comfortable he seemed, so totally at home. Jenna turned back to her aunt. "So what were you two discussing again?"

"Harry is going to protect us," her aunt said. "I feel ever so much safer just knowing he's around."

"What do you mean by 'protect us'?" Jenna asked.

"We need a bodyguard of sorts, someone to ensure that no one comes along and knocks either of us off in the night."

Jenna turned to Harry. "And how's that supposed to work?"

Aunt Clair answered. "He'll sleep in the second-floor guest room, of course."

"Surely that's not necessary?" Though she understood her aunt's fear—had enough of it of her own, in fact—but Harry as bodyguard? "I mean, Harry, don't you have school to attend? Economics at London University, isn't it?"

"Night classes, yes, but that's no problem," the young man said, slipping to the table with a plate of mac and cheese in hand. "I'll go to my classes, as usual, but I can be back here in minutes, if you need me, and I'll sleep here to keep an eye on you two at night. This street has become murder central, what with that actress being knocked off and you being attacked and all."

"And you really think Dunn is the killer?" Jenna asked. She was so sure he wasn't but couldn't remember why.

"I don't know—I'll leave that up to the cops—but there's lots of rumors on the street. You know, like people seeing him with Suzanna Lake and loud arguments heard."

Jenna pressed a finger between her eyes as if seeking a reset button. *Loud arguments heard.* She knew something about that but couldn't remember that at the moment, either. Memories kept flashing in and out.

"Anyway," Harry continued brightly, "my job will be to keep you two safe so you can rest easy. I'm just going to collect my things from my flat but I'll be back soon. Keep the doors locked in the meantime. Cheers."

Jenna watched him leave.

"Don't look so puzzled, dear. It makes perfect sense that we have someone stay with us until this is over, besides which, he can help with things I can't manage, especially while you recover," Aunt Clair said.

"If it makes you feel safer," Jenna said, picking at her food. "How much does Harry know about what happened the night I fell?"

"What do you mean?"

"Does he know about my roofing excursions? Does he know I fell through Nicholas Hewitt's skylight?"

Aunt Clair placed her hands palms down on the table. "Of course he knows, Jenna. Both my boys do. Jake carried you from the yard into the house. I couldn't do it alone, could I? And Harry's been ever so helpful since you've been laid up—fetching the groceries, taking out the trash, plus all those little things your uncle used to do that I can't. If it weren't for him, I'd be lost, and frantic. He calms me down, makes me believe that we'll get through all this, that *I'll* get through it. He's like the son I never had, and, Jenna, he lives right here in London, so he's not going to leave me the way you will. I made him promise."

❧ 14 ❧

One hour bled into the other throughout the next day. Jenna tried to read properly but found that impossible so settled for skimming through the online news instead. Speculation regarding Nicholas Hewitt still raged and, so far, it seemed he remained suspect number one, though police had released him from custody.

There was no mention of her. She figured the police kept their cards close to their blue serge chests. As long as Hewitt remained unaware, she still had time to scheme a way to explain her involvement directly to him. Which seemed unlikely in the present circumstances, but still mattered to her.

The doctor dropped in after lunch to prescribe pain medication and to check her wound.

"The police interviewed me," he told her as he removed the bandage. "We'll just let the air get at this. Meanwhile, I've arranged a scan for you at St. Pancras this afternoon at 2:00 p.m."

"Fine. I'll take a cab." She looked up at him. "I suppose you told the inspector about the blunt trauma thing?"

"I did indeed. In my humble opinion, whoever attacked you meant you harm."

"And he succeeded."

"And yet he did not kill you. Another blow most likely would have completed that task, had it been his intention."

"Maybe he was interrupted or distracted." She stared down at the bedspread, searching for eyeprints but coming up with the same fractured scenes.

"Physically, you are coming along well, but the amnesia will take time. The brain can be startlingly unpredictable. A trigger may provoke total recall in the near future, or it could take years before you remember what happened that night. In the meantime, do continue to rest."

"Doing nothing is provoking symptoms of another kind," she remarked. "I'm irritable."

"A sure sign that you are regaining your strength. Irritability is natural for your kind of injury."

After he left, Jenna prowled the house, tentatively at first, but slowly gaining confidence in her ability to bend over without tipping, in her capability to fix herself a cup of tea unassisted, and to stand upright for increasingly longer periods of time.

With Aunt Clair holed up in her study with the Whiz Kid, she tried doing as much as she could herself. For some reason, Sara had not been up to check on her that morning. And still no word from Annette, though a brief email message from the editorial assistant advised her to call the office ASAP. For some reason, she felt disinclined to do anything quickly, especially that. That world seemed surreal to her now. Everything did, for that matter.

She wandered into the kitchen, stood for a moment squinting into the sun flooding the room. Pots sat stacked in the sink with mugs and dishes scattered over the kitchen table. And poor little Mac had been tied up on the steps again. He stayed close to the conservatory door, his little ears keened into the wind, his body tense. He needed a walk and nobody was going to give him one. Probably needed food, too.

Opening the conservatory door, she spied Jake planting something leafy. "Jake?" she called.

The young man bolted upright, dropped the spade, and lumbered over, stopping within feet of the steps to peer up at her while Mac barked furiously. "Ms. Elson? Are you doing all right? You look knackered, if you don't mind me saying."

"I don't need a confirmation of how awful I look, thanks," she told him while shooing Mac into the conservatory and shutting the door. "I just want to ask you a couple of questions."

Jake shrugged. "Sure, shoot."

"You carried me into the house the other night, I understand."

He looked down at his muddy boots and poked a stone with his toe. "Yeah. Miss Elson called, so I came over and carried you in."

"And you found me here in the yard?"

He bent down, picked up the stone, and flung it onto a raked heap. "Yup."

"Where exactly?"

He pointed to a spot to the right of the debris pile.

"Was I on my back or face-first?"

He looked startled and briefly met her eyes before looking away. "Um, face-first, in the mud, like." Then he added, "So, I'd best get stuck back in or the Japanese grass will die."

"Wait. You made it look like I fell into the pond pit?"

"Yeah. Miss Elson wanted it to look like an accident."

"Meaning that when you found me I'd obviously been struck or something."

"Or something. Dunno. Couldn't tell. Hope you're feeling better. Sorry about saying you looked knackered. Didn't mean anything by it."

Shit. Jake was lying and she didn't have the energy to force the truth out of him. Returning to the kitchen, she fed Mac and then eyed the mess. After plugging in the kettle, she slowly began moving the dishes to the sink. She was just running the water when Harry came bounding into the room. "So sorry! Meant to do that but got tied up with your aunt. You doing okay? Can I fix you a sandwich or anything?"

Turning to face him, she needed to grasp the counter to steady herself. "Where's Sara?"

He raked a hand across his red curls. "Gone. Quit."

"Quit? But she's worked here for years."

"Aunt Clair's okay with it. I mean, she was going to give Sara her notice, anyway, and I'm going to help her find somebody more suitable."

"More suitable how?" Jenna demanded, her last nerve strung taut. And since when had her Aunt Clair become his Aunt Clair?

"Not so grumpy, you know, more pleasant. Aunt Clair needs someone upbeat, right? Besides, I can fill in for the short-term. I can even cook. I used to work as a short order cook in a restaurant when I was younger. Anyway, if you don't need me, I'll just be off." He shot her a charming smile. "If you need me to pick up anything on the way home, just give me a ring."

He called this his home now? He was halfway down the hall when she stopped him. "This is only temporary," she said. "As soon as this killer is caught, you can return to your flat, or wherever."

He grinned. "Well, sure, but your aunt likes having a man around the house. Catch you later."

She stood watching as the door shut behind him. Knowing he was right didn't make it easier. She was returning to Toronto. What Aunt Clair did with her life from here on in was up to her.

On the way back to the kitchen, she ducked into the parlor with the house phone and called her office, counting the seconds as the call clicked through across the miles. Miranda, the editorial assistant, answered.

"Miranda, it's Jenna Elson. I've been trying to get through to Annette but getting nowhere. Is she in today?"

"Jenna, are you all right? I heard you had a bad fall."

"Who told you that?"

"The email you sent, of course."

"Oh, right. Anyway, yes, I did fall—a stupid accident, but I'm on the mend. Is Annette around?"

"She's gone, Jenna, off to Cambodia, I think—retired, flying free, and all that."

"But she said she was going to stay to the very end." Her voice sounded dangerously close to a wail.

"She did, Jenna. Friday was her last day. We've been trying to contact you, but with your accident and everything ..."

Jenna pressed a finger to her temple. "Of course. Time's a bit scrambled for me at the moment. And she's traveling now, isn't she?"

"That's what she said—heading for 'parts unknown,' she told us. Do you want to speak to Hellen? I know she'd like to speak to you."

Hellen? Who was Hellen? Oh, right, that Hellen. "No, I'll phone back. Something's come up." She returned the phone to its stand. Staring down the darkened hall, another kind of dread thickened around her. They'd hired Hellen, that had to be it. The magazine needed somebody on the spot to muster together the next issue, and what good was she in her present state? She'd lost her shot.

What was worse, right now she didn't care. She didn't care about anything but getting her head back.

By the time she'd wandered back into the kitchen moments later, she'd forgotten all about it. Aunt Clair was there pouring tea and turned as she entered. "How are you, dear? You look ever so much better without that bandage, but still so very pale. Did you make the tea? It's a bit strong but still drinkable. Shall we share a cup?"

"I hear Sara left," Jenna said, lowering herself into a chair.

"Yes, she handed in her notice and I told her to just finish up and not come back. Never mind, Harry thinks he knows an excellent replacement, and we can manage just fine for a few days. Were you doing the dishes? Just leave them. Harry can take care of them when he returns."

Today Aunt Clair was freshly turned out in another new blue dress. She always could manage her personal care splendidly, her bedroom and bathroom being filled with the latest accessibility features. "How could you let Sara go?"

"I didn't let her go, Jenna, she left."

"And Harry's calling you 'Aunt Clair' now?"

"I asked him to. I like the sound of it, and the idea of extending my safety net. He's such a nice young man, and has been so good to me. Really, both of them have. Jake even brought me flowers this morning. There's a posy for you, too." She pointed to two bouquets of peonies each in a blue glass vase on the counter.

Jenna closed her eyes, forcing her heart to steady. Her emotions were such a roiling mess. "How sweet. But, Aunt Clair, your relationship with Harry is one between employer and employee. It's a paid relationship."

"What does that have to do with anything?" her aunt asked in a low voice. "Are you jealous?"

"Jealous? Not jealous, just concerned, that's all."

"Well, don't be. Now that Dan is gone and you will eventually be leaving me, too, I must take care of myself, and I do need help to do so. Living on a street of murders doesn't help. Thanks to both those young men, I rest ever so much better. Just knowing that Harry's in the house at night is such a comfort."

"I know, I know. Sorry. Anyway, I have an MRI scan booked at St. Pancreas this afternoon so I'm just going to get dressed now."

"Oh, you shouldn't go alone, Jenna. Let me call Harry and he'll go with you."

"No," she said too quickly. "I'm fine." She continued more carefully. "I'll just take a cab and come right back home."

But she didn't expect stepping out into the daylight to be so chaotic. It wasn't just her unsteadiness, or even the intense sunlight glinting off chrome surfaces that startled her, it was the commotion. Marlytree was crushed with news wagons and rubberneckers, and Hewitt's end of the street had been completely blocked off.

As her cab did a three-point turn, Jenna stared behind her at the barrage of cars parked next to the barricade. It appeared that a kind off media stakeout was in progress as the police herded back gawkers. A uniformed officer was busy instructing all traffic to detour.

For the first time, she realized how horrible all this must be for Hewitt, who had to be as much a captive inside his house as she was in hers. Simultaneously, she understood that, even if she had been fit, there was no way she could get to him. The lane was barricaded with do-not-cross police tape and the whole street was a murder scene.

"A right mash-up, if you ask me," the cabbie said. "A zoo. Did you see or hear anything the night that actress died, miss? I know you're not supposed to say anything, but I was just wondering, like," he asked.

"Me? I live way at the opposite end of the street," Jenna told him, using a technique she'd learned from her journalism experience which deflected questions with an honest answer. Better than constantly lying. He tried prodding her further before giving up.

At the hospital, the X-rays and scans passed in a blur. She answered the medical questions with more nondisclosing statements pertinent only to her injuries and not to the circumstances that caused them until, finally, she caught another cab to the police station. Though Chief Inspector McKinnon and Constable O'Reilly weren't in attendance, she submitted to fingerprinting and more questioning by an officer, much of which was in the same vein as the previous line of questioning.

By the time she exited, exhaustion hit hard. The cab pushed along through the traffic, delivering her home at 5:35. She noticed the time flashing on the dashboard as she paid the driver and trudged up to her aunt's door.

"Pardon me, miss."

She turned. On the sidewalk behind her stood a woman holding a microphone accompanied by a cameraman. "Mind if I ask you a few questions? Did you see or hear anything on the street the night that Suzanna Lake died?"

"No." Jenna turned away and continued fumbling for her key. Oh, shit. She must have left it on side table upstairs beside her cracked phone. Pressing the doorbell, she could hear Mac's barking in the hall beyond.

"Just a couple of questions. We won't take long." The newscaster was actually trotting up the walk towards her—one of those aggressive kinds. Jenna had always prided herself on being a different breed of journalist entirely—the kind that invaded one's privacy in secret. She'd laugh at that irony but she wasn't in the mood.

Slowly turning, she faced the woman. "Go away."

"Now, don't be like that. We only want to ask you a few simple questions. Think of yourself as participating in a murder mystery. How does it feel to live on Marlytree now? We'll even turn the camera off, if you'd rather." The woman—a young, perky-looking elfin creature with cropped black hair and a big engaging grin—was literally in Jenna's face.

"How do you think it feels? What an idiotic question. Can't you do better than that? Are you fishing for the human interest angle or pretending to be an investigative journalist honing in on a real story? Either way, I suggest you alter your approach because no sane subject likes to be plummelled with insensitive questions. Back off."

The woman paused, regarding Jenna intensely. "Is that accent Canadian or American? And what happened to your head?"

"None of your damn business on both counts. I'm not answering your questions." Stupid, stupid response. She should have just played along, said something banal, deflected. Instead, here she was tackling this smiling Doberman head-on while her head throbbed. She needed one of those painkillers, something to eat, plus a good nap, though right then she'd settle for a Taser gun or a can of mace.

"It'll only take a few minutes," the Doberman continued. "Were you at home when Suzanna Lake was murdered?"

"Hey, you, bugger off, do you hear?" A tall redheaded man came barreling around the corner brandishing a shovel, his biceps impressively straining against his black Guinness T-shirt. "You're on private property. Don't you get that? I'll call the police on you lot and boot your sorry asses off the property. Get lost!" he bellowed.

The Doberman, startled, jerked her head at the cameraman and scampered off down the walk.

Jenna sighed, sagging against the door. "Thanks, Harry."

"No problem. Here." In seconds he had the door unlocked and was ushering her into the house while Mac jumped up on her in a fury of tail-wagging welcome. She scooped him up and held him close, happy for the licks and doggy breath. The terrier turned in her arms and barked at Harry.

"Hush," Jenna cautioned him.

"Jenna, dear, are you all right?" Aunt Clair asked as her wheelchair lift slowly made its way downstairs. "Harry, fetch her some tea and something to eat, will you, dear?"

"Already on it," he said, peeling off his sneakers and padding into the kitchen.

Somehow Jenna ended up at the table being coddled by her aunt, the tech dude, and the dog, and not minding any of it. Feeling hellishly vulnerable, she was so grateful for the support she yearned to cry. It had been years since she felt this lost. It was unbearable.

After a chicken dinner, which had manifested from somewhere, plus a little port poured into a crystal glass, and lots of tea, she shuffled over into her uncle's favorite chair in the corner and dropped off to sleep, vaguely aware of Harry and her aunt talking in low voices.

When she awoke later, the kitchen lights were dimmed and her aunt sat at the table under her earphones watching something on her iPad. Harry had gone and Mac was whimpering softly at her feet. She leaned forward, rubbing her eyes. "You need to pee, don't you, Fuzz-face?"

Hoisting herself to her feet, she shuffled into the conservatory and opened the door. "Make it quick and I mean it."

She stood for a moment inhaling the moist air, and gazing out into a blackness laden with threat. Poor Zanna, poor everybody. Could Nicholas Hewitt really have killed her? He was frustrated but had seemed able to keep his temper in check both times she'd heard him, but what did she know? Now that Dunn was out of the running, he did seem the likeliest perpetrator. Then she paused at her own thought. Now, why did she know Dunn was out of the picture? She couldn't remember.

Meanwhile, Mac scrambled to the right towards the old shed and settled down to do his business. Watching him didn't seem decent somehow so she returned inside to wait by the door.

"Jenna, dear, are you feeling better?" Aunt Clair appeared in the kitchen doorway.

"I am, thanks, Auntie. It's just been a tough day."

"Poor dear. You've had such a blow."

Jenna noted her aunt's iPad in her hand.

"Are you watching the news or something?"

"No, I'm adding to my journal. I still keep one just as I did when you were a girl, only now I put it all on the cloud. Do you still keep a journal?"

"No, I lost the habit when I started writing professionally. Ran out of time, I guess. Where's Harry gone?"

"Back to the university. Tonight is his advanced statistics class."

"Oh.

"Jenna, you don't mind about the money thing, do you? You have lots of money of your own, as do I, and some are just not as fortunate as we are."

"What money thing?" Still sleep-fogged and brain-battered, nothing quite made sense. "You mean how much you pay Jake and Harry? Of course not. Besides, that's none of my business."

"Harry's so ambitious. He wants to get his degree and become an entrepreneur like Richard Branson."

Jenna rubbed her temples. "Ah, my head's started pounding again. Excuse me while I go upstairs and get my pills."

She longed for the time when she didn't need props. Though she felt stronger day by day, she still wasn't strong enough, not by a long shot.

Upstairs, she washed down a pill with a glass of water and returned to the kitchen to find Aunt Clair back under the earphones. Pausing at the kitchen door, she tried to remember something that escaped her, something important. *Mac!*

❁

WITH HER HEART BANGING AGAINST HER CHEST, SHE FLEW TO THE garden door and called. No Mac. She called again and again, until she finally pulled on her rubber boots beside the door and stepped out into the mud. My God, the gate was open again! Shit! She could not, would not, leave Mac alone in the lane that night. She'd go as far as the gate and he'd be there, same as before.

But once she'd navigated the muck and reached the gate until she stood staring down the lane ... nothing but rustling leaves and shifting shadows down there. Behind her, she could just see the strip of black-and-yellow police tape blocking off the street entrance. The police were probably within yelling distance.

Pulling her sweater closer, she took a few steps forward and called again. She'd go as far as Mrs. Chester's. Uncle Dan had found Mac in her yard once, though that was back in Mac's puppyhood.

Mrs. Chester's broken fence seemed a mile away. When she

reached it, her voice stuck in her throat. "Mac?" Still no answering yap, no scurry of little paws.

Her feet kept moving as if on their own volition. Every few steps, she'd turn around to check behind, but nobody followed, that she could tell. And yet, as always in that lane, she felt watched.

It was deadly quiet, all the residents having double-locked their gates and drawn the curtains. She scanned the surroundings for possible escape routes. She might not be in top form but she could run if she had to, at least for a few yards. And she knew a couple of self-defense moves, too, but God help her, she couldn't imagine using any of them right then. This damn headache owned her.

And no phone, either. And once Aunt Clair realized she wasn't in the house, she'd panic. She really should go back and tell her what she was doing. But by the time she negotiated the hassle that would follow, Mac could be in her arms and both of them back home.

Nothing to do but carry on. All the house owners had their gate lights on, probably in some unspoken decision to chase away the lane's dark secrets. Even so, the shadows glommed as thick as ever between the lampposts. She hurried by, imagining herself a little fish slipping through shadows towards sunny pools ahead.

She was almost where Uncle Dan had died when she caught the sound of a man's voice followed by Mac's little yip. It was coming from up ahead. It was coming from Brian Dunn's yard!

She bolted forward, past more police tape, reached the gate, and shoved it open, calling for Mac. The garden beyond was flooded with light, revealing a yard nearly as churned up as her aunt's—tools everywhere, mounds of dirt, plants. Up on the patio stood the lean form of an older man bending down.

Picking up a spade, she cried: "Don't hurt him or I'll slug you!"

"Hurt him?" The man straightened. "Why ever would I hurt him?"

She halted, stunned, as Mac bounded up to her wagging his tail. Her gaze slipped from the dog to Brian Dunn. A cigarette glowed against a face that took on an almost cadaver cast in the light. "I've been calling but he wouldn't come," she said, not quite restraining the accusatory tone.

"Well, it's not as if I've held him hostage, is it? The little fellow used to visit me all the time, so I presume he misses me, as I do him. You must be Jenna. Your late uncle and I were friends."

"You were?"

"And why does that surprise you? Would you mind lowering that thing?"

She tossed the spade aside. "How could you and my uncle ever be friends?" It sounded stupid but she didn't care.

The man stood as lean as a bagged bone and coughed up a dry chuckle. "Oh, yes, I see. How could a fine upstanding man like Daniel Elson befriend such a reprobate as I? Fair enough. Some may think that the best friendships are the stuff of mutual likenesses, but I would counter that it is the differences that often spark the most interest between humans."

"I get that but I still can't picture you two as friends."

"Nevertheless, I found your uncle's opinions fascinating, as I dare say he did mine, but, in truth, we shared another bond. I would love to explain further. May I? It's important that you know, and I have been searching for a way to explain everything to you but present circumstances have made it all so difficult." He stepped towards the edge of the patio. "Please, do come up."

Jenna slowly climbed the five stone stairs to the patio, no less uneasy because Mac appeared to be totally comfortable in the man's company. "You saw him on the night he died," she said.

"I did, sadly. I had meant to give him a gift but it wasn't quite dry. Now I shall never again have the opportunity."

"And yet you lied to the police and said you didn't know him."

"Who told you that?" He gazed at her, perplexed.

"I've heard rumors." She had reached his level and met him eye to eye.

"Ah, rumors—a fabrication of scuttlebutt, in other words. This is a neighborhood rife with them. Rest assured, I told the police everything, a fact that can be easily attested. Shall we discuss the horrible occurrences of Marlytree Terrace further, perhaps in the comfort of my kitchen? Care to step inside and out of this damp air? You look rather the worse for wear yourself, Ms. Elson."

"I've had an accident."

"Fell through a roof, perhaps?"

Jenna stared at him dumbfounded. "Why do you say that?"

"It is an occupational hazard of roof-climbing, you must admit. I caught you on my security camera clambering over my roof days ago," Dunn continued. "I thought it was you so I chose not to report it."

"You knew it was me?" This was all too much.

"Your uncle once told me that you had done such a thing as a child and I figured you might be retracing past steps. And poor Nicholas recalls a woman falling on him, though to date he still believes that might be a factor of his fractured skull. I, however, put two and two together, no pun intended." He paused to cough.

"And did you share that theory with him?"

"I did not, but the police told him that they have a witness to his argument with Suzanna the night she died. He wonders how that could be, and then there's the little matter of his demolished skylight, and his memories of a woman dropping in on him unannounced."

Jenna leaned against the side of his house. "I need to talk to him."

"Indeed you do."

"Do you believe he killed Suzanna?"

"Certainly not. Though she infuriated him, he would never do a thing to harm her. Besides, since he was himself whacked on the head, he was hardly in a position to axe Suzanna."

"*Axe* Suzanna? How the hell do you know she was axed?"

"Because my sister found her body just outside our garden gate the next morning." Something like a sob escaped him.

"Your sister—Fran?"

"Ah," he said, trying to compose himself. "You know about Fran."

"Eavesdropping, remember?"

He turned away. "Ah, yes."

"I'd better go," she said, gazing down at him as he appeared doubled over in grief. "Sorry about Suzanna. Sorry for everything. This whole thing is just such a mess."

He straightened. "No, please stay. You see how much we have to discuss, you and I? I would so like to become better acquainted. In fact, I have longed to do so since your uncle's passing ... but circumstances have been beyond my control—dear Suzanna's death, my own illness. But there are things ... you must know, and we are now both entangled in this terrible business. Perhaps together we can sort some of it out. Please let us talk."

"No, I mean, yes, but not now. I must get back. If my aunt finds out I am missing—"

"She will panic. Yes, I know, but you must see how important it is. There are things ... I need to tell you."

"Yes, I get that—just not tonight."

"Very well. Wait a minute. This, I believe, is yours." He handed her the missing flashlight. "I intended to return it personally."

She clutched the flashlight. "Thanks. I've been spying on you for weeks and trying to get it back."

"I know."

"I thought you might have killed my uncle."

"Never." He took a deep breath before carrying on with difficulty. "I am losing my friends far too quickly these days to hasten ... any of them along. And, I assure you, I am no threat to you, or ... to anyone, and I do miss your uncle terribly, and Suzanna also, for vastly different reasons. I would never harm either. Why would I?"

"Your paintings tell a different story."

"My art is just show. You understand show, don't you, Ms. Elson?"

"Yes, I understand show, and I also know that there's a killer on the loose. You can't blame anybody for making assumptions based on those slasher paintings of yours."

He began coughing. "Point taken. But ... we need to discover his ... identity before he strikes again. Will you come back ... perhaps tomorrow after supper?"

"Make it 10:00. I'll drop in as close as I can to that hour." Aunt Clair was usually fixed to her television by then. She picked up Mac and turned to leave.

"Wait!" he called after her. "Do you mean 'dropping in' ... literally or figuratively?"

She paused by the gate, arms full of dog, and smiled. "I'm hardly up to doing any more dropping at the moment."

"I only ask because ... it is unwise to just ring my front doorbell under present circumstances—too many gawkers about—and the alley is hardly safe. You really should not be ... back there alone, not tonight, either. I can't believe I'm saying this but I believe the roof is safer, only not in your condition obviously. Say I leave my roof studio open should you be well enough ... to take the high road, so to speak?"

She turned to go. "Thanks."

"Otherwise, I shall have to ... escort you."

She swung around. "You cannot come knocking on my back door or Aunt Clair will come after you brandishing a bread knife or something."

"I believe it. Nevertheless ... Hold on. Permit me to walk you home now. Just let me fetch my cane." He tossed his cigarette away and slipped inside.

Fetch his cane? Jenna waited until he returned encased in a winter jacket grasping a carved walking stick that could have come straight out of *The Lord of the Rings*. He hobbled down the steps and around the piles of earth and gravel.

"Look, Mr. Dunn, I appreciate the offer, but you're in no condition to walk me anywhere," she pointed out. "I'm perfectly fine on my own."

"We shall take our time, if you don't mind."

She knew she'd be safer without him but she let him take her arm, making progress even slower. Then a sudden thought hit. "Were you in the hospital the night Suzanna was murdered?" By then, she'd deposited Mac on the ground and let him bolt ahead. "I think I overheard Suzanna tell Hewitt just before I fell. I don't remember much after the fall and my memory keeps flashing in and out."

"Amnesia?"

"Partial, yes."

"Yes, I was in the hospital."

"What's your affliction, if you don't mind me asking?"

"Fine word, 'affliction.' My affliction is acute emphysema. Had I been home when ... Zanna was killed, she might still be alive."

"You don't know that."

"I do. Fran or I would have let her in, as we always did. Once Nicholas ... locked her out, she had nowhere to go."

She stared at him in the half-light. "She seemed distraught."

"She was always distraught ... an addict. Nicholas and I could not help ... her." Jenna paused, bearing his weight as he wheezed softly beside her.

"She made an easy mark but who would have killed her and why?"

"Ah, there's the rub. If only ... we knew."

"No theories?"

"None that ... make sense."

"And do you believe my uncle's death was accidental?"

"I have asked myself that ... a thousand times. Certain things disturb me ... and Suzanna, dear girl, believed someone was following her...and here she is murdered. But what motive?"

"That's what I'm trying to figure out—who has motive to kill both Suzanna and my uncle, or are they even connected?"

"No idea," Dunn replied, pausing to cough into a tissue. "Not you, not me, and not ... Nick," he wheezed. "He was her ... staunchest supporter ... despite everything."

"What do you mean by 'despite everything'?"

But Dunn was too consumed by coughing to answer.

"Here, sit down for a moment." Jenna looked desperately for a seat but saw none. She leaned him against a wall.

"I am due to be nebulized ... that's all. When Fran comes home. I sent her to see a film, get her mind off ... things. Carry on ... please. Not far now ..."

"I'm not leaving you here. Does your sister live with you?"

"Lately ... yes."

She looked down the lane from the direction they'd just come, relieved to see a familiar figure bounding towards them. "We have company. Don't mention about our appointment tomorrow night."

He nodded.

The man stopped within feet of them, looking from one to the other. "You guys okay?"

"Hi, Jake. My aunt called you, I presume?"

"Yeah, a few minutes ago. Said you'd gone missing."

"You must live nearby," Jenna asked.

"Over a pub on Kensington High Street."

"Could you help Mr. Dunn back home? Make sure he's fine before you leave, all right?"

"Sure thing," the young man replied. "Mind if I carry you, sir?"

Dunn nodded and Jenna watched as Jake hefted the frail form easily into his arms and headed back towards Dunn's yard.

15

"I can't believe you were alone with that creature, in the lane, of all places, and you still recovering from your injury!" Aunt Clair wailed the moment Jenna finished explaining.

"Aunt Clair, it's fine, I'm *fine*. Calm down. Dunn walked me home—limped me home, more like it."

"If I hadn't sent Jake, you may have wound up like Suzanna Lake."

"But I didn't, and Dunn's in no condition to knock anybody off, believe me. He is not the killer. He couldn't be."

"How can you be so sure?"

"He was in the hospital the night Suzanna died."

"How do you know that?"

"He told me. Suzanna herself told Nicholas that, too. I only just recalled that piece." Jenna lowered herself into the chair. "I keep remembering things, then forgetting them all over again."

"Which makes you very vulnerable with the killer loose. If it's not him, then who?"

Jenna leaned forward. "I don't know. I only know it wasn't him."

"Then who?" her aunt demanded again.

"I don't know, I said. Please keep your voice down. It's hurting my head."

"I don't mean to badger you, but I'm so worried. Admit you were glad Jake was close at hand tonight."

"He was helpful, I admit."

"To think of you out there alone after all that's happened ... " Aunt Clair let the sentence trail away while she sat studying the little dog sitting on the floor between them, his paws caked with mud. "And all because Mac ran away. Bad dog." She shook her finger at him.

Mac flattened his ears and whimpered.

"It's not Mac's fault. Jake left the gate open again. I meant to tell him that, but hell, I can't recall my own name half the time." Jenna patted her leg. "Come here, boy. There's a good dog." Mac slipped over to her and pressed himself against her leg. "You were just obeying your own instincts, weren't you, Fuzz-face? And you and Brian Dunn are friends, aren't you?" She looked up at her aunt. "Dunn is a sick man and I doubt he has the strength to whack anybody over the head. He was in the hospital the night I fell. And besides, Mac actually went to visit him tonight. He and Uncle Dan were friends, too. Scratch him off your list."

"I will not! No one's going off my list until we catch the culprit. Does this bring Nicholas Hewitt to the fore now?"

"That makes even less sense."

Aunt Clair straightened. "But who else can it be?"

"I intend to find out, I promise you." Jenna propped her head in her arms on the table. Now she was even more certain that she must keep tomorrow night's rendezvous a secret from her aunt.

At that moment, in strode Jake, pausing long enough to wipe his boots on the conservatory mat before entering the kitchen. He glanced from one woman to the other. "Hi ya. Everything okay in here?"

"Just fine. Did you deliver Mr. Dunn back safely?" Jenna asked.

"Sure thing. Poor old wheezer was in bad shape, but after I hooked up that breathing thing, he was doing much better. I stuck around just to make sure."

"Thanks for that," Jenna said, assessing the man anew. She could smell the beer on his breath from where she sat. "And did you lock our garden gate behind you before you left tonight?"

"Yeah, of course," he said, looking surprised that she'd even asked. "I always do."

"And yet I keep finding it open," she said. "It's annoying. And dangerous."

"Just double-check next time, Jake. We can't be too careful," Aunt Clair said. "Thank you, dear. You can return to your mates now."

After he left, Jenna turned to her aunt. "So where's our bodyguard tonight? It's already pushing nine o'clock."

"He has a study group at 8:30 and I'm not sure I like your tone, Jenna. He'll be back as soon as he can, which would be fine if we keep the doors locked and remained inside."

"I had to let Mac out for his wee."

"Put Mac on a lead next time, won't you? I'm just off upstairs to watch my show. Would you like to join me? It will help take your mind off this horrible business."

"No, thanks. I'm just going to clean up Mac's paws and head for bed."

"Very well, dear. I love you."

"I love you, too. Good night." And she gave her aunt a quick kiss on the cheek, before watching her zoom off. "Come on, Mac, let's clean up those paws of yours," she said, gazing down at the terrier.

The dog followed her out into the conservatory where a sink and a long counter had been installed next to the kitchen door. Her uncle had it built for potting and watering plants but Jenna remembered him using it for dog-washing, too.

Over the years there had been multiple West Highland terriers under this roof, though this one was special. There was comfort in doing these little dog-tending tasks the same way as her uncle, even though she changed things up a bit. He'd never stick Mac's paws under the faucet, for instance. Mac, however, didn't mind at all and tried to lap the water.

Jenna had just finished drying Mac's paws and lowering him to the floor when the dog erupted into furious barking and hurled towards the conservatory door. Jenna froze. How in hell had that gate got open again? But she forgot that the instant she saw the pale face of Nicholas Hewitt through the glass, his striking features accessorized by a bandage and an expression sour enough to bleach the ghost off Hamlet's bones.

Shit. She couldn't move. She stared at him staring at her. He knocked again, the flickering anger in his eyes shooting spikes of fear through her body. Mac kept yapping while fresh pain hammered at her skull. She tried hushing the dog, taking his squirming body in her arms as she stepped up to the door. The safety chain looked flimsy, nothing to really prevent anyone from barging in.

Maybe he *was* the murderer, maybe her memory had gotten everything wrong. But she couldn't just leave him standing out there, either. She had to explain what happened, try to plow through his anger somehow, anger which was justified. My God, she fell on the man!

"Step away," she said through the glass.

He straightened and took one step back.

Jenna put Mac into the kitchen and shut the door before returning to the conservatory and unlatching the lock, flicking the chain, but blocking the entrance with her body.

"It's true, then," Nicholas said through his teeth. "Jenna Elson is the woman who fell on me and killed Suzanna Lake."

"Are you crazy? Why would I kill Suzanna Lake? I didn't know Suzanna Lake, but yes, I fell on you by accident."

"What the hell were you doing on my roof?" He stepped forward, one hand gripping the edge of the door.

"I'll make whatever amends you feel necessary, plus I told the police everything I remembered—I have nothing to hide—but I did not kill Suzanna Lake."

"How do you know, if you can't remember anything?" His large green eyes fixed on her with chilling intensity. He knew how to use that face.

"What would my motive be?"

"How the hell should I know?"

Her gaze dropped to the shoe wedged in the door, a buffed lace-up the color of melted caramel. Her eyes met his. "Maybe you killed her. You had motive and opportunity. You two were arguing and she was driving you crazy. Maybe you'd had enough," she whispered.

"Would that be while I lay unconscious, slugged in the head by an axe handle?"

"Was that the same axe that killed Suzanna Lake?"

"You're asking me? The police found the murder weapon in my yard wiped clean of prints."

"I saw that axe." It was as if a curtain lifted, an eyeprint revealed clearly. "I saw blood. You were on the floor. Glass everywhere, and the axe was lying beside you." She met his eyes. "How did it get in the lane?"

"You're still asking me? That's bloody rich."

She backed away from the door, her hands gripping her head, trying to recall the eyeprint. "I can't see it anymore. It keeps coming in and out."

"What does?"

"My memory, my eyeprints."

"What the hell are eyeprints?"

"They're like vivid memories—like visual recall, only mine keep disappearing."

"Dunn told me you'd hurt your head during the fall."

"Not from the fall," she said, still gripping her head. "Somebody slugged me."

"I'm coming in." He shoved his weight against the door and stepped inside. "All I need is for the paparazzi to catch me here."

"You'd better lower your voice, then. You're projecting all over the place." She took two steps back as he stepped inside.

At that moment, Aunt Clair flung open the kitchen door and whizzed into the conservatory, Mac bolting ahead of her in a fit of yapping. "What is this? How dare you come skulking around my house at this time of night?" The wheelchair squealed to a halt. "Nicholas Hewitt?"

Mac had stopped inches away from the actor, looking up at him expectantly. Jenna captured an eyeprint on the absurdity of it all—her aunt in a blue housecoat staring at the handsome bandaged actor in a mix of awe and anger while the little terrier wagged his tail in friendly delight.

"Sorry to disturb—Miss Elson, I believe?" and to the terrier

Nicholas added: "Hello, little fellow," and crouched to offer the dog his hand. Mac sniffed and wagged his tail while Nicholas rubbed his ears. Jenna knew at that moment that whatever this man did or did not do to Suzanna Lake, he was in no way responsible for her uncle's death.

Aunt Clair must have reached the same conclusion. She eased her chair forward, nodding as she went. "I watched you once on *Masterpiece Theatre* and thought you made a passable murderer in *The Wiltshire Affair*, Mr. Hewitt."

Nicholas stood up, his mouth quirking. "Only passable? Well, perhaps that will do, since I in no way wish to be mistaken as the real thing."

"But I did think your heroics rather overdone in that comic book film you made."

"Blame Hollywood," Nicholas said with a half-smile, "and the fact that I never could do an even passable hero."

"Your Sir Lancelot wasn't bad," Aunt Clair added.

He returned his large green eyes to Jenna. She almost flinched. "Pardon me if I cut the small talk, but I am not in a gracious mood. Comes from having one's head smashed in, not to mention the little matter of being a suspect in a friend's murder—a murder, Ms. Elson, for which you are responsible, one way or the other. If you hadn't fallen through my bloody skylight, knocked me senseless, and then left the scene, maybe Suzanna would still be alive. How many crimes does that make? Let me count the ways: trespassing, break and entry, assault, possible homicide. I count four. How's that for a start?"

"Don't you dare speak to my niece in that fashion," Aunt Clair said. "You're the one they suspect, not her."

"I'm sorry about Suzanna, sorry for your loss, and hers, but I did not kill her," Jenna said.

"What the hell were you doing on my roof, then? Answer me that. Dunn says you have a roofing habit, whatever the hell that means. Are you one of those slimy reporters who creep over people's lives sucking on juicy bits to just to prompt a feeding frenzy? You're a journalist, aren't you?"

"Not that kind of journalist."

"She's a world-class travel journalist," Aunt Clair said.

"Is spying on me a travel assignment now?" he boomed.

Aunt Clair drove her wheelchair forward. "She was searching for my brother's murderer, Mr. Hewitt. My brother, Daniel Elson, was felled in the same alley just three weeks previously. Somebody must find evidence necessary to nail the true murderer."

Nicholas's eyes widened. "You were climbing on my roof looking for Dan Elson's murderer? But his death was an accident."

"We think not."

"I'm still not sure," Jenna said quickly. "But I had to start at your end—"

"Because I let Jake cut down the trellis," said Aunt Clair.

"But I was attempting to make my way to Brian Dunn's to retrieve my uncle's flashlight and—"

"And I thought Brian Dunn was the real murderer," Aunt Clair announced. "Still do, in truth, because we have evidence."

"We do not have evidence and he couldn't have done it, I said," Jenna insisted, lowering herself on a chair. Why did she feel as though she'd fallen into a hideous farce?

"Those pictures clearly show a connection between Brian Dunn, Suzanna Lake, and my brother. The police won't listen."

Jenna lifted her head from her hands. "A picture of a dog painting is not evidence, Aunt Clair. That may have been the gift Dunn told me about. He meant to give it to Uncle Dan before he died."

"A painting of a dog, a trellis, and bloody Brian Dunn as a killer? Are you two ladies out of your effing minds?"

Jenna gazed up at his six foot-something height. "Keep your voice down."

"Watch your language," Aunt Clair admonished, and then she beamed. "Shall I fetch us a spot of tea?"

"No, you should not! This is not a bloody social call. I came here looking for answers and I'm sure as hell not getting any from you two. This isn't over, not by a long way." And he left, slamming the door behind him.

🕸 16 🕸

"**N**ow what?"

Jenna was busy making breakfast for her aunt. "Are scrambled eggs okay?"

"I don't mean about breakfast, Jenna. I mean concerning this murder business."

"I know what you meant." Jenna continued whisking the eggs, revelling in how much stronger she felt. She'd only awoken once the night before, and then only long enough to figure out where the noises were coming from. She'd heard Harry moving around in the kitchen. Now that he'd commandeered the guest room, nocturnal noises were to be expected but they still kept her awake. "I suggest we do nothing at all and leave it to the police."

"The police are useless."

"But they're still in the business of catching killers and we're not." And yet, Jenna could go places where they couldn't. She was in a much better position for catching this guy, or at least identifying him—that is, after she'd recovered. How could she stay out of it? "Right now, let's concentrate on breakfast."

"You know I can cook for myself and would be happy to make something for you, dear. I am not helpless."

"Yes, but I feel like doing it for you this morning."

"That's sweet of you. I never liked Sara's eggs. She used far too much ground pepper."

They ate in silence for a few minutes before Jenna casually asked: "Do you remember phoning me the night I fell?"

"Of course I do," Aunt Clair said. "I was most worried."

"Do you remember what you said?"

"I told you to come home. Why do you ask?" She gazed across the table at Jenna.

"The police were inquiring, that's all, and I didn't remember all of our conversation."

"Does it matter exactly what I said?"

"Yes, of course."

"Well, I don't remember. I was distraught. Are your memories still mangled?"

"I vaguely remember talking to you that night, that's it."

"Understandable. You must be patient. Maybe it's a blessing that you don't recall everything."

A blessing? It made her so frustrated she could scream. "Aunt Clair, what do you really know about Harry and Jake? Have you ever done a background check on them?"

Aunt Clair's fork clattered to the table. "What are you saying? Are you implying that one of those two boys is the killer now?"

"I didn't say that. I'm only asking a perfectly reasonable question, given what's been going on around here."

"I'll have you know that your uncle found Harry himself. He was recommended by someone on the street, and Jake worked at various gardening companies before he went off on his own. He, too, comes highly recommended."

"Okay, forget it."

Twenty minutes later, Harry shuffled into the kitchen wearing what looked to be the same clothes he'd had on the day before. He'd probably slept in them.

"Hard night at the study group?" Jenna asked.

"Pardon?" He stood at the counter peering into the empty coffeepot as if waiting for a brew to magically appear, his mouth turned into a tight line.

"I asked if you had a hard night at the study group. You look kind of tousled," Jenna asked.

"We studied late. Have a big test later today. Are there any more eggs?"

"Sure," she answered brightly. "In the fridge." She picked up her cup and sipped, keeping her eyes averted. If he expected her to cook for him, he'd be waiting a long time.

"Shall I fix you something, dear?" Aunt Clair asked.

"No, you should not, Auntie," Jenna said quickly. "Harry used to be a short-order cook, didn't you, Harry? And you certainly don't need Aunt Clair fussing after you, since it's supposed to be the other way around." She didn't care how pointed that sounded.

"Right," Harry said, flashing Aunt Clair a grin. "I'll fix something quickly. Can I make more toast for you two ladies?"

They both refused and, as much as Jenna longed to hang around to make sure Harry didn't maneuver Aunt Clair further, the desire to escape won out. She headed upstairs, determined to get moving. By the time she had showered and dressed, her aunt was under the headphones with Harry by her side and did not hear Jenna knock.

Harry, however, turned and waved. "Everything okay?"

"Sure. I'm just taking Mac for a walk. Are there many still hanging around outside?"

"A few, but nothing like a few days ago. Police still have the lane blocked off at both ends, though. Very cool disguise, by the way."

She'd put on a black fedora, more to protect her head than anything else, but she knew the sunglasses put the look way over the top—black jeans, black turtleneck, black leather jacket, hat, and sunglasses. Black had always been her look for practical reasons.

As soon as she stepped outside, she regretted her choice. Almost immediately, the two newshounds who had accosted her previously broke away from the group at the end of the street and began barreling towards her. Jenna tugged on Mac's lead and headed in the opposite direction. She wouldn't even make it to the end of the street before they'd catch up. And her stomach started churning as soon as she quickened her pace. Damn, she should have taken a dose of her aunt's lurid goo. Maybe when she got back to the house.

Bolting across the street, she thought she'd escape into the park. Only when she reached the gate did she realize she'd left the garden key behind. For one crazy moment she considered climbing the fence, but that would abandon Mac. Turning, she faced her tormentors.

"Ms. Elson, may we have a word?"

"No, you may not. Back off."

"We only want to ask you a few questions."

"And I refuse to answer."

"Is it true that you know Brian Dunn and Nicholas Hewitt?"

"What?" she gasped. "Where did you hear that?" Mac was barking and barking.

"Is it true?" the elfin-faced reporter asked, stepping forward.

"Get out of my way!" Jenna barrelled through the bloodsucking knot, heading back across the street. "Back off," she said again as she pushed her way towards her front door. At least she'd remembered the house key.

After that, Jenna resolved to stay indoors and bide her time napping and scanning the news until night finally fell. Harry dropped by with Indian takeaway shortly after 6:00 and left just as quickly. She chatted with her aunt over supper, keeping the conversation carefully neutral.

The hours ground by. Finally, Aunt Clair retired upstairs to watch TV, leaving Jenna to pretend to head to bed early. Moments later, she tiptoed downstairs with Mac in her arms.

Though she'd donned her usual black-on-black—leggings, hoodie, a loose black kerchief that wouldn't hurt her healing scalp, plus her second pair of black sneakers—she had spent time on the details. What assets she had—shapely figure, fine bone structure, thick shoulder-length hair—had to shine. She'd allowed herself to look scruffy for far too long. It was a matter of pride.

Downstairs, she kept only the night-lights on and lowered the dog to the floor. "Wait for me here." Mac whimpered, watching her anxiously. Deep down in some beyond-words connectivity, she believed he understood.

She'd already decided against going the street route. She'd glimpsed the car parked on the other side of the square, recognized a paparazzi stakeout when she saw one, and knew the police were on regular drive-by. On the other hand, she wasn't quite up to roofing, either, which left the service lane. She managed yesterday and would do so again. Besides, Dunn would be keeping an eye out for her and surely the murderous bastard wouldn't try anything again so soon.

She eased open the conservatory door and slipped into the dark, pausing to test the air for movement, animal smells, anything, the way she'd done on her wilderness treks. But the city was different. Here, everything seethed, scents glommed together in a miasmic goo, and the dark seemed populated by every possible danger. But only one danger interested her now.

And in her imagination, she could feel him waiting.

Stepping out into the yard, she paused, the hairs prickling the back of her neck. What kind of killer sneaked up behind unsuspecting victims and banged their skulls in? A coward, that's who. The hell if she'd be afraid of a coward.

But when the twig snapped from somewhere in the shadows to the right, her response was pure adrenaline. She shot across the yard, into the alley, and sprung towards Mrs. Chester's, seeking the quickest route to higher ground. Footsteps pounded the earth behind her. She couldn't risk turning around, couldn't slow down for a second.

She counted the houses as she ran—one, two, three. He was behind her but not gaining. She bolted across the widow's weedy yard, focused only on the shed, thinking she'd be up in seconds. Only she couldn't see a shed. It had disappeared! No way. Her brain had to be playing tricks, yet once she was closer, she saw that what was once a shed had been reduced to a stack of rotting lumber. The house was dark, this being past Mrs. Chester's bedtime.

And a shape darker than shadow was moving stealthily towards her. Turning back, she launched herself at the side of the house, fingers grappling with the brick sill as she levered upwards. Her sneakers gripped crumbling mortar, one foot finding support on a nail left over from the shed, her hands grasping the top of the kitchen extension, both of which gave her enough leverage to leap for the second-story dormer.

There she dangled, peering up into the dark for the next handhold but seeing none. The basic structure of these houses were all built the same, and she knew that nothing but a straight drop of ten feet separated this level from the next. She was too far away from the drainpipe, which looked to be too rickety, anyway. Shit.

He stood below her now. She could hear him breathing. "Who are you?" she cried. "What the hell do you want?"

No answer, as if he were assessing her predicament. Was he waiting for her to fall? Damned if that was going to happen. She strained her neck upwards and realized the window was ajar. It should open onto a hall. If she could get inside and bolt upstairs to the third-story window, it would be a quick leap to the dormer roof to the main roof. *If.*

She felt him move below, and in a sudden burst of fury, she kicked her weight upwards, hitching one leg onto the ledge and hoisting herself up by gripping the inside of the lower sill. Then she shoved her other leg through the opening and in seconds had the window pushed further open and had wiggled into the darkened hall. By the time she turned and looked through the window, he'd already disappeared. Bastard.

Trembling, her head pounding, she bounded down the hall. Snoring rattled the air from a room to the right and everything reeked of cat and litter boxes as she climbed the next flight. The third-story dormer was wedged shut from disuse but she banged it open, cringing when the snoring below stopped briefly. When it resumed seconds later, she strengthened her assault. Once the window was open, it took only minutes to climb out to the dormer and stretch up to the roof where safety enveloped her at last.

She wedged herself in among the chimney sentries to steady her heart. What had just happened? She hadn't seen his face, hadn't even caught a sense of his height and weight—nothing—and yet he'd been there. Maybe he would have killed her had he had the chance. But no, he had the chance. He could have caught up to her while she was still in the alley, grabbed her earlier. So, why hadn't he?

He was taunting her, playing with her. She shivered, her strength reserves severely taxed. Even her legs trembled.

It was past 10:30 and she was already late. If talking to Dunn brought her closer to answers, the risks she took that night would be worth it. Time to worry about the return trip later.

She continued slipping up and over the range of peaks towards Dunn's at number 48, careful to steady herself where necessary. Occasionally, she paused to listen, but her pursuer was now keeping well out of sight. Onward she went, passing all the usual inhabitants, while keeping her eyes away from their worlds. Her head still ached but was bearable.

After scrambling over the chimney wall of number 47 and down the other side, she noticed the light from Brian Dunn's rooftop shone like a beacon. From there it was an easy climb down the trellis to the studio. Thank God. And the door was unlatched

Stepping inside, she stared hard at the near-empty studio. Where had all the paintings gone? Dropcloths lay strewn on the floor amid the empty easels. It was as if the place had been cleared in a hurry.

A set of narrow stairs led down to the third-story hall. Removing her sneakers, she padded along the wooden floors. Devoid of furniture, the white walls displayed large pieces of modern sculpture at either end, with bright slashes of abstract paintings everywhere else. But the men's voices downstairs interested her more.

It only took a few seconds to follow Hewitt's baritone downstairs, along another hall, and into a large, book-lined den. Nicholas stood over Brian Dunn with his back turned. "Are you kidding me? Why didn't you tell me this earlier?" he was saying. Tall and broad-shouldered, something about the real man hit Jenna's senses in all her secret places. Damn. It was like an ambush.

"Well, Nick, old boy, it's not as if we were having regular tête-à-têtes at the time. You were filming in New Guinea or some god-awful place, and Suzanna was mooning around being miserable."

"You should have delivered her to detox."

"I tried, but I could not persuade her the way you could. She—"

"I'm here," Jenna said.

Nicholas swung around. "Bloody hell, you didn't seriously just climb over the roof again?"

Jenna stepped into the room. "I did. Seemed the most expedient path, considering some bastard chased me in the lane."

"What?" Dunn struggled to stand.

"He's playing with me. He was out there," Jenna continued, pointing towards the lane. "He could have had me but didn't. It's like he's toying with me. I bolted in through Mrs. Chester's second-story window and, from there, up to the third-story window to the roof. I have no idea how I'm going to get back."

Nicholas swore under his breath. "I'm going after the bastard." He sprang for the door.

"Wait. He's already evaporated into the night. He knows this street too well. You'll never find him."

Nicholas turned, staring at her. "Then we'll call the police."

Jenna shook her head. "Go for it. We'll explain that I'm back to roofing while colluding with you two. Besides, he's been operating right under their noses all along."

"She's right," Dunn said. "Whoever this is has had a leg up on us the whole time."

"I think he lives on the street," Jenna continued. "He's always here, yet can disappear in an instant. What other explanation is there? He didn't try climbing the roof after me, either, which means I'm safer up there than on the ground."

Nicholas bored into her with those green eyes. "What are you saying?"

"I may be the only one who can find him, that's what I'm saying."

Both men stared at her for a moment. "You can't possibly be serious?" Dunn said.

"That's ludicrous," Hewitt agreed.

"Who do you think you are, my girl, one of those comic book heroes that can climb buildings with a single leap?" Dunn asked.

"And crash to the ground with equal ease," Hewitt muttered.

"Look, he's killed two people and I doubt he's finished yet. What choice do I have?"

"But what about your injury?" Dunn inquired.

"It's on the mend. I just need my memory back."

"Don't be hasty. This man is ruthless. Nevertheless, I'm so happy you came, Jenna. Sit down, please, let us talk," Dunn said. "I was afraid you'd think better of coming," he continued, propping himself to his feet. "May I offer you a drink? I have every possible alcoholic potion on call."

Jenna followed the direction of his hand to an impressively stocked bar, complete with a thick oak counter and stools. "You have a pub in your den?"

"It's from *The Crown and Tuppence*, to be exact," Nicholas said. "The only antiques of which Brian approves are those associated with his pet vices."

"Nonsense, you won't find a cigarette dispenser on the premises. Nicholas, don't be churlish. Pour the lady a drink. I'll just remain seated, if you don't mind. I've been instructed not to stray far from my nebulizer, I'm afraid."

Hell, the poor man sounded as though he was living on borrowed time. "Water's fine for me, and I can get it myself," Jenna said.

But Nicholas moved swiftly to intercept, his arm brushing hers. "Water, it is. Take a seat, Ms. Elson. I'm not that much of a brute."

Jenna perched on a chrome-and-leather chair next to Dunn. "You said you had something to tell me."

Nicholas turned towards her, a glass of water in one hand and a refill of his own wineglass in the other. "And we have plenty to ask you in return," he said, passing Jenna the glass. "I expect you to explain your actions more fully." His large green eyes still sparked anger.

"Nicholas, stop—" Dunn began.

Jenna straightened. "That again? I'll tell you everything you want to know, but I'm not being interrogated, so cut the tone." Really, she wasn't in the mood for this shit. Zero patience. "The only people able to figure out this mess and possibly catch the killer are in this room. If I'm not the murderer—and I assure you I'm not—and both of you claim to be innocent, too, then who murdered Suzanna and my uncle? Who's out there in the alley stalking me tonight?"

"Bravo! You tell him, Jenna," Dunn said.

She turned to her host. "Let's get to work. Each one of us has pieces of the puzzle. Let's put them all out on the table. Suzanna Lake knew both of you, let's start there."

Nicholas kept his gaze fixed on her but she couldn't bring herself to meet his eyes. "And you fell on top of me the night she died. Let's start there."

She couldn't resist his gravitational pull any longer. Slowly, she turned. "I told you why I was there and what happened. I was initially investigating my uncle's murder," she said, locking her gaze with his. Those damn eyes. "Well, possible murder. My aunt suspected you, Brian." She snapped her attention back to her host.

"I understand, and you were playing the old game. Your uncle told me all about your childhood."

"What game?" Nicholas asked.

"I told you, Nick: Jenna's aunt kept herself entertained by prodding her young niece into climbing roofs and spying on the neighbors. Jenna would then feed her with the details."

"That's bloody child abuse," Nicholas said.

Jenna turned to him, hoping her face didn't betray how much his words hurt. "She didn't have to prod me, I loved it. We called it 'be my eyes.'"

"You were a child," Dunn said. "You didn't know any better. Your aunt should have."

Why did it sound so harsh coming from a stranger? "Did my uncle really tell you all this?" she asked quickly.

"He did indeed," Dunn replied.

"I can't imagine him telling anyone anything so personal. He was such a private man."

"He was, but the time came in his life when he craved companionship, and we struck up such a thing over our gardening one summer's day. It began with a discussion on trimming hedges and ... developed from there. Every man needs someone to talk to once in a while. Don't you need a friend also?"

She thought of Annette, now out of reach. "Don't be an asshole, Mr. Dunn. I get your point."

He gave her a sly grin. "Yes, well, we had much in common, your uncle and I. Both of us had single sisters, for example."

Jenna swallowed. A nude montage lay right in her field of vision. She couldn't imagine her uncle befriending Brian Dunn under any circumstance, but it had to have been true. "Are you saying that he discussed our private lives with you, too?"

"Exactly what I am saying. We old farts had a few things in common—more than you'd suspect. You wouldn't begrudge us that, would you?"

"I'm not begrudging him anything, I'm just shocked."

"Excuse me for interrupting, and you two will need further time to cozy up, I'm sure—maybe over tea and scones with violins playing in the background—but do you mind if we keep to the topic at hand?" Nicholas said, slapping the top of the bar with his palm. "You were on my roof playing an old childhood *game* while supposedly checking out Dunn as a possible murder suspect for a death that had already been declared accidental by the police. Am I getting this right so far?"

Jenna shot him a sour look. "Yeah, so far."

"And did this visual memory of yours serve to provide something crucial that night or was it all for entertainment?" Nicholas pressed.

That stung. "My memories are fractured like my skull. They keep flashing in and out, but not in any way that makes sense."

"And you were eavesdropping on my conversation with Suzanna. You are, in fact, the witness who overheard our argument the night she died?"

"I heard most of it. Can we get to what happened next? This is the part that's crucial: someone hit you *after* I fell, and whacked me on the head *after* I left your house. Maybe before, too, for all I can remember —and I can't remember much, at least not coherently. There's that business with the axe. Maybe he intended to kill us both or just confound the police. What makes more sense?"

"Nothing makes sense, Ms. Elson, that's the bloody point," Nicholas said through his teeth.

"Who has a motive for axing Suzanna, besides you, I mean?" she countered. "She was, after all, your girlfriend, or maybe 'wanted to be your girlfriend' would be more like it."

"Are you trying to play Chief Inspector McKinnon now?" Nicholas demanded, his hands plunged deep into his pockets and his face flushed. "Does you spying on my conversations somehow make you some kind of expert?"

"Look, I'm trying to figure out what happened—why I have this bash on my head that refuses to let my eyeprints align; why you have a cracked skull; why somebody chased me in the lane just now; why two people are dead!" Jenna cried.

"Children, stop!" Dunn pleaded. "Enough. Nicholas, cease the attack." He coughed, steadied himself, and continued. "She's ... here to get information, the same as we are, and she is *not* responsible for what happened to ... Suzanna. You know that."

Nicholas paused, gazing up at the ceiling. "I'm just so damn frustrated and angry, but more with myself than anyone, except maybe Suzanna herself."

"You were trying to help her," Dunn said with a wheeze.

"Well, my god-awful tough-love plan didn't work, did it?" He strode towards the opposite wall, his hand pressed to his temples. "And then, the one time I wouldn't let her in—*the one time*—she's brutally murdered."

Jenna studied him. Was this an act, Nicholas Hewitt in dramatic persona?

"Stop beating yourself up, Nick, old boy. You weren't to ... blame," Dunn said. "Only Suzanna could help herself. You were not her keeper."

"I am still guilty," she heard Nicholas say, the words wrenching out from some deep-down place. If he was acting, he was damn good at it, even offstage. "She told me someone followed her home on more than two occasions, but I put it down to drug-induced hallucinations."

Jenna leaned forward, following his every move. She eyeprinted his expression—the high color, the flashing eyes. Maybe she could study the images later and catch a flaw in his presentation. "Somebody was watching her, watching us all."

Nicholas swung to face her. "But why, who?"

Their eyes met again. She almost flinched. "That's what we have to find out. Maybe I'm to be next, or maybe you, or somebody else. I'm not going to just cower in a corner and let him get away with it. This is personal. My uncle died, and so did your girlfriend, and I think someone is trying to set one of us up."

Nicholas pulled back. "Fiercely stated, but Suzanna was my friend first, the girlfriend role only a temporary aberration on my part—an error in judgment, one bloody night I wish to hell I could take back. We went to drama school together. We were mates first, good mates. God, I miss her." He swung away, his anguish too raw to be an act. She had the sense that he wasn't really talking to them, but to himself: a soliloquy of the conscience.

"*That* Suzanna has been gone for a long time, Nick, old chap," Dunn added. "Once she started in on the drugs, there was not much any of us could do. You just became one more addiction."

Jenna couldn't stand this. "So, what could be the motive linking both?"

"Maybe this isn't about premeditated murder that requires a motive," Nicholas replied, turning back towards her. The planes of his face were sharp and tight like a man holding himself together with fraying bits of resolve. "Perhaps there's a serial killer out there who just likes to kill."

"I'm no expert in murder," Dunn said with a cough, "but I have seen a few films and read the papers. Don't serial murderers favor a type?"

"A profile, you mean?" Nicholas said, still gazing at Jenna. "But your uncle, presuming he was even murdered, has nothing in common with Suzanna, in terms of type."

Jenna shook her head, which had, not surprisingly, begun to throb. "I think this is personal, but I don't understand why or how. I think I was being followed that night, and probably Suzanna, too. I think someone hangs around the lane, watching and waiting—the same guy that tailed me tonight. That still doesn't answer the question of why he would want to kill any of us. There has to be a connection we're missing." She reached for her water glass, excruciatingly aware of Nicholas's scrutiny weighing down upon her. "What and who are the common denominators besides you, Mr. Dunn?" she asked, trying to break Nicholas's gaze.

"Brian, please," Dunn said, taking a deep draw of oxygen from the machine by his chair. His face, too pale and thin, looked like a death mask. "Pardon me, yes, well, I have no motive for killing anybody. Both were friends and, trust me, I treasure my friends ... more now than ever. Suzanna was a beautiful, damaged woman ... who tried to retain her fame by ... commissioning me to paint her ... in a variety of salacious poses ... based on the one movie ... that sent her to fame a decade ago."

"*Neon Blue*—a gory B movie that mashed sex with violence," Nicholas remarked, swigging back his wine. "And you didn't have to encourage her, damn it. She was a fine actress. You should have seen her play Cordelia—bloody brilliant! If she had stopped trying to use her sexuality instead of her talent, she might have acquired better roles."

"Suzanna believed her ... sexuality *was* her talent," Dunn said, waving his hand.

"Bollocks! That's what you fed her. I knew better. I encouraged her to be the woman she was meant to be, not some goddamn nudie poster!"

"In any case, she would often drop around to see me, especially ... after Nick activated his tough-love approach. I'd always ... take her in. However, I was in the hospital the night she died," Dunn said, gazing over at Jenna.

"So you have the perfect airtight alibi," Jenna agreed. "But where does my uncle fit into all this? He knew you, Mr. Dunn—*Brian*—but not Mr. Hewitt or Suzanna."

"Ah, not true, my dear. Your uncle knew both Suzanna Lake and Nicholas," Brian Dunn said.

"What?"

"Hold on, Ms. Elson, you're in for a shock." Nicholas reached for the wine bottle and refilled his glass. "You'd better get this over with, Dunn, but be gentle on her. 'And weigh'st thy words before thou giv'st them breath.'"

Jenna glanced from Nicholas to Dunn. "What?"

Dunn sighed. "Your uncle was in love with my sister."

❧ 17 ❧

"Uncle Dan was having *an affair?*"

"*Affair* is a bit strong for two well-into-their-seventies seniors sharing wine twice weekly. Take a seat, please." Nicholas tossed back the rest of his wine and proceeded to refill his glass.

"You will meet her," Dunn explained between coughs. "She is coming tonight. Suzanna was here a few times ... when they met ... and—"

"And, Brian, get your bony old ass back under your nebulizer." Nicholas leaned over to pull the apparatus towards Dunn's face. "I'll explain the rest while you focus on breathing. I can't stand your bloody gasping."

Dunn acquiesced and replaced the mask.

"And stay there this time," Nicholas ordered.

Once Dunn was breathing regularly, Nicholas turned to Jenna, who had climbed to her feet and stood grappling with everything she'd heard.

"I met your uncle only once but heard the whole story from Zanna," Nicholas explained, "who thought it sweet but amusing—imagine two seniors getting it on under Brian's roof?"

"Getting it on ..." Jenna mumbled.

"Zanna was under the impression that life ceased after the age of thirty, and in her case, it did." He paused, gazing down at his wineglass for a moment before continuing. "Apparently, they met while Fran was here visiting Dunn, though I wouldn't put it past Brian to have set the whole thing up. Your uncle was a regular here, used to swing by while walking his dog. And Fran—who is a gem, I might add—is very close to her brother. Dunn, despite his appalling art, is a bred-in-the-bone romantic, so you can see how it transpired."

"But Uncle Dan had been a bachelor for seven decades. I can't imagine them having, ah ..."

"Sex?" Nicholas asked. "Why ever not? I certainly hope they did the deed, but what do I know?"

Brian shook his head vehemently from under his mask, the machine rattling away at his side.

"Looks like they did not," Nicholas said. "Pity."

Dunn lifted his mask and said: "Not before the wedding."

"Wedding?" Jenna cried.

"I was getting to that. Yes, your uncle asked Frances Dunn Hardy to marry him," Nicholas said, shooting back the last dregs of his wine "They had yet to set a date, but I believe there was some talk of summer nuptials. Suzanna asked to be maid of honor. Now, that would have been something. I'm not certain that Fran and your uncle agreed to such a request, for obvious reasons." He studied her for a moment while swaying slightly on his feet. "Think I need another glass. Are you sure you wouldn't like something stronger than water, Ms. Elson? You look like you need it. Oh, wait—scratch that: never climb and drink."

"Never drink with a head injury, more like it!" She was back on her feet and, for some unaccountable reason, her face was wet with tears. "My uncle and Dunn's sister were going to marry?"

"Calm down, Ms. Elson," Nicholas began, one hand reaching out to steady her but missing by an inch.

"Oh, for God's sake, call me Jenna, and you're drunk!" she cried, slapping away his hand.

"And you should be, too, after what you've just heard."

Jenna ignored him. "But how can Uncle Dan have fallen in love after all these years? How could he even think to make such a massive change?" *Without me knowing? Without telling Aunt Clair?*

Dunn lifted his mask briefly. "Hope for happiness, Jenna. Everyone has a right to some."

"But my uncle *was* happy!" she cried. But he wasn't, she knew he wasn't. Why did she still cling to that lie?

Nicholas set his glass down and looked at Jenna. "The man only yearned for a little comfort in the winter of his years. He and Fran got on famously."

Dunn lifted his mask. "Soul mates," he rasped.

"Yes, soul mates," Nicholas said. "Do you believe in soul mates, Ms. Elson?"

"*Jenna!*" she cried. This was all too much. Maybe it was her injury, but her emotions were clawing at the surface like caged animals and she couldn't stand it.

"Are you all right?" Nicholas asked in that smoke-and-whiskey voice.

But Jenna didn't answer, only stepped past him and strode to the opposite wall where she found herself face-to-face with that hideous montage—not brutal, not violent, but still painful to view. She swung around to face Dunn. "Uncle Dan would hate your art. He was a good, kind man. This would *appall* him!"

"And so it did," Dunn said, lifting his mask. "I want people to recoil, to protest, to ask ... what in our society would ever make this ... acceptable ... for women, for anybody."

"Bollocks!" Nicholas boomed. "You wanted the money!"

"It's true ... they paid well ... and delivered me ... fame." Dunn took a deep, labored breath. "How I wish I'd never painted them."

"You have pictures of Suzanna *sliced*," she said.

"*Had.* I destroyed ... them all. I am not that person." And then the man crumpled into sobbing heaves. "I was a ... slave to ... economic expediency. Shameful ... it wasn't real."

"The man is a reprobate, but he really isn't as bad as he's painted himself to be over the years, pun intended," Nicholas said, and to Dunn he added more gently, "Pull yourself together and reapply your mask, man. I'm just going to take Jenna for a bit of a stroll while you compose yourself."

Nicholas took Jenna's arm and steered her out the door. He was unsteady on his feet while she was an emotional mess. She considered shaking him off but didn't have the will. It was as if the world had collapsed all over again and she couldn't see her way through the rubble.

He led her down the hall and up the stairs to the roof.

"Where are all his paintings?" she asked as they stepped into the glass studio.

"Cut them up and sent them out with the trash apparently. He thinks his art is in some way responsible for her death, but that's not true. Poor Suzanna ... was bashed on the head—" his breath caught in a half-sob "—bashed, not slashed." He tried to laugh but couldn't pull it off.

God, what a trio they made: all grieving, all beating themselves up for one thing or another. And Jenna had to be the biggest mess of all. Why couldn't she accept that her uncle wanted a life beyond his suffocating existence with Aunt Clair? His life had been nothing but sacrifice and trying to do the right thing. And here somebody squashed his chance for a happy ending. Somebody wanted him dead, but who, why?

She took a deep breath, expelling it slowly. Poor Uncle Dan. She would have come to his wedding. She would have been a bridesmaid. It was then that her gaze landed on a small painting of a little dog leaning by the stairway door.

There were two paintings of the same terrier side by side. One, an expertly realized oil of MacTavish, was so vivid she half expected the terrier to trot over and lick her hand, while the other was clearly one of uncle's loving but amateur watercolors. The sight almost broke her down again, but she refused to succumb. Damn it, she had to pull herself together and fast. "I feel like everything is cracking me open," she whispered. "I'm battered and raw."

"As am I," Nicholas said behind her. "The only consolation is that we may need to be broken to become whole again. Sounds trite, I know, but it's irrevocably true."

But she was crying now, sobbing uncontrollably.

"Oh, hell, wait a minute, there must be a tissue around here somewhere for you to slobber into." He turned, stumbled over to the glass, and returned with a box of tissues.

She grabbed one and she blew into it noisily.

"Sound effects are a nice touch," he remarked.

She stifled a laugh and blotted her eyes. So much for not falling apart. Even her dreams were in pieces. "Would you go check on Brian and leave me alone for a minute?"

He peered at her for a moment as if assuring himself that the tears were real. "Certainly."

After a few moments of grappling with new truths in solitude, Jenna took a deep breath and headed out the door to the hall. She was halfway to the den when the front door opened and in walked a woman Jenna recognized as Fran. For a moment, they just stood staring at one another.

Fran broke the silence first. "Oh, dear, Jenna. I am so sorry for your loss."

"Our loss, I understand."

Fran stepped forward. "Brian told you. Yes, our loss. I adored your uncle. I still can't believe he's gone." And the two of them embraced, both crying.

Nicholas poked his head out and quickly withdrew.

"How long have—had—you been engaged?" Jenna asked.

"He proposed to me on May Day, so not awfully long." Fran stepped back while pulling a tissue from her pocket. "He called you to discuss it all. He wanted your advice on how to tell your aunt."

"So she doesn't know?" How could she? She would have said something.

Fran shook her head. "I don't believe so. He kept putting it off, poor dear. He was so worried about how she'd respond, but he wouldn't have just deserted her, you understand that, don't you, Jenna?"

"Of course."

"We purchased a little Georgian town house across the park so we could stay close—he to his sister, me to my brother. Sounds so perfect, doesn't it? So cozy. That's what we believed for a while, that all our dreams had come true. We had found one another after all these years.

Once everything was lined up properly, he planned to introduce me to Clair, and ease her into the idea of our marriage slowly. Do you think she would have accepted me?"

"I don't know," Jenna answered. "She can be unpredictable, but if she thought she'd have more freedom, maybe. Uncle Dan kept her on a tight financial chain apparently."

"He did? I didn't realize that. We always decided on things together, so I assumed matters would be handled in a similar fashion with his sister."

"It was a stipulation my father put in place."

Nicholas appeared at the doorway. "Would you ladies care to join us?"

"Yes, of course," Fran said.

The moment they entered the den, Fran strode directly to her brother. "I am sorry, Bri. I tried to come earlier but the traffic is horrid tonight with these terrorist scares." She turned to Jenna. "I stay here most nights but still have my flat in Chelsea, at least until it sells."

"You can sell the new place and move here after I'm gone, Fran," Brian told her, lifting the mask.

"You're not going anywhere, you silly man. Have you been following the doctor's orders?" Fran asked.

Dunn dropped the mask, his eyes sunk deep into the sockets, a patch of stark red on each cheek. "Yes, of course. Do stop fussing. I see you've met Jenna."

Fran turned to Jenna and smiled. "Yes, we have been getting acquainted."

"It's a lot to take in," Jenna remarked. "I'm having trouble processing it all."

"Did you see the paintings?" Dunn asked.

She nodded.

"We were to make a trade, your uncle and I. We each painted a portrait of Mac. He brought me his the night he died but mine ... was still drying. I would like you to have it, but if you don't mind, I'll keep my ... gift."

Jenna sighed. "Of course, and thank you. I'll leave it here for now."

"Are you all right, Jenna? I know you must be hurting," Dunn said.

"We all are," Nicholas muttered behind her.

"Yes, we are," Fran agreed. "It's all so heart-wrenching."

"And still no suspects," Jenna said. "We need to get back to our discussion over who could have done this thing, who had motive to kill both Uncle Dan and Suzanna Lake. What does that man chasing me tonight have to do with it? Either the deaths were crimes of passion or someone stood to gain from Suzanna's and Uncle Dan's deaths. Or maybe the two deaths aren't even related, but I doubt that. They *were* killed in similar ways—a blow to the head—the same injuries as Mr. Hewitt and I suffered."

"*Nicholas,*" she heard him say behind her.

"*Nicholas,*" she said, liking the way the name moved in her mouth but not liking the man. He was so different from her dream lover, so flawed. Why must life be so damn messy and complicated? "They must be linked—all of this is—but how?"

Brian Dunn fixed her in his gaze. "I have an idea, but you won't like it."

"What could possibly be more of a shock than what I've already heard?" she asked.

"Let me pose a question to you, Jenna," Dunn began. He paused for a moment to take a deep, wavering breath, fixing her with his bleary eyes, now so deeply sunken she could barely see them. "What do you know of ... your uncle's will?"

She straightened. "My uncle's will? Everything. I mean, I was there during the reading, and all of it went to Aunt Clair, as it should. I have money enough of my own."

"And the monies left to your aunt is a substantial amount, I understand."

She didn't like where this was heading. "A substantial amount, yes, in the millions of pounds. When my father died, he divided his assets so that half went to me and half to my aunt and uncle equally, and Uncle Dan was a whiz with investments."

"Actually, that half went to your uncle fully, did it not, with the stipulation that he, in turn, take care of your aunt in a kind of trust?" he asked.

"He told you that, too?" she said slowly. "I didn't even know that part until recently."

"Your uncle was quite torn up about it. Apparently, his older brother, your father, insisted it be so."

"Yeah, he would. He worried about Aunt Clair's ..." She paused. Aunt Clair's what? "Her buying *impulses*," she said finally.

Of all the years she'd known her uncle, of all the days she'd spent with him growing up, never once had he raised his voice or spoken a negative word about Aunt Clair. Not until she was an adult and had moved far away had her Uncle Dan tried to communicate his anxiety. She remembered it now as if it were yesterday, and remembered brushing off his concerns with a laugh. She didn't have time for that, after all. Aunt Clair was Aunt Clair.

"He needed someone to talk to, and I, after all, would soon become part of the family," Dunn was saying. "He said he tried to call you to discuss the details but no one answered."

"I was away," Jenna said, faltering. "He never would call my cell. It always had to be my home phone. By the time I got the message he was gone."

"So sad. So your aunt now inherits the estate fully without restrictions?" Dunn returned briefly to his mask to take several lungfuls of air.

"What are you implying?"

Dunn coughed. "Only posing ... questions, nothing more."

Fran turned to her brother. "It's more than that, Brian. What are you trying to say?"

"Yes, what are you trying to say?" Jenna demanded. "Aunt Clair would never have Uncle Dan harmed for money. She loved him."

"Of course she did. That's not the point," Brian wheezed.

"Then what the hell is?"

"That we look at every possibility," Nicholas responded, "you said so yourself. This is only one avenue and we're only brainstorming here, aren't we, Dunn?" He had found another bottle of wine and was helping himself to a glass.

Brian lifted the mask. "I only ask because ... it's a possible motive. Money is always ... a motive."

"Money would never be a motive for Aunt Clair!" Jenna cried.

"Spoken like one who has always had plenty of it," Nicholas muttered.

Jenna turned to him. "What the hell is that supposed to mean?"

"Only that money is a time-honored motive for those who never feel they can have enough," he replied.

"Are you suggesting that my aunt killed her brother to get his money? That's utterly preposterous!" Jenna didn't care that she was shouting.

"I'm only ... posing a perspective ... I—" Dunn offered.

"Dan did tell me that he would have another will drawn up after we married," Fran said, "but I never gave it another thought."

Jenna stared at her for a moment. "I can't talk about this anymore tonight," she said, turning away. "I'm done." She turned and lunged for the door.

"Wait, Jenna ... please. I'm sorry. Let's do exchange ... cell numbers. Let's meet again ... soon," Dunn called.

But Jenna wasn't listening. She pushed past Fran and headed for the stairs. All she wanted was to escape from them all.

"Wait!" Nicholas called, following behind her. She was at the door to the studio stairs when he grabbed her arm.

"Let go of me," she cried, shaking him off.

He held up his hands. "Calm down. I'm just going to give you our numbers. Hang on. I don't suppose you've got a pen or paper?" He patted his pockets. "Shit. I've come unarmed." He stood swaying, his mouth twisted into a wry smile. "Why not give me your phone so I can input the numbers?"

"I don't have a damn phone." She turned and strode upstairs. "It got smashed during my fall."

"Wait." He scratched a couple of numbers on the back of a receipt with a blunt pencil he unearthed from his jeans pocket. "Don't know if it's legible. One can only hope." He passed it up to her. "After you process, we'll need to talk further. Please call."

She wadded the paper up and shoved it under her waistband, catching the way his eyes followed her hand.

"Pardon if I don't climb with you home but I'm afraid of heights," he said. "I make a pathetic hero."

"You also make a pathetic drunk."

"Ouch. I thought I managed that much rather well."

She stared down at him as he stood two stairs down. Handsome face with those made-for-matinees cheekbones in high relief, the curly hair tousled, the fine mouth turned down in a wry smile—or was that a grimace?—he looked as gorgeous as ever, yet different. Real. Totally imperfect, flawed. And he scared the hell out of her. "Your head's going to feel like shit tomorrow."

"It's my soul that's wounded," he said, calling after her as she climbed the stairs to the roof. "My head can bloody well heal itself!"

❧ 18 ❧

Jenna scrambled up the trellis to the roof without thinking. So much to take in, so many assumptions cracked, and now her brain throbbed insistently—whether because of her injury or the news she'd just heard or both, she didn't know.

Time to face the facts: Uncle Dan, the mild-mannered man who'd raised her and sacrificed everything for his sister, had fallen in love with a woman and planned to escape to happiness.

He deserved it, he really did.

That didn't mean that her aunt had killed him for it. Aunt Clair would never kill her beloved brother over money—*thud, thud, thud.* Shit, it was like some battering ram splintering her skull with the force of her assumptions.

But Aunt Clair did have those two rent-a-dudes working for her. Either one of them *could* have killed Uncle Dan at her request.

Jenna squeezed her eyes shut. No, no, no. She couldn't think like that. But what did she really know about those she loved, let alone those two? How many whacks in the head did it take to start asking the really hard questions?

The traffic hummed far away, the rustling breeze lifting her hair, that sense of being above and away from it all comforted her. While she remained cocooned in this world that was dark and strangely hers, every thought became clearer. Maybe if she stayed up here long enough, she'd understand all of it, put all the broken pieces together. Perspective was everything.

The last thing she wanted was to descend back down to earth but she had no choice.

When she reached Mrs. Chester's, all she could do was stare into the shadows, her heart so heavy she could barely move. She had to know the truth. Time was running out. Soon she'd have to leave England and return to her job or, worse, the killer might kill again.

Suddenly it struck her that she had no idea how to get back down. Getting up always seemed easier, though this one hadn't exactly been a breeze there, either.

But once she dropped onto the third-story dormer, all she needed to do was crawl down through Mrs. Chester's open window, into her house, and down to the open second-floor window. That wasn't the problem. It was the length from the second story to the kitchen extension that worried her—ten feet of unbroken drop.

She took a deep breath, sensing the darkness below. The night felt empty but that didn't mean the killer wasn't waiting. And yet, she couldn't stay up there all night based on a possibility.

Finally, she swung over the edge, hands gripping the eaves. If she fell, it wouldn't be the first time, and she'd done this kind of fool thing before, only under vastly different circumstances—like with a rope and minus this broken skull.

She landed on the dormer, twisted around, and shimmied inside the open window. So far, so good. Standing there for a few seconds, she tried sussing out the atmosphere. Everything felt still, too still, and yet she could here a cat mewing from somewhere below so it wasn't as if the house was empty. Oh, hell. Just get this over with. Heading downstairs, she almost tripped over a white tabby.

"Sorry, kitty," she whispered as she tiptoed down to the second level. *The second level.* She stared down the length of the darkened hall to where curtains billowed streetlight from the open window. For a moment she had been afraid that Mrs. Chester had awoken in the night and closed it, but no. Yet something was still wrong.

Then she realized the snoring had stopped, that the house was deadly still despite the cat noises. *The cat noises.* One of them was meowing tense and plaintively like an animal in distress.

A chill hit. Someone moved below, someone heavy trying to be soundless, someone who couldn't resist kicking an animal out of the way. She sprang for the window ahead, finding it wide open when she had left it only partially so.

She'd climbed into a trap!

Footsteps were racing down the hall behind her as she dove through the window and kicked her way up to the dormer. Only, before she reached safety, a hand grabbed her leg. She tried kicking herself free but he held fast while she clung to the eaves above, her fingers digging into the rotting wood.

"Let go of me!" she cried, but he didn't. Instead, he started pulling her as if trying to dislodge her grip.

She kicked furiously, slamming the hand that clutched her ankle hard against the window sill. She heard him curse as he released her, which provided all the time she needed to spring for the roof. Once there, she huddled, trembling, and stared down towards the dormer. Was he going climb out after her?

"Move over to your right a bit," said a smoky baritone far below.

She froze. "Nicholas?"

"I've got a ladder. I thought you might be able to use it."

"Bring it over to the side, away from the window. The killer's in there, he's after me!"

"I'm calling the police!" he bellowed. "Hear that, you bloody bastard?"

She sensed her attacked pulling himself away, heard footsteps pounding through the house. Her body went limp with relief. Moments later, she made herself scramble down the ladder.

Once her feet touched the ground, Nicholas grabbed her hand and pulled her to the mouth of the lane.

"What are you doing?" she cried.

"Getting you to safety. I called the police."

"But he's still in there! We've got to go nail the bastard."

"Like hell we do." He tugged her away. "Leave it to the cops. I'm no bloody hero."

"Then why did you even come after me?" she asked.

"Why do you think? You said you had no way to the ground level."

"If you hadn't come, I might have ..."

"You might have what?" he asked, turning towards her.

"I might have fallen." Her voice sounded too hoarse.

And then she saw the police car zooming towards them. She stood there, still holding Nicholas's hand as the constables ran up to them.

"You're too late," she told them. "He'll be long gone by now."

"Who? Did someone attack you?"

"I was on the roof when he chased me," she said wearily.

"You were climbing the roof?" the constable asked in disbelief. Now there were three of them clustering around them.

"I had to," she explained. "The killer was chasing me. Are you checking inside to see if Mrs. Chester is all right? He was in there with her!"

"We are investigating the house." Two police cars had their lights pulsing along with an entourage of press bloodhounds arriving at the scene. Cameras sparked like bullets in the night. Shit! She and Nicholas's faces would be plastered all over the news the next morning.

And she still had to deal with more police at the station. More police, more questions, and no action. In the end, the events leading to that evening made a long and tangled story that sounded no better when Chief Inspector McKinnon arrived.

"You were instructed to remain off of the roofs," the inspector stated.

"He was chasing me when I tried to take the lane earlier," she explained, after which she launched a detailed account of why she went to Dunn's in the first place, with Nicholas adding further details between gulps of coffee.

"Brian Dunn's sister was engaged to be married to your uncle, Ms. Elson?" McKinnon asked, jotting down notes.

"Yes, I said. I only just discovered this tonight. You see, there is a link between my uncle and Dunn, not that anything becomes clearer."

"We're not the bloody killers here, Chief Inspector. That bastard was in Mrs. Chester's house, we said. I caught sight of a shadow while I was positioning the ladder," Nicholas said, glowering into his foam cup.

It was then that the inspector informed them that Mrs. Chester was found deceased, apparently suffocated with a pillow as she slept.

"What?" Jenna gasped. "He *killed* her, too? But she's just a poor lonely old woman! Why did he have to kill her?" And then she started to cry, sobbing into her hands like the emotional wreck she was. Nicholas tried to comfort her but she elbowed him away.

"Did you catch the bastard?" Nicholas demanded. "He was right there! How far could he get with the place surrounded by police?"

"Mr. Hewitt, as of this moment, and prior to further investigation, there was no sign of anyone else having been in that house with the exception of Ms. Elson."

Jenna removed her hands from her face. What? Was that the plan all along, to make her look guilty? "So he's trying to pin this death on us, on *me*?"

"No such conclusions have yet to be reached," the inspector told them, "but while we're on the topic, where were you when your uncle, Daniel Elson, died?"

"What? I was in the Antarctic on assignment. You can't seriously accuse me of killing my uncle?"

"We're not accusing you of anything, Ms. Elson, merely posing questions. And is there someone who can verify that you were in Antarctica?"

"Yeah, try my passport, my employers, my bloody camera trail, and a shit-load of penguins!" She couldn't believe this. They couldn't be serious?

They were escorted back to their houses in separate cars, Jenna pulling up the hood of her sweatshirt trying to avoid the prying cameras.

She bolted from the street into the house, finding Mac at the front door wagging his tail. Scooping him up, she sprung for the stairs and into her room. Oblivious of Aunt Clair's calls, she locked the door behind her.

❧ 19 ❧

How could they ever think that she'd murder her uncle, let alone poor Mrs. Chester? Would they accuse her of killing Suzanna next? Jenna paced the narrow confines of her room, wanting to just kick down these damn walls and spring for the roof to stay there forever and ever.

Mac was watching her from the bed. Whimpering low in his throat, he suddenly barked.

Someone knocked hard on her bedroom door. "Jenna, let me in. I must speak with you." Her aunt's voice.

Oh, shit. Like she needed that. "Aunt Clair, not now," Jenna pleaded. "Hush, Mac."

"Yes, now."

"Give me a minute," she called.

"Then meet me in the kitchen in five. I mean it, Jenna. We must talk."

Jenna no more wanted to talk to Aunt Clair than she wanted to swim the Thames in January, but she knew she'd never hear the end of it if she didn't. Moments later, she entered the kitchen, Mac by her side.

Her aunt sat as if welded to her chair, her knuckles white on the armrests, her lips pursed.

"Aunt Clair, before we begin, just stay calm," Jenna began.

"Stay calm? You were brought home in a police car. They tell me Mrs. Chester's been murdered in her bed, and that you were there, inside that very house, with the killer, and I'm supposed to stay calm? You weren't supposed to leave the house! It is too dangerous, and yet you went, and to see Brian Dunn, of all people! We're not safe, nobody's safe in their beds!"

"You're safe with us around," Harry pointed out from where he leaned against the doorjamb. "Nothing's going to happen to you. We can install a full-sweep security system with cameras and hardwire it to the cops."

"I'll install new locks, bolt the windows. There's lots of things we can do but haven't yet," Jake added, looking down at the dog who kept barking.

"Mac, hush," Jenna said before swinging to the boys. "Where were you two tonight?"

"Jenna, that's enough," her aunt demanded. "I won't have you interrogating them under my roof. Be quiet, Mac!"

Harry shrugged. "We've talked to the cops already. I was walking home from class with my mates. Jake here was getting pissed in the pub, as usual—"

"I was not getting pissed. I had a few pints, that's all," the gardener protested.

"Point is, we both have alibis. You can't really suspect us as the killers?" Harry continued, his face flushing. "Hey, look, can we tie the little mutt outside so we can talk in peace?"

"No, you can't," Jenna snapped. "He lives here, you don't."

"Jenna, don't be rude!" Aunt Clair said. "Put Mac in the other room, then. Forgive her, boys, she's just overwrought, that's all."

Jenna scooped Mac up in her arms. "Can't we discuss this in private, Aunt Clair?" If things weren't bad enough, her aunt had summoned both rent-a-dudes.

"No, we can't. They stay, Jenna. They're here to help us, whereas you—" Aunt Clair began.

"Whereas me what?" Jenna asked, staring at her aunt. God, were they actually fighting? They never fought. They could always talk things out. "Let's just stop there. We're both too wound up to discuss anything rationally tonight. I'm exhausted and I'm just going to bed. See you in the morning." And with that, she pushed Harry out of her way and bounded for the stairs with Mac in arms.

Once in her room, she could not settle down. She continued to pace and fume until exhaustion forced her to sit, and then finally stretch out on top of her bed. What was she going to do? How would she escape this mess? The situation was like some vicious quagmire that kept dragging her deeper and deeper.

"I feel so trapped," she whispered to Mac. "So trapped ..."

She hardly slept, but what little she managed came just before the dawn and held her fast late into the morning. She awoke with Mac licking her hand as she lay still dressed on top of the covers.

Sunlight poured through the leafy curtains as she stared at the window, struggling to align her thoughts. Mac nuzzled her fingers.

"You need to pee—got it." Then her eyes landed on her broken phone on the bed table. Something stirred and shifted. She remembered holding the ringing phone. She remembered bringing it to her ear, hearing her aunt's voice say: "Get out of there right now!" *Get out of there right now!* But how did Aunt Clair even know where she was?

Mac whined again.

"I know, I know. Just let me get dressed and then I'll let you out." She grabbed a fresh set of clothes and headed for her en-suite bathroom. Hot water might jolt her thinking. Something had to.

Minutes later, she opened up the bedroom door and headed downstairs, Mac dashing ahead. Shuffling through the empty kitchen, she followed voices through to the conservatory. Her aunt was sitting by the open garden door talking to Jake as he installed a new security lock. She swung her chair around at the sound of Jenna's footsteps. "There you are," she said.

Jenna gazed from Jake to her aunt. "Here I am. How are you this morning, Aunt Clair?"

"Very well, thank you, Jenna, and you?" her aunt said, studying her intently.

"Fine. I see we are installing a new bolt."

"It is long overdue. Have you seen the news?"

Oh, hell. "Not yet, but I can imagine the headlines."

"You and Nicholas have apparently been lovers all along, and you no doubt bumped Suzanna Lake off in a jealous rage," her aunt told her.

"That makes sense. And did I kill Uncle Dan because he was attempting to stop the affair while knocking off poor Mrs. Chester because I didn't like her jam?"

Jake snickered as he wielded his screwdriver, caught Jenna's pointed look, and dropped his gaze.

"This is no laughing matter, Jenna Elson," Aunt Clair said.

"No, it isn't—" she sighed "—and yet those jokers are making up stories so ludicrous what else can we do but laugh?" She looked down at Mac, who was making no move to go outside. When she looked up again, Jake and her aunt were watching her. "Well, I'll let you get on with it, then. I'm going to make breakfast. Where's Harry?"

"He's off investigating a security system. He'll be back soon, but he dashed out earlier and bought a bag of croissants from the bakery," her aunt called behind her. "They taste delicious once nuked for a minute in the microwave."

Nuked. Jenna marched right through the house to the front door, eased it open, and shooed the terrier outside, watching while he dashed down the steps and anointed the side of the wrought-iron fence. He was back inside within minutes, but not soon enough, since the gawkers caught sight of her. She slammed the door as they surged towards the house. Returning to the kitchen, she put out Mac's food and dashed back upstairs, heading straight for her aunt's den.

She only had a few minutes before Harry returned. What was she looking for? Anything, something that might give shape to her vague suspicions. She began pulling out every drawer, finding notes, packages of colored pencils, flash drives—flash drives, five of them. She paused.

Everything must be stored electronically. She'd go through the drives one at a time, put them back, and take another until she had scanned all five. But as she pocketed a memory stick, she realized that any tech-savvy person would password-protect an important file and save everything to cloud storage. Breaking into that would be more of a challenge.

She lightly touched the keyboard of the nearest terminal. The machine slipped out of sleep mode and requested her password against a mountain vista background. Would a password be of her aunt's devising or Harry's? Her aunt could be endlessly inventive and she hadn't a clue what Harry would choose. In fact, she hadn't a clue about Harry—that was problem enough.

Taking a deep breath, she tried a few possibilities that Aunt Clair might consider—her uncle's birthday, her birthday, plus a few of her aunt's favorite books and films. Nothing worked—too pedestrian.

Voices downstairs. Mac barking. Someone entering the house. She backed out, switched off the light, and prayed that the terminal returned to sleep mode within seconds. Slipping into her uncle's den, she shut the door and stood there with her heart pounding as footsteps strode down the hall. Harry had arrived.

Three days after she'd landed in London, she and Aunt Clair had presided at the reading of Uncle Dan's will at his lawyer's office. It had been a dry, painful affair, no less excruciating because they already knew the contents: all of her brother's assets, half of which were hers, anyway, went to Clair Elson.

Uncle Dan had added a codicil leaving Jenna whatever personal effects she wanted. She'd briefly discussed with her aunt that she'd like a few of her uncle's paintings, his den furniture, his old watch—all things associated with warm memories but not particularly valuable. Aunt Clair had told her to take anything she wanted. There had been no mention of a second will devised for a pending marriage or any indication that Mr. Crosby, the barrister, even knew of such a thing, let alone her aunt.

But maybe the lawyer did know and that was protected under client confidentiality? Seeing as Uncle Dan had not only predeceased his sister but hadn't yet married, a second will would become redundant, anyway. Or maybe Uncle Dan had prepared a draft but hadn't disclosed it to anyone, seeing as the wedding was months away. That was more likely. He was meticulous. If he and Fran had gone so far as to buy a house together, he'd have drafted an alternate will.

Jenna stared at his desk—a lovely eighteenth-century mahogany roll-top. She and her uncle had picked it out together in an antique shop on Portabello Road decades before. If he'd ever drafted a second will, he'd have stored it in a traditional place like that desk or a safe, but certainly not on a computer. As far as she knew, he didn't own a safe, or even a strongbox. After his death, Aunt Clair had sent Jenna to the bank to close out his safety deposit box, which contained nothing but the deed to this house and an old gold watch.

Both she and her aunt had gone through all the obvious places that first week, the desk drawers included. They'd been seeking paperwork like unpaid bills, the usual stuff. "I keep all the household accounts on my system," Aunt Clair had said, "but your uncle always clung to the paper copies." And Uncle Dan, in his typical organized fashion, had left that paperwork in perfect order, right down to his checkbook with all the bills ticked off, his will tucked into a brown envelope in the middle drawer. But what if he'd drafted another and needed to keep it safe? What if he needed time to work out the specifics before revealing his plans to his sister?

Jenna locked the door behind her and slipped up to the desk. Crouching beside it, she reached deep under the central drawer to the back, letting her fingers seek the little latch she remembered the dealer showing them all those years ago. "Those eighteenth-century gents loved their secrets, they did. Thought to keep them safe in hidden compartments." The desk had two such hidey holes—one under the main drawer and one at the rear of the fourth pigeonhole on the right-hand side. Her nail caught the latch, she felt it give, and seconds later she was lifting the fold of paper from its slot. Hell, it was too damn easy. She'd hoped she wouldn't find anything.

Perching on the chair, she opened up the page and read her uncle's cursive script penned in one of his favorite fountain pens:

I, Daniel Ellis Elson, being of sound mind, do bequeath half of my investments and annuities to my wife, Frances Louisa Hardy nee Dunn, and half to my sister, Clair Kathleen Elson, with the total portion outlined in my brother's trust to go to Clair solely, as was his wish. In addition, the house and contents of number 40 Marlytree Terrace becomes the sole property of my sister, whereas the house at 19 Marlytree Place goes to Frances Louisa Elson.

JENNA RAN HER EYES OVER THE SCRIPT, ABSORBING EVERY DETAIL, hearing his voice as an overlay to each word. Though unsigned and unvalidated, it was no less true: Uncle Dan intended to bequeath half of his assets to his wife-to-be, which made perfect sense. That would have hardly left Aunt Clair destitute—far from it—but it sure as hell offered a possible motive for murder.

Only, Aunt Clair would never have had her own brother killed over money—wouldn't, couldn't. Surely Jenna knew that much? God, she hoped she knew that much. But her aunt had been spending a lot of money, though that was nothing new, and no one would kill a brother in order to pave the way for skylights and a koi pond, surely?

Jenna hunched over her knees, the thought of her aunt murdering Uncle Dan hitting like a physical blow. *No, no.*

There had to be a missing piece. Her fingers trembled as she returned the paper to its hiding place. Next, she popped the flash drive into her laptop, thrumming her fingers on the desk as the directory scrolled onto the screen. Documents, folder after folder worth. This was going to take a while. An hour later, she had scanned nothing more interesting than PDFs on subjects ranging from software manuals to *How to Grow a Shade Garden*. Shoving the drive into her jeans pocket, she resolved to return it later.

When she opened her door, Mac was waiting amid sounds of *Carmina Burana* rolling from the speakers about the house. Jenna slipped down the hall to her aunt's den. At the door, she was surprised to see Harry at one of the terminals working alone. He turned as she stepped through the door.

"Hi ya, Ms. Elson," he greeted.

"Hi ya, Harry. You may as well call me Jenna. So, have you installed the security system already?"

"I ordered the components. They should be here in a couple of days."

"Good. That will help Aunt Clair rest easier, I hope, but it seems too long to wait, under the circumstances."

He studied her. "Yeah, I know what you mean. Best to play it safe in the meantime."

"Like how?"

"Like not going anywhere after dark."

"Ah," she sighed. "You mean like me staying locked up inside."

He shrugged. "Just saying. I can get anything you need. You going off and meeting with Nicholas Hewitt and Brian Dunn like that didn't seem too wise, to me."

"I'll take that under advisement." *But I don't plan on adding you as a handler any time soon.* The kid had the nerve.

"Anyway." He turned back to his computer. "What can I do for you this morning?"

You can tell me what the hell is going on. "Actually, I wanted to thank you properly for helping my aunt since I've been indisposed." She liked that word *indisposed*, especially since it struck her as so ridiculously understated, under the circumstances. "I know I've seemed a bit testy lately, but with all that's been happening ..."

He swung back, the smile fixed back on his face. "No prob—totally understandable. Anything you need at any time, just ask. I can give you my cell number, if you'd like. Are you going to get your phone fixed? I can pick one up for you."

She smiled. "Thanks, but no thanks. I'll take care of it today." She took the card he offered and shoved it into her pocket.

"But those bloodsuckers on the street will swarm you."

"I'll find a way around them." She turned to leave. "Hey, do you know Mr. Dunn?"

"Yeah, sure, but not personally. I mean, he's kind of famous."

"I mean, did you know him before?"

"No way."

"Does Jake know him?"

"You'll have to ask him, but I think he's worked for a couple of gardening crews along the street, so maybe. Why do you ask?"

"Just wondering. Anyway, I'll let you get back to work studying or whatever it is you're doing."

"I enjoy the break." He sat there beaming, his freckled face all sunshine and bonhomie. He enjoyed the break, did he? What exactly was he taking a break from?

"And your parents don't mind you staying here?"

If possible, his smile broadened. "I know I look really young, but I've lived on my own for a long time. My parents are both gone. I'm sort of like you in that respect."

Like hell. "Sorry to hear that. Well, all right, then," she said, backing out. "Catch you later."

In moments, she was downstairs, finding her aunt at the kitchen table sipping tea while sniffing into a tissue and typing into her iPad. Jake could just be seen through the windows planting something, and the shiny new safety lock gleamed in the light.

Jenna slid into the chair across from her aunt. "Aunt Clair?" she whispered.

Her aunt looked up. "Yes? Oh, Jenna, poor Mrs. Chester. I can't believe she's gone, and to die so horribly. I'm just adding it to my journal but it's so hard to write when all I can recall are our neighborly years together. She used to visit me once upon a time, you know?"

"Did she? Mrs. Chester's death is tragic, and totally unnecessary. It's crazy to think whoever the killer is knocked her off for no good reason, unless she woke up and saw him." Jenna paused. "Still, whoever he is, he's growing bolder, thinks he can't be caught, and kills because he enjoys it."

"You're right: she must have seen him. Had you not been in her house—"

"Look, I am not responsible for Mrs. Chester's death just because I used her house to escape my own. That bastard has to be stopped, do you understand?"

"Yes, of course, Jenna, I was only saying—"

"Forget that for a moment, we have to talk privately while we can."

Aunt Clair nodded. "I suppose so."

"What do you mean, 'you suppose so'? We've always been close—confidantes, really—for years," Jenna continued, balling a paper napkin in her fist. "Now is not the time for us to fall apart. With everything crashing down around our ears, we need to be straight with one another. We can't afford games."

Aunt Clair arched her eyebrows. "Games, Jenna?"

"Secrets, games. You've always played them, and encouraged me to play along, but what used to be fun when I was a kid just isn't anymore."

"I'm not the only one keeping secrets in this household."

Touché. "No, you're not. I've been keeping things from you, too, especially things that could upset you. I went out last night and didn't tell you because I knew you'd be frantic, especially since I didn't have a phone."

"It was a crazy thing to do, Jenna. Surely you realize that?" her aunt said, her voice trembling. "I was so worried."

Jenna grabbed her aunt's hand. "Keep your voice down. Yes, I do know but these are desperate times. Look, what we're discussing here is between you and me—no telling Jake or Harry. Promise."

"But I—"

"*Promise.* Say the words like you mean them."

"I promise. Why are you making me say this?"

Jenna gripped her aunt's hand tighter. "Because we've always held to our promises, you and I, and this one could be the most important one of all. Something's not right under this roof. I don't trust either of those worker-bees of yours, and intend to discover the truth. What haven't you told me?"

"Oh, Jenna, dear girl, you *are* jealous! I knew it!" She exclaimed in delight.

"I'm not jealous, Aunt Clair, I'm suspicious, and for good reason. You had Jake follow me down the lane the night I fell, didn't you? That's how you knew I'd crashed into Nicholas Hewitt's house. I remember that phone call now, and you knew exactly where I was before I told you, before I even knew myself. You lied to me."

Aunt Clair tried to tug her hand away but Jenna held fast. "I had to. I couldn't let you go out there with a murderer loose, could I? Jake kept an eye on you, protected you. He couldn't climb the roofs like you, but he could patrol the alley and keep you safe from predators on the ground. It was him who brought you home after you collapsed in the alley. You should be grateful."

"Grateful? And since when did I collapse in the alley? I thought I collapsed in the garden? And I was whacked on the head, remember? No, I am sure as hell not grateful. That was a murder scene and he was there, don't you get it?"

"I get it, but he wasn't there. In fact, he probably scared the real murderer away before the hatchet man could finish you off. Don't look at me that way, it's true! I asked Jake to keep an eye on the ground that night while you climbed and he followed along right up until that terrible rainstorm, when he took cover in that abandoned house. Then he called me to see if I'd heard from you but, of course, I hadn't. I told him to get back out there and keep looking, and that's when he heard the crash. He couldn't tell where it was coming from. He thought it was thunder at first. By the time he reached the middle of the lane, you were flat on your face covered in blood. He thought you were dead!"

Jenna gripped her aunt's other hand, holding both tight. "Don't you see how suspicious that makes him look?"

"Of course I know. Why do you think we haven't told the police?"

"But you must tell the police."

Aunt Clair squeezed Jenna's hands so hard she winced. "You must *not* tell the police or my boy will end up in jail before we ever discover the truth! He'd become the prime suspect."

"Because he is," Jenna hissed. "That fact can't possibility have escaped you."

"He was never near the crash site. He only got as far as where you collapsed in the lane, at which point he brought you home."

"So he says, but somebody messed with the crime scene."

"But not him! Jenna, he is not a killer!"

"Then who? And if Jake keeps hiding—if both of you keep hiding evidence—you'll look like suspects and end up in jail. At the very least, he needs to explain what he's seen." Then a thought struck. "Wait, you had him follow Uncle Dan, too, didn't you? He's become your new 'be my eyes,' hasn't he?"

The blue eyes widened. "He's not half as good as you, but yes, he goes where I tell him—both of them do. Dan was behaving differently so I had Jake follow him."

"And?"

"And what, Jenna, what are you implying?"

"And what did he discover? And why did Uncle Dan wind up dead?"

"Jake did not kill him, if that's what you're implying. Do you think I would just sit here if I thought for a moment he was the killer? But I knew you'd think that, which is why I couldn't tell you, and we still don't know why your dear uncle wound up dead."

Jenna pulled away. "Maybe we do."

The older woman jerked back as if she'd been slapped. "What are you saying? You must be jealous! Why else would you behave this way? And you wonder why I keep secrets from you."

"Keep your voice down," Jenna said.

But Aunt Clair wasn't listening. "You've been so different since the fall, so quick to judge and accuse. No wonder I don't tell you things."

"What else haven't you told me? What did Jake find out about Uncle Dan? Tell me."

Aunt Clair opened her mouth to speak but then Mac started barking. In seconds, Harry had bounded into the room. Shit. How much had he heard?

"Everything okay in here?" he asked, looking from one to the other.

"No, everything is not okay," Jenna said. "Aunt Clair and I were just discussing more security features. She'd like cameras, like as in a security depot set up right here in the house, don't you, Auntie?"

Aunt Clair hesitated but then nodded. "He knows what I want, don't you, dear? But Jenna insists we speed up the process."

"Maybe I can jerry-rig something temporary until the equipment arrives," Harry said. "Just let me write my exam this afternoon and then I'll get right on it."

Aunt Clair looked at Jenna. "We can wait a bit, can't we, Jenna?"

"I guess we'll have to." Jenna climbed to her feet. "Meanwhile, I've got to get going. I have some errands to run. Can I pick anything up for you?" she asked her aunt.

"That's all right," Harry said. "I'm around for a little while and I can get anything she needs. I wouldn't go outside, if I were you."

Jenna just smiled and headed upstairs, Mac trotting after. Was Aunt Clair really that blinded by her own neediness? Couldn't she see what a pair of manipulative liars these boys were? But if they were involved in this, what could their motive be?

And could her aunt really have lost patience with the financial restrictions Uncle Dan placed upon her enough to have him killed? Could she really have discovered Uncle Dan's marriage and plotted to take all the fortune for herself?

No, no, no. She could not, would not, believe that her aunt had anything to do with her uncle's death or any of these deaths. Besides, why Suzanna Lake and poor Mrs. Chester?

Still, the longer Jenna remained under this roof, the more vividly she recalled the tension between aunt and uncle. They were not like a happily married couple the way she'd liked to remember them, but more like two people entwined in a throttle of love and obligation. What would Aunt Clair do when she found out about Uncle's Dan engagement?

Unless she already knew.

On the top landing, she saw that a photo had slipped from the wall. She stooped to pick it up, returning the ornate brass frame to the hook amid the series of other family photos. In this one, Dan Elson circa 1962, stood with his brother, George, in the center, with her grandmother and grandfather flanking either side. Aunt Clair sat in her wheelchair before her two elder brothers, her face scrunched into a reluctant smile.

Jenna studied the scene for a moment. It had been taken outside her grandparents' Dorset estate, back in the days when her grandfather still ran his textile mills and the money still poured in by the bucketful. Jenna hadn't been born yet, and her father—the handsome man in the middle standing hands taller than anyone else—had yet to seek his fortune. But they were all rich at that point, the bankruptcy not occurring until five years later, when their new circumstances sent them scurrying into the city, and to this very house. That was about the time George Elson determined to acquire a gorgeous wife and strike out on his own to regain the family fortune. He accomplished both within five years.

Other photos in that vignette included one of her parents on their wedding day, her mother looking so radiant, so hopeful. She must have believed that she was marrying her prince charming, that being the fairy tale that generation embraced so absolutely. Certainly George Elson was to become a prince of commerce. Her mother's own family had been much more humble, Jenna's maternal grandfather being a history professor and her grandmother, a teacher. Look how far they'd all come—and gone.

Damn this whole mess. Her brain still only squeezed out snippets of information instead of the whole picture that she so desperately needed. Jenna continued upstairs, praying her aunt would keep her promise and not disclose Jenna's suspicions.

20

Jenna stood on the back patio, staring at the canker-shaped pond in the center of the yard. It was raining softly, one of those gentle spring rains that conjures growth and greenery while turning the world into a misty scum. Over the fences and walks, she could hear the chatter of voices on the street. The police would no doubt pay another visit to their house very soon.

"Jake?" she called.

The young man poked his head out of the shed, his red bandana like a smudge of blood in the gloom. "Ms. Elson?"

She plowed across the muck towards him. "We need to talk."

He backed up, letting her into what was once her uncle's old garage but now had turned into a work storage shed. He pulled up an old stool for her to sit on but she preferred to stand.

"Would you like some water? I've got a couple of bottles here." He pointed to a workbench where four bottles of water and two soda pop cans stood in a row. God, he was acting like this was his living room and she a lady come to visit.

"I'm fine, thanks."

"Mind if I have one?"

"Why would I? I see you've made yourself comfy here."

He shrugged. "Yeah, well, I'm usually so dirty, didn't seem right to mess up the house." He popped the top of a can of ginger ale.

"I'm sure my aunt wouldn't mind. She seems pretty fond of you."

His face split into a big grin. "Yeah, she's all right, your aunt."

He didn't act like a murderer, not that a murderer was a breed with specific characteristics, but he dressed almost as if he wanted to look tough but couldn't quite pull it off—the bandana, the jeans, the studded boots. It was as if he was all wannabe tough.

For some unaccountable reason, this amused her more than put her on guard. Who was all that outward toughness for, anyway—the girls? She almost felt sorry for him. "So, my aunt just told me that you were following me on the night I fell, that you picked me upon from the middle if the lane, and not the yard like you said. It's time you told me the truth."

His face, leaner than she remembered, almost hollow-cheeked, took a moment to register her words. "Oh, shit, she told you? I'm relieved I can finally say the truth. It's been burning a hole in me, you know? She asked me not to say anything to anyone, made me promise."

"Hell, Jake, don't you realize how much trouble you're in?"

He rubbed his eyes and swung away. "Yeah, I know, but what could I do? I need to keep working for her. I *need* the money."

"Yeah, well you won't stay employed in jail, will you? Tell me exactly what happened, and I mean everything."

"That night, you mean? I was trying to keep an eye on you, like she asked, but it started pissing down and I lost sight of you, so I went for cover in that new reno down the street."

"Number 46/47?"

He wiped the hair from his eyes, "Yeah, that's the one. I've been using the basement as a flophouse for the last couple of months— couldn't afford a place of me own—and then she called and told me to get back out there, so I went, but I couldn't see anything on the roofs, so I kept going and going until I reached Mr. Hewitt's yard. The gate was wide open so I crept up to the back door and into the house, and then I saw you there, facedown beside Mr. Hewitt—glass everywhere, the skylight above destroyed, rain coming in—and Suzanna Lake standing over you both. I thought you were dead or he was dead. I thought maybe you'd killed him by accident or Suzanna killed you both. She was sobbing and sobbing. I panicked, okay?"

"Did you see an axe?"

"Shit, no—no axe, no blood, though you both looked cut up pretty badly."

"And Suzanna was just standing there?"

He turned to face her. "Yeah, just standing and bawling."

"Did she see you?"

"No way."

"And then what did you do?"

"Look, I'm chicken-shit, okay? I ran. I didn't know what the hell had happened, but I thought maybe you accidentally killed him, you know? So I ran halfway down the lane and called your aunt to see what she wanted me to do. She said to go back, but I didn't want to. I wanted to call the cops, get an ambulance. Look, I've been to jail long ago for carjacking. I have a record, you know? I don't need to get wrapped up in this shit, don't need to be implicated in any way."

"As if you're not. And then what happened?"

"She talked me into it eventually, so I went back, only by then you were facedown in the center of the lane, covered in blood. I saw a guy running away and I ran after him but didn't get very far before she ordered me home."

"What did he look like?"

"About my height, in black pants, black hoodie, and a ski mask—too far away to get a good look."

"So you didn't recognize him?"

"No, how could I? It was pissing down, I said, and dark. Aunt Clair ordered me to pick you up and bring you home, so I did."

"And you didn't tell the police any of this? Hell, Jake, obstructing justice is only the beginning."

"I know, I know, but I don't want to go back to jail. I'm trying to remake my life, trying to play it clean. Now look at me, smack-dab in this bloody mess."

Jenna's eyeprints were cascading through her brain like a kaleidoscope. "You have to tell them what you know and you'd better do it soon. If what you say is true, and you help them find the real killer, you may not be charged."

"But if they don't nail the guy and blame me?"

"If you're innocent, how can they? Look, do you want this bastard caught or let him keep on killing?"

Jake hesitated. "Of course I want him nailed, but I'm scared, and I'm not fooling. I feel like, if I trip up, I'm dead meat. That's what I think happened when poor old Mrs. Chester woke up last night and saw him: he killed her. So, like, Suzanna saw him the night you fell, so he killed her, too, see? As long as you don't see his face or can't identify him, you live. The moment you can identify him, game's over."

"But you're big and strong, and all the victims have been weak and vulnerable."

"So? What if he jumps me when I'm not expecting it?" He wiped the back of his mouth with his hand and looked away. Hell, he was actually frightened.

She studied him closely, noting how the hand holding the can trembled. If he was a killer, he wasn't a particularly brilliant one, nor did he seem to possess the fortitude to pull off multiple murders. "Where were you last night?"

He turned to face her. "In a pub trying to get piss-eyed drunk. You can check."

"And what about Uncle Dan? How does he fit into all this?"

"Dunno, that's the problem. His death started it all, didn't it?"

Yes, it did. That was the key. Taking a deep breath, she continued. "Aunt Clair had you tailing him, too, didn't she? What did you find out?"

He met her eyes again, his dark brown gaze catching the light from the open door. "Only that your uncle finally made a couple of new friends. I didn't blame him, either, poor chap. God knows he could use a few since all he and your aunt ever did was fight."

Jenna caught her breath. "Really, you heard them?"

"Well, your aunt was always yelling at him but he never said anything back."

"But she wanted you to tail him?"

"Yeah, 'cause he started going out for walks at night, at weird times, you know? So I'd tail him as far as Mr. Dunn's and then take off. She wanted me to get right up to the house and spy on their conversations and stuff, but I don't have the patience for that shit. Most times, I'd take off to watch football at the pub and only pretend to stay with him."

"So what exactly did you tell my aunt, then?"

"Only that he was friends with Brian Dunn. She didn't like that but it was the truth."

"And that's it?"

"That's it, I swear. What else would I say?"

"I don't know, that's why I'm asking. And which pub were you in last night?"

"In the bloody Crown of Thorns off Bayswater. The cops already checked it out. Lots of peeps saw me."

Jenna took a deep breath. Everything he'd said sounded like the truth and yet she sensed he was holding something back. Nevertheless, she knew she'd get nothing more from him that day. Yet, she didn't feel in any danger at that moment. If he was the killer, she couldn't imagine he'd be so stupid as to slaughter her here in the garage when the finger would point so obviously to him. "Do you know who the killer is?" It was a desperate bid but she was nothing if not desperate.

He kicked a nail away into the corner. "Me, no, why?"

"You'd better talk to the police today, you hear me?"

"Yeah." He kept his head down.

"Look, I have to get to the high street. Think you can take me there on your bike?"

"Sure," he said, relief washing over his face. "So, you're not going to tell the cops on me?"

"It's better that you tell them yourself I said." While the pieces were still coming together, she'd give him a chance to do the right thing. "Don't tell Aunt Clair that we spoke, understand?"

Moments later, she was fastening on his spare helmet and climbing on the back of his shiny new bike. She didn't have to ask to know that he'd purchased the motorcycle with the proceeds from Aunt Clair's largess. So what if he'd rather have a set of shiny wheels than a place to stay?

She clutched his waist as they zipped down the lane, splashing through puddles towards the opposite end. Jenna cast a quick look up to Nicholas's ruined skylight, now tented under a tarpaulin. What was he up to today? Had Brian heard about Mrs. Chester?

No one tried to impede their progress, though knots of onlookers clustered at this end, too. Luckily, motorcycle helmets made excellent disguises.

Once on Kensington High Street, she nudged Jake to pull over. At least three phone depots were along this stretch and nearly every department store also sold them. He pulled to a stop and she dismounted. "Keep an eye on Aunt Clair," she told him. "If she should chance to figure out the killer, she could be next."

He nodded grimly and pulled away. She didn't really trust him but it seemed a good idea to pretend to trust everybody for now.

In minutes, she was wedged inside a little phone depot and, twenty minutes after that, had a new smart phone complete with a different number. Thank God. It was as if she'd regained an amputated limb.

Slipping away from the bustle of the main drag, she strode down the quiet lane of Drayson Mews. Leaning against a wall, she dug into her bag and plucked out the paper Nicholas had scribbled on the night before. The numbers were nearly illegible. She despaired at ever making a connection until finally, after several wrong numbers, the call connected to that rich husky baritone.

"Hello?"

She closed her eyes. That melodious tone could still ignite a firestorm in her belly. Stupid. "Nicholas?"

"Yes, it is he." As if that voice could belong to another.

"It's Jenna. I need to speak to you as soon as possible. Can we meet?"

There was a pause and then: "Jenna, shit. Where are you?"

"On Drayson Mews."

"You're bloody kidding me? Wait there and I'll pick you up." The phone clicked off and left her staring up at the converted stable cottage across street, wondering how he could reach her in his recent state of scrutinized captivity. The answer arrived minutes later when a black Bentley cruised down the lane, driven by what appeared to be a blond shaggy-haired man. The window lowered as she stepped forward.

"You look like you're wearing a cocker spaniel," she remarked.

His mouth quirked. "Wardrobe assistants are never around when you need them. Please get in, Ms. Elson."

She slipped into the seat beside him, wrinkling her nose against the smell of stale cigarettes. "I thought we were on a first-name basis after last night?"

He removed his sunglasses and looked at her fully, the green eyes bagged with fatigue and the fine mouth tugging downward. "My apologies, Jenna. I'm knackered. This has been such a hellish few days."

My, weren't we formal in the sober light of day? And testy. Jenna stared straight ahead. It had finally stopped raining.

"I have plenty of new information to share, if you're interested."

"Of course I'm interested. Do you mind if I smoke?" he asked, one hand reaching for his breast pocket.

"Yes, frankly. It's hell on my lungs."

He withdrew his hand. "So, what have you learned?"

"For one thing, I discovered that my aunt hired one of her rent-a-dudes to follow me every time I go off on a roofing excursion, including the night I fell. In fact, we've just had a good long talk and it seems we do have a new most-likely suspect, though in many ways he doesn't fit the profile." She quickly filled him in on her conversations with both Aunt Clair and Jake.

Nicholas swore. "Your aunt is sounding creepier and creepier—the spider at the center of a dark, tangled web."

"Oh, come on. She's just a brilliant woman forced to live under her brothers' thumbs all her life."

"One who manipulates others to do her bidding, including a child, and now may have had one brother killed to pave the way for her new life. What she had you do as a kid was nothing short of child abuse."

"Oh, please. I didn't do anything I didn't want to do."

"Listen, Jenna, I know that she's your aunt, and that this must be difficult for you, but let me ask you one thing: how many guardians do you know encourage their young charges to do dangerous things— things that could get them killed—just to keep them entertained? You could have fallen during those climbing episodes of yours. You were a kid."

Jenna stared straight ahead. "I did fall, many times, but I always got back up again and climbed the first chance I got. Nobody could stop me." She rested a hand on her gut, which had begun to churn.

"Shit."

"Look, this isn't about me, or my aunt; this about a killer."

"This *is* about you *and* your aunt, but you just don't want to see it. You're at the center of this mess somewhere, and if we dig deep enough we'll find it."

She turned to face him, startled to find him watching her. "Are you saying that I'm somehow responsible for these deaths?"

He swung his gaze back to the road. "Of course not. Calm down, will you? We're only talking."

"I'm talking, you're accusing." She fell back against the seat and squeezed her eyes shut, her head pounding, her emotions shattered. She heard him take a deep intake of breath beside her as if wrestling with his own frustrations.

"Look, Jenna," he began more gently, "family loyalty aside, you must realize that your aunt could have hired this Jake to do her dirty work. That's the only thing that makes sense."

Jenna stared out into the traffic and swallowed hard. "I found the draft of my uncle's second will in his antique desk."

He slammed on the brakes. "Shit! Why didn't you say that first off?" The car lurched forward as he waved an apology to the driver who almost rammed into them before swerving past with an angry honk.

"He planned to leave half of his estate to Fran and the rest, including the house, to my aunt."

"The part that was hers already?"

"Yes," she said, suddenly cross again. "But it doesn't prove that she had him killed. Why would she when the remaining funds would be still more than enough for her to live on forever, even with her spending habits?"

"You really don't get it, do you?" He shot her a quick look, his face all hard angles in the light. "Because people who have money always want more, that's why. It's a fact of life."

"A fact of whose life—yours? Not mine. It's a generalization that doesn't apply to everyone, especially not to my aunt. She's different, in more ways than one. She would never do that."

"Are you really so sure? Jenna, open your eyes. Try to at least consider the facts. She fits any murder investigator's 'most likely to succeed' profile: she has motive and opportunity, considering those two nobs she has working for her."

"But she's the one who's been calling my uncle's death murder all along, remember? The police have been content to label it accidental." She was shouting at him, her eyeprints rising before her in one slamming vision after the other: Aunt Clair sending a sidelong look at the boys; Jenna's broken phone that hadn't been damaged the night of the fall. She kept hiding evidence, sidetracking the investigation. Oh, hell. Jenna's throat tightened.

Nicholas was still talking, his hands gripping the wheel, his mouth tight. "Which would make an excellent cover, don't you think? And, from what I understand from both Fran and Brian, your uncle was wary where his sister was concerned, maybe even a little afraid of her."

"That's crazy!"

"Is it? What do you really know about them, Jenna? You've been away for how long?"

They had arrived at a stoplight but Jenna couldn't focus on the traffic streaming around them. His words were burning her brain.

"Just consider that your aunt might have paid Jake to knock off your uncle," Nicholas continued more gently. "Just consider it, that's all I ask."

As if she hadn't. Damn him. He was forcing her to stare down what she'd tried so hard to avoid. And at that moment she hated him for it.

She sat further back into the seat, the buttery leather oddly comforting and annoying all at once, and took a deep breath. She had to regain her balance; she had to defend her borders. "I know how guilty that second will makes her look, especially if it could be proven that she knew about it in advance, and I know that having both me and Uncle Dan followed is equally damning, but I also know she's innocent. Call it faith, call it instinct, call it whatever the hell you want, but there's something else afoot here."

Forcing her heart to steady, her blood to ease its pressure on her temples, took everything she had. She found herself literally pressing her hands to her heart as if that could keep all her emotions in check.

"'Money is the root of all evil, as they say."

"Don't tell me you quote the Bible as well as Shakespeare? Are you even capable of an original thought?" Nasty but she didn't care.

He just laughed. "I quote from a range of sources and occasionally do emit my own ideas, though apparently not today. All compliments aside, is there any way your uncle's death could benefit anybody other than your aunt?"

"Not that I know of."

"What about those two nobs?"

"Their employment increased significantly after my uncle's passing but that's no reason to kill anyone. So what if my aunt has them on call? She relishes having employees of her very own, it's true, and it's true that her 'be my eyes' obsession has always been carried too far, but I always went along with it. She's always wanted more control because her existence is so stifled, but does that mean that she'd kill her brother to get it?"

"The question stands."

She turned towards him. "There's something else amiss but I can't see clearly enough to figure out what. Why would Jake even tell me all this if he was the killer? It's like he had a need to confess."

Nicholas swore. "Maybe a good Catholic lad from way back, but I suspect it's to more likely to win your trust. I'm not the only actor in this world, you know. Maybe he killed Suzanna because she saw him the night you fell, and this bit about him saying that anybody who recognizes the killer dies is a subtle warning. He may be a lot smarter than he appears."

"Maybe."

He turned to meet her eyes. "What about this pub bit. He said that the police verified his alibi?"

She stared hard into his large green eyes, thinking ridiculous things like agate orbs and green pools. "Apparently. He was with his friends at the Crown of Thorns in Bayswater. Why lie about it if it can be checked?"

"Maybe he paid off a few blokes to back him up."

Jenna fell back against the seat. Somebody was playing them all, her especially. Somebody was out to slaughter anyone in his way. She'd get the bastard, she swore she would. "Well, if he is the killer, I swear I'll make him pay."

"Whoa, roof lady, you are not in this hellhole alone. We've both lost someone. If he's the killer, we'll bloody well get him together. Look, let's find a quiet pub somewhere, burrow into a dark corner, and talk this out."

"You make us sound like a pair of wood beetles, but okay." They were speaking in normal tones now, and it was a relief in more ways than one. She added: "Will your disguise hold up with you looking like a tall Labrador retriever?"

He flashed a quick grin. "So, I've changed breeds, have I? I assure you, no one will give me so much as a second glance even if I were to start barking. This is England, eccentrics still rock."

"Mad dogs and Englishmen," she muttered.

Moments later, Nicholas had parked the car on a quiet street in some outer borough. Jenna hadn't paid attention to the street signs so had no idea where they'd ended up, but the old pub reflected against the slick street like an apparition from another century, all cross-timbers and stucco with a wooden sign creaking in the breeze.

They wove through to the back of the main room and tucked themselves into a velvet-upholstered booth. Nobody seemed interested in either of them.

"Have you eaten recently?" he asked.

"Not since breakfast."

"Right, so we'll order lunch," and he called for a menu. "What do you feel for?"

"I don't care. I'll have what you're having." Not her usual style but it really didn't matter what she ate right then. Checking through a menu didn't seem worth the effort. When he ordered pot pies, chips and a couple of beers, she almost protested but managed to keep her mouth shut.

"So, tell me as much as you know," Nicholas prompted as they sipped their ale and waited for their meals.

She began to relax. This, at least, was nothing sexual—her mind was too consumed by threat to go there—and she couldn't relate this Nicholas to her dream lover, anyway, or even to the public image the man projected. No, here Nicholas was someone else entirely: a multifaceted, richly nuanced individual to whom she was bound by a common trauma.

"Turns out that Jake has been sleeping in the basement of that reno next to Brian's. That strikes me as the most damning thing of all, since he has total access to the lane day or night and repeatedly leaves my aunt's gate open." She gazed into her beer. "He has a record for carjacking, by the way, but claims he's a coward. I always figured that whoever our murderer is, he's got to be the worst kind of coward." Slowly, she realized, she was putting Jake firmly back on the suspect list.

"So can we agree that he's our prime suspect as it stands?"

"I guess so, but there's also Harry."

"The other nob?"

"The network guy. Thing is, he's never around in the evenings."

"That doesn't mean anything." Nicholas set his mug on the table. "Watch both of them. Stay on high alert at all times, not that you aren't already. You must be adept at survival skills while pursuing your, ah, activities."

She arched her eyebrows. "My activities?"

"Your climbing proclivities," he clarified.

"My roofing, you mean?"

"Is that what you call it?"

"That's what my aunt and I named it over the years, yes." She found herself filling him in on the details of her childhood, as well as on the series of events that caused the child she had been to break out of captivity again and again. It had to be the beer that loosened her tongue but she didn't care. She needed to talk and he was a surprisingly good listener.

When she finished, she found him gazing at her intently. "Poor little dodger," he said gently. "Broken homes and philandering fathers can smash a kid's life to pieces," he said.

"Oh, stop it. I don't need your pity." Her beer glass was empty. How'd that happen?

He held up his hands. "God, you're prickly. I was only commiserating as one piece of damaged goods to another."

"I'm not damaged goods," she said, looking around for the bartender. "I want another beer."

All Nicholas had to do was signal the bartender with his eyes, and the guy game running.

"How'd you do that?" she asked after the guy left to fetch another round.

"It's all in the facial action." Nicholas demonstrated.

"All in the gender, more like it. I'd practically have to drape myself over the table and show a leg before I'd get that kind of attention."

"Like hell," Nicholas murmured. "You just have to learn to use what you've got instead of hiding it under ..."

Jenna met his eyes. She got his drift but wasn't about to pursue it. "So why do you say you're damaged goods?"

"I was the little bastard who couldn't stay in school long enough to get my O levels, that's why. I drove me mum to distraction trying to curtail the criminal activities of her wayward son. My dad bolted when I was ten, leaving his two sons at the mercy of the streets as our mum worked like a dog just to put food on the table. My brother found succor in the computer industry but not me. I got in with a bad lot and turned to crime."

"You?"

"Me." He pulled a sneer so pronounced his high cheekbones slashed into a mask of villainy. "I was a bad little bugger, I was," he growled in a parody of some Dickensian character. "I pilfered, I vandalized, I was a destructive little menace. This Jake has nothing on me."

Something like a laugh escaped her. "But you have such a plummy accent. I could have sworn you were educated at Oxford."

He grinned. "Testament to the superior education I gained at acting school, and by studying the great masters of dramatic literature until I could drag myself out of the mire by the scruff of the neck." Spreading his hands, he added, "I had to take responsibility for myself in the end, so I found my gift, and stayed there until I grew into some-body I could live with."

Until I grew into somebody I could live with. "I understand that," she whispered, dragging her eyes from his face to the fresh beer that had just landed before her. So why was it that, after all this time, she was still trying to find a way to live with herself? Why wasn't she happier, and why only now did she realize she wasn't? "What about your mum?" she asked.

"I bought her a mansion in the country to thank her for putting up with me for all those years."

"Nice," Jenna remarked. "I can't buy my aunt stuff since she takes care of all that by herself."

"It's not money she wants from you obviously," Nicholas said softly.

Jenna took a deep draw of beer. "No, she wants me, wants my time. That's why she's so smitten with these guys. Both of them are like her little puppets willing to do her bidding, to be her eyes. It's my fault, and maybe my uncle's, too," she said, taking another sip.

"How so?"

"Because she needed her brothers to acknowledge her as an intelli-gent, if eccentric, individual in her own right—something I always did as a child in my own way. When I got older, I struck out on my own, and avoided returning home. I just left her. It's always been all about me, see? I always keep insisting that my career is more important than the people I love. I had to keep returning to my empty shell of a life in order to keep up the pretense of being someone important." Stunned by her own admission, she stared unfocused at her mug and suddenly burst into tears. *Oh, God, oh, God, here I am falling apart over a beer, in front of this man.*

"Jenna," Nicholas said softly. "There's the crux of what ails you, isn't it? It's yourself you're running away from. Escape artists have to be running away from something."

"So you're acting the psychologist now, are you?" she said with a sob. She had to rein in her emotions, but everything inside of her just kept galloping wildly. She heaved in more breath, demanding the tears to stop, but they wouldn't.

"You can't be an actor and not know something about character. Human nature is my life," he said softly.

She stared at him. "I told her I'm not sticking around. It's my fault Aunt Clair's being suckered in by these rent-boys of hers." Reaching out, she grabbed the beer and downed it all in several gulps and then stifled a belch behind her hand.

"You probably don't mean *that* kind of 'rent-boy—'" he smiled "—unless your aunt is paying for all kinds of services."

"Pardon?" She wiped her mouth on the back of her hand. "I didn't mean that kind of rent-boy. I shouldn't be drinking on an empty stomach. In fact, with my head injury, I still shouldn't be drinking at all." Had she really just spilled her guts in front of Nicholas Hewitt? "Oh, damn. I feel like barfing."

❧ 21 ❧

"Jenna, wake up."

Jenna roused herself from her doze. "Pardon?"

"I said that maybe we should go to the police," Nicholas said as he maneuvered the Bentley through the traffic back towards inner London.

"Um, and say what?" She yawned.

"We can tell them our suspicions."

"But suspicions are worth ... nothing without proof." Did she just glimpse an eyeprint of a parking lot from a weird angle? She sat up. "Um, did I just get sick back there?"

"Yup, upchucked into the bushes just outside the public house. Luckily, I got you outside before you entertained the guests. Woman, you can swear. You were punctuating every heave with a mouthful of sailor curses. Good on you, girl!"

"Shit."

"Where did you learn that?"

"Film crews. They're the worst. I had to be one of the gang."

"Well, seems you are a cheap drunk, after all."

"No doubt because of that cheap beer you forced down my throat along with all that greasy crap you fed me."

Nicholas laughed. "Yes, that was me spoon-feeding you all that pie, plus all of your chips and half of mine."

"Oh, hell." She sank back into the seat and squeezed her eyes shut. "I need coffee."

"I poured two cups down you back there. That's all that's revived you. How's your stomach now?"

"The stomach's empty, so fine. It's my head that hurts."

"Pop the glove compartment. I carry headache pills for just such emergencies.

She did as he suggested, washing down the pills with the remains of a takeaway coffee he had apparently purchased for her.

"Anyway, back to the police: you found a second will, remember? You could deliver that to the police."

She tried to focus but the moving car wasn't helping. "Not yet." She'd thought about speaking to Chief Inspector McKinnon, of course she had, but what good would that do at this point? She rubbed her temples, willing the headache to subside. They needed real evidence, not just theories. And then there was her aunt, who looked so very guilty. "I have to keep looking. Aunt Clair transcribes everything on her iPad ... and stores it on her network. She's obsessed about it. That's where I'll begin."

"And look for what?"

"I don't know, but I might be able to discover if my aunt knew about the second will."

"That still won't explain why Suzanna was killed. If Jake's telling the truth, she came upon us after you fell on me."

"Maybe she saw the killer so he murdered her?"

"You mean, she was just at the wrong place at the wrong time. That would be Suzanna."

"Well, that's what Jake said." Jenna sighed.

"Like he's the most reliable source."

Jenna stared out at the traffic. "He admits he was there—that's something. He also claims that there was no blood and no axe when he came upon us."

"Then he must be lying. I mean, how long would it take to kill Suzanna, dispose of the body in the lane, bash us both on the heads, *and* get back in there and disturb the scene? Probably a lot longer than he implied when he spun his story."

"His timing does seem off."

"So, maybe Jake is our killer, after all. Maybe he's setting us both up," Nicholas suggested.

"He must be a really, really good actor, then."

"They do exist," he remarked.

Jenna smiled. "So I hear. Anyway, we need hard evidence. I have to keep hunting."

"*I?* What's with the first person singular?"

"Look, I'm in the best position to find evidence, and you know it. By the time the police get the necessary search warrants, the evidence could be destroyed. All I need is a chance to dig around further." She downed the rest of the cold coffee.

"You mean, inside your house?"

"Not the house exactly, but the computers. Aunt Clair has everything she cares about recorded online. She even showed me a map she created of the roofs so she could climb with me virtually."

Nicholas whistled through his teeth, his eyes fixed on the road. "Getting creepy and creepier."

"She's wheelchair-bound as well as agoraphobic, so technology helps spread her boundaries, kind of like our 'be my eyes' games, plus she has this fantasy that the two of us can work together as covert spies."

"Are you kidding me? Spy on what, on whom?"

"I never asked," she said, wiping her eyes. Shit, not the tears again. "Don't you see: *I never ask.*"

"Good Lord, Jenna, don't tell me you're blaming yourself again? Stop with the self-recriminations and stay fixed on whether she knew that second will existed. The very existence of the will alone is pretty damning."

Jenna focused unseeing on a bus whizzing past. "I know that," she said softly.

"And how do you expect to find the answer to that on the network?"

"Because she keeps a journal—always has. She used to encourage me to keep one when I was growing up. Since she tuned into technology, she mentioned that she's scribed it all virtually, through scanning."

"Well, hell."

"Yeah, hell. The answers could be locked in that network somewhere because she seems to use that for everything, all password protected and lockbox safe."

"Do you have the skills to hack into her network?"

"Not exactly."

"What the hell does that mean? You either do or you don't. Sounds like a waste of precious time. Let me ask my brother Alex and speed this thing up. Now, he has the skills."

She shot him a quick look. "Your brother is a hacker?"

A wry smile tugged at his lips. "He wouldn't call himself that. I believe the term is a 'data security consultant' but he's a hacker by any other name. In any case, he never can resist a challenge. What are we getting him to search for?"

Jenna looked away. "Ask him to look for something out of the ordinary, something suspicious."

"Could we be a bit more specific?"

"No."

"Good thing he's suspicious by nature. Perhaps he can dig around for those journals?"

"A good place to start. Can he keyword search the words *will* and *marriage?*"

Nicholas arched his eyebrows. "You'd be surprised what these guys can riffle through when you're not looking. Lately, he's been contracted to work on banking security and the like."

"The killer's plan must be coming to a head soon. I have to keep digging the old-fashioned way."

"And risk getting caught the good old-fashioned way, too. We need to stay in close contact. I'll give your number to Alex. Oh, and I texted it to Brian in the pub, by the way. He wants to talk to you."

"Good. I need to talk with him and Fran again soon, but under the circumstances I think it's best not to leave the house for anymore nighttime assignations."

"I was going to suggest that."

They had arrived in the Kensington area, Jenna watching the traffic slide by in a blur of colored lights.

"You realize how bloody dangerous this is, searching that house alone, especially if Jake is on to you? If he catches you at it, it could all come crashing down around your ears."

"Technically, it already has," Jenna said.

"Jenna, I'm serious."

She took a deep breath. "Think I'm not? Look, just let me off at the corner, all right? It's better that we're not seen together."

Nicholas swore. "How are you planning to get back to the house without being recognized?"

"I'll figure something out. Can I borrow your cocker spaniel?"

"Be my guest. I have a shaggy kennel full where that one comes from."

The wig was curled up on the seat like a sleeping pup. Jenna pulled it down over her hair and adjusted the look in the vanity mirror. "Makes me look much curlier. Hopefully it will fool them long enough for me to get inside the door."

"There's a hat in the backseat. It'll probably come down around your ears, but it's worth a try."

Applying the hat, she studied her reflection. "Even worse, but it will have to do. You can let me off here."

Nicholas slapped one hand on the steering wheel. "Shit, there's a bloody bus behind us. I can't stop."

"I'll make a run for it."

"But we need time to set up a plan." Even as the car slowed to a stop, the bus started honking.

"I'll text you. Talk to you soon."

"Wait, Jenna—"

But she had bolted onto the sidewalk, giving him a quick wave before striding away into a stream of pedestrians.

Turning the corner, she strode towards Marlytree, her mind churning. The dregs of the day were casting an eerie orange-tinged glow through the mist, and it was as if the light set fire to her eyeprints. Blood, axes, glass, and Nicholas, all floating in a sickening orange miasma. She definitely should not have had that beer—*beers*, she amended.

But at least the crowds had dissipated, though a police car still sat outside poor Mrs. Chester's. Suddenly, she felt the urge to cry again.

Quickening her pace, she bounded down the street, turned the corner onto the lane, and tried the garden gate—locked. Good. Returning to the front, she unlocked the door and stepped swiftly into the hall.

The silence was chilling—no yapping Mac, no Aunt Clair. But this late in the day, she reminded herself, the house was often quiet. Jake generally left at suppertime, Harry disappeared to class, and Aunt Clair often napped between 4:00 and 6:00 o'clock if the boys weren't around. It was 5:15 and the boys weren't around.

But her heart still thumped in alarm as she carried on into the kitchen where she saw Mac tied to the garden railing, where he'd probably spent the day. "Poor little guy, you've been neglected again, haven't you?" She unfastened his lead and let him inside. "I'll take you for a little jaunt before dark tonight, I promise."

After filling his food and water bowl, she left him to his meal and crept upstairs. As she thought, Aunt Clair's bedroom door was closed. Carefully, she opened it a crack to assure herself that her aunt's steady sonorous breathing meant that all was well. She considered waking her so they could talk but it was too good an opportunity to pass. Carrying on down the hall, she stepped into the den, switched on the light, and gazed around.

Five terminals sat around the room, each networked and doubtlessly holding their secrets elsewhere, like in a cloud drive, maybe. She'd never be able to penetrate that digital fortress by herself. Hopefully, Nicholas's brother would come through.

Every terminal was locked by password protection but she spent a few futile moments testing passwords before giving up. That left the remaining flash drives to go through. Returning to her study, she locked the door and settled down to work.

This time it took only minutes to scan each drive because she had a better idea of what she *wasn't* looking for: she had no interest in file after file of saved articles covering a range of her aunt's many interests. Aunt Clair would probably have happily shared every detail, anyway, had she only asked. They used to talk about everything. It had been Aunt Clair who had encouraged Jenna's passion for exploring, for photography, and for writing. When had she become so busy that she had shut her down? But there was no time for guilt right then. Now she needed answers.

She was about to return the drives to the drawer in her aunt's den when her pocket vibrated. Nicholas: *Phone Alex now. He's expecting you,* followed by a number.

She tapped the digits and her phone rang through. "Hello?"

"Jenna?" Another deep baritone, but this one came with an East London accent.

"You're Alex."

"Right. Is this a secure line?"

"It's my new cell phone. Nobody else has the number but your brother and one other."

"Not secure, then, but will have to do. In order for me to investigate, I need the IP address. Text it back to me in five." And he clicked off.

A man of few words. So, where would she find an IP address? Once she'd Googled the topic, she returned to her laptop, and followed the instructions until she had the necessary number string to text back to Alex. In minutes, he phoned back.

"Do you have a cloud drive where I can send files securely? You'll need to go through this stuff yourself. I'll export whatever looks like it needs further scrutiny."

So she texted him her Dropbox link and password. So much for not giving your password to a stranger. All she had stored there were articles and work emails, anyway.

That done, she checked the time—7:00 p.m., much later than she expected, and far too long for her aunt to be still napping. She rapped on her aunt's door and stepped inside, the room pressing in around her, dark and close.

"Aunt Clair?" She could see the shape of her aunt's body under the covers. Slipping to the bed, she shoved away the wheelchair and gently touched the older woman's arm. "Auntie?"

A moan followed a sigh before Aunt Clair whispered, "Jenna, is that you?"

Jenna's relief swelled only long enough for her to switch on the bedside lamp. "You're so pale!"

Mac had arrived, jumping up on his hind legs to lick Aunt Clair's hand. "Hello, boy," Aunt Clair murmured. "Dear little Mac. Jenna, please do take him for a walk tonight. He's been such a good little fellow but he barks so much that we all find it quite annoying. I'm afraid we left him outside all day."

"I plan to take him for a quick walk around the block if the news suckers aren't too thick. Now back to your health..."

"Oh, it's nothing—upset tummy, nothing serious." She propped herself on her elbows while Jenna adjusted her pillow behind her head.

"But you never get sick."

"Of course I get sick. I'm only human. I just ate too much of that Thai takeaway Jake brought home today. Red curry always causes me upset, yet I never take heed. Few enough pleasures in life to deny myself the occasional treat, isn't that so? Here, pass me that pink stuff in the bottle—that's it. I shall just take another swig."

Jenna watched as her aunt took three gulps of the thick pepper-minty goo. "You say Jake brought this takeaway home to you?"

Aunt Clair rolled her eyes and replaced the cover on the bottle before passing it back to Jenna. "I asked him to. Today is Harry's big exam day. He writes two tonight from 7:00 to 10:00 and has been quite uptight about it all day, so we decided upon an early supper so he could take off to the library."

We. "And you asked Jake to get your supper?"

"Jenna, do stop." Aunt Clair leaned back against the pillows. "The demons always lay outside our borders, remember?"

"That was one of our old fantasies, Aunt Clair. This is real, this is murder, and the killer could be right under this roof."

"Oh, for heaven's sake! I haven't been poisoned. We were growing annoyed with the Gilded Orchid after they shorted us on the spring rolls a second time and refused to take responsibility, so we took our custom to a new place where they use far too many spices. Lesson learned."

"When was this?"

"When was what?"

"When did you eat?"

"Maybe fiveish. Don't worry, Jenna. We all ate the same thing, so if anyone laced the curry with poison, we'll all be on our way to the great beyond by now, including Jake. In any case, by tomorrow I'll be back to my old self. And what did you do this afternoon?"

Jenna pulled up a chair. "I met Nicholas Hewitt for lunch."

"Oh, did you now? Did you discuss the murders?"

"Of course. And did you keep your promise not to say anything to anyone?"

"How could you even ask such a thing? I said nothing to no one, even the tiresome police. They wanted to know where you were but I said I didn't know."

"Did they interrogate Jake and Harry?"

"Yes, of course."

"But Jake still didn't tell him the truth about that night you sent him out after me, did he?"

The older woman closed her eyes, suddenly looking much older. "I have no idea what he told them. We didn't discuss it, and your manner upset me to such a degree, Jenna, that I cried all day, what with dear Mrs. Chester gone, and you acting so harshly."

"Stop it, Aunt Clair."

The blue eyes flew open. "Stop what?"

"Stop the emotional manipulation. I'm not buying it. I know you too well. I want the truth and I want it now. It's time."

The older woman turned away to focus on the wall in front of her as if trying to hide within the thick undercover of her leafy Morris wallpaper.

But Jenna wouldn't let her go. "Aunt Clair?"

"All right, all right—I do have things to tell you, many things, and for the longest while I've been trying to decide how best to broach the topics, seeing how touchy you are—"

"Stop making this my fault. I have a few things to be accountable for but let's stick with your secrets first."

"Very well, but you must promise not to overreact and to try to understand my perspective."

Jenna flattened her palms on her thighs and inhaled deeply. "I can't promise anything until I hear what exactly it is I'm promising. Supposing you tell me the truth and I promise to listen fully. How's that? The more open and honest we are with one another, the better it will be."

"Yes, yes, that much is true." Aunt Clair sighed. "I am trying to be more forthcoming after a lifetime of maneuvering just to keep my soul alive, but it is challenging. Your uncle was quite hard on me, in his way."

"And maybe you were equally hard on him, in your own way."

Aunt Clair sighed again. "Yes, perhaps. We did quarrel so."

"But you wanted him to release your money and treat you like an adult."

"I did."

"But he wouldn't agree?"

Aunt Clair turned to her then. "That's just it, Jenna. I think he was considering it, I really do. He said he had something important to talk to me about, and to just hold tight, but then he died and I never did learn his big news."

Jenna stared down at her hands twisting in her lap. "You have no idea what he wanted to tell you?"

"No, nothing. I have always tried to be truthful to you, but sometimes it is like we're strangers."

Jenna stared straight ahead. Oh, God, but that was true. "I know. I'm sorry."

"Sorry for what exactly, Jenna? Let me hear it."

"Sorry that my father and uncle financially shackled you; sorry that you've spent your whole lifetime trying to ..." She gazed into her aunt's palm frond lampshade—crosshatchings of green blades against a haze of tropical sunshine trying to push light into some jungle darkness. Why did she think like that? "Trying to keep your imagination and spirit alive, despite all the rigidity of your life with your brothers ... for all these years. And, more than anything else, I'm sorry I never noticed."

Aunt Clair smiled sadly and grasped Jenna's hand. "Oh, you do understand, then, dear. But aren't we all just weak humans in the face of it all? I used to say that to you as a child, reminding you that even though we're all flawed, and that we hurt those we love when we don't mean to, it is still the love that lifts us above."

"Always," Jenna whispered, grasping her aunt's hand.

"I want you to forgive your father."

Jenna almost flinched as she tightened her grip on her aunt's hand. "Not yet, not now. Right now I need you to tell me what you've been hiding."

"I will, but I fear it will roil my stomach more than a bit and I do just wish it to settle some first. Humor me. Let us give the bismuth a chance to do its magic. Why not take our little trouper for his walk, and when you return, I shall be feeling ever so much better, and we will talk. I'll tell you the one thing I have been holding out on you, and can only hope that you will forgive me for it."

"Tell me now."

Aunt Clair laughed. "No, not now. Give me a few minutes, dear. Now go and be careful out there. It's still light. Stick to the main street and don't take any risks."

"Not knowing what you want to tell me is going to drive me crazy," Jenna said, getting to her feet.

"You'd best get on with it, then, hadn't you?"

"I'll be back in fifteen minutes."

"And I'll be waiting."

❧ 22 ❧

Mac's squirming said it all. "Okay, I get it," Jenna whispered as she steered him out to the sidewalk. "So, we'll jog."

She'd have loved to let him loose in the gated garden but too many shadows thickened on the perimeters this time of evening and who knew where the killer stalked tonight?

Dusk would fall soon. As it was, the street had almost cleared. A police car sat parked at Nicholas's end but otherwise Marlytree was near-empty.

She broke into an easy run, letting the dog keep up with his little legs. She'd jog along the four streets that formed the square, returning to her aunt's in what she estimated would be close to fifteen minutes. Maybe the exercise would stifle the itching curiosity. Maybe it would help her think. But the nature of her aunt's big secret chewed away at her and every scenario seemed too ugly to bear.

It's times like these when she'd love nothing better than to climb higher and higher, escape the world and all its problems, but that refuge seemed impossibly far away these days. Her troubles followed her everywhere and always had. They were always there waiting the moment she returned to earth. Why hadn't she realized that years ago? It was so damn obvious.

Marlytree looked deceptively innocent predusk. The gawkers had evaporated, the sidewalks nearly empty, leaving the terrace much like its old self—a quiet enclave in an inner London borough with rows of tidy houses sporting window boxes fronted by tiny manicured gardens.

But behind, above, and below, they seethed with secrets and fear. Jenna sensed the watchfulness of a neighborhood in lockdown. Nobody who lived here could experience anything else. Residents didn't linger on the streets or even dawdle in the garden anymore. They all hurried inside to bolt their doors.

She crossed the street to Kenmore Walk, a long stretch of road that linked several terrace squares that ran parallel to Kensington, and immediately turned the corner onto Upper Oakley, the street that faced Marlytree across the garden. Her pace was brisk. She was halfway along when her phone pinged in her pocket. Reining Mac in, she pressed her back against the wrought-iron fence and pulled out her phone.

A text from Alex: *Check your files.*

Jenna logged into her Dropbox account to find reams of new files occupying her storage, most bearing innocuous labels like *Household Expenses 2010-2011* throughout multiple years. A quick check revealed scanned documents of bills, invoices, and even bank statements. Jenna continued until she found special folders listed for each person in Aunt Clair's life, going way back to her parents, all dated. Everyone had a series of folders with the more recent files labeled *Sara, Jake, Henry, Daniel*, even *Jenna*. Fear wormed into gut. What the hell?

Holding her breath, she opened the first, Sara's file. It was no more than a litany of brief entries describing some slight her aunt felt the housekeeper had inflicted upon her, ranging from taking her brother's side in some argument, to refusing to do some requested task.

Next, Jenna opened her uncle's file, which was considerably longer and would take far more time to study than Jenna had at that moment. And yet, a brief scan revealed a kind of virtual scrapbook of her uncle's life, some entries which, like his retirement from the bank, were detailed and contained annotated conversations. Scrolling to the end, she read the words dated only a month earlier: *Where is Dan going on these walks? I have asked Jake to follow him and now know he visits Brian*

Dunn regularly, but why, and why won't he tell me? No entries followed after that except the date of Uncle's Dan's death.

What else had Aunt Clair asked the young man to do beside stalk her brother? Jenna needed to go through each of those files, discover what her aunt was thinking, what the hell she'd been doing, and why. Jenna shoved the phone deep into her pocket, a cold sweat prickling her skin. What did it all mean? She needed to know what her aunt had compiled about the two young men, about *her.* But not now. Now she had to get back and hope to God the woman who raised her would finally tell her the truth.

Mac whimpered at her feet.

"I know. Let's go."

Jenna bounded into a jog. Jake had to be involved. Regardless of what he said, he must have been the shadow she'd seen after the fall and the one who dodged her last night, Mrs. Chester's murderer—a coward. Maybe he'd been working with Aunt Clair all along, the two of them plotting together on how they would off Uncle Dan and split his fortune between them. Wasn't he driving a new bike? Hadn't he stopped working so hard on the renovation? She hated how her brain was working, thought her heart would break in two.

Then her phone rang. If it was Aunt Clair, she didn't want to answer it, but it was from Nicholas. "Nicholas," she breathed into the phone, her heart thumping from exercise and alarm. "I'm thinking more and more that it could be my aunt behind this, after all. She says she's going to tell me the truth finally."

"Bloody hell. Is Jake home?"

"No, she's alone and I'm heading back there now. Where are you?"

"Making my way across London. I had to drop by the theater. Can you wait until I get there? I'm only a few minutes away."

"No, I have to get back before one of the guys returns or she changes her mind. She promised to tell me what she's been hiding."

"I'll be there as soon as I can." And he clicked off.

Jenna only made it as far as the corner of Upper Oakley and Pembroke when her phone pinged again. She stared down at the text in alarm. It was from Dunn. *Having an attack. Fran not home. Nick not home. Come now.*

Shit. With Mac's lead in one hand and the phone pressed to her ear with the other, she bounded around the block towards Dunn's. Nicholas wasn't picking up. "Nicholas, Dunn just texted. Said he's having an attack. Meet me there!" she yelled into the recording. Then she speed-dialed her aunt to say she'd been delayed, only Aunt Clair didn't pick up, either. Maybe she was in the bathroom. Jenna finished leaving her a message seconds before arriving at Dunn's house.

Dunn's town house wore the same brick face as the others minus the careful grooming. No topiaries or flower boxes for Dunn, only a trim boxwood hedge on the inside of the iron fencing that badly needed a touch-up, and an exuberant yew near the door.

The gate creaked as it swung open. She walked forward in a brisk stride, trying to restrain Mac's tug. She was halfway up the walk when the dog barked and shot ahead so quickly that the lead slipped from her grasp.

"Get back here!"

The dog scrambled up the stairs and stood before Dunn's front door yapping in agitation. God, what was wrong with him?

"Stop that!" She lunged for the lead but the dog leaped against the door before she could grab hold. The door fell open and the dog quickly entered the house, trailing his lead behind. She pinned the lead with her foot, keeping Mac close. "Settle down!"

Why would Dunn leave his door open? What was Mac on about? She turned to gaze down the street. Empty. For once, she wished it wasn't.

"Dunn?" Mac barked even harder. "Mac, hush!"

The darkened house yawned silent as the dog strained against his lead towards the stairs. No lights on up there, either. Jenna hesitated. Something was very wrong. Why hadn't Dunn called the emergency number first instead of her?

Because Dunn couldn't have been the one who texted.

She could hardly breathe. She'd call 999, tell them to send the police and an ambulance. To do anything else was crazy. She was just thumbing in the number when Mac jerked the lead out from under her sneaker and bolted for the stairs.

23

Mac's frantic bark traveled up the stairs and deep into the top level of the house.

"Mac? Come back here now!"

The barking turned into a low growl. Her neck hairs prickled. And when the growl turned into a yelp, she bolted for the steps.

"Mac! Brian?" she called. She tapped in 999 while jolting upstairs. When the dispatcher answered, she gave the address. "Hurry!" she cried, before clicking off and using the phone as a light.

She tracked Mac down the shadowy central hall, feeling a draft as if from an open door or a window, but Mac's whining took her straight to a back bedroom.

At the door, she beamed the phone light ahead while her other hand found the wall switch and light flooded the space. The scene burned an eyeprint into her brain: a blue-lipped Dunn fixing unseeing eyes in her direction as he slumped sideways in a chair, his nebulizer sprawled in pieces at his feet.

She fell back against the doorjamb, her mouth opening in a mute scream. And then Mac crawled into view, blood trickling from his jaw but baring his needle teeth in her direction.

"Oh, Mac," she cried, springing towards him. "My poor little Mac."

She knelt beside him, trying to decide whether to pick him up or leave him until she could get help. Shocked seconds passed before she realized he was growling at someone behind her.

Slowly she turned. The hall seemed empty, the opposite rooms dark. "You sick bastard!" she shouted, getting to her feet.

A black-on-black shape lunged towards her from the opposite room, sending her reeling backwards before she realized what hit her. Her skull slammed against a marble statue, which crashed to the floor, taking her with it. Her attacker spun her onto her stomach and pressed his knee into the small of her back, forcing the breath from her lungs while he wrenched her arms behind her.

Dizziness hit so violently that she struggled not to faint. And she couldn't breathe! Her legs kicked out in helplessness, raw panic hammering her chest. The pain in her arms intensified as she heaved breath into her aching lungs.

Her attacker seemed strung with a wiry, vicious power. Muscled legs squeezed against her body as red pain blurred her vision. Her head spun. She couldn't move.

Through the haze of pain and shock, Jenna realized that Mac was trying to crawl towards her assailant. She could see his hind quarters inching past where she lay with her cheek ground to the floor. He was tugging at something or someone, though one of his hind legs jutted out in a wild angle. *No, Mac, leave him alone!*

And then a gloved fist shot out that hurled the dog across the room. She heard Mac hit the wall, whimper, and lay still. *No!* She hauled breath back into her lungs and bucked her body in a desperate attempt to get free. No one would do this and get away with it! But her anger did nothing to dislodge her attacker and only provoked a low chuckle—the first sound she'd heard him make. The voice sounded familiar, yet strange, too.

And then she pushed hard enough to raise her torso a few inches from the floor, far enough to see the top edge of the bureau mirror where the reflection of a hooded figure grasped a hunk of marble ready to crash down on her skull.

She twisted her body to the right seconds before the stone slammed into the floor. The attacker's weight shifted. He was looking for another weapon. He'd see what she saw—the broken arm of a sculpture a few feet away. Then the sound of her name bellowed through the house.

"Jenna? Dunn? Anybody home?" Nicholas.

"Here!" she choked. As the weight lifted from her back, she managed to roll herself over in time to see a black-garbed figure dashing from the room.

Jenna stumbled to her feet, wobbled briefly, and fell to her knees screaming as Nicholas burst into the hall. "Catch him! Catch the bastard! Down the hall!"

Nicholas hesitated, eyes swerving from Jenna, to Dunn's body, to the dog. "Jesus Christ!" He took off in pursuit.

Jenna rolled to her knees, thinking she was done, bested, finished, yet wild with fury. Poor Brian, her dear little Mac.

Her eyes landed on her phone lying where she'd dropped it. A text from Alex blazed on the screen: *Found a copy of your aunt's will.* She tried to process that but couldn't. Her *aunt's* will? No time to think.

Nicholas returned moments later and tried enveloping her in his arms but all she could do was sob her fury and pain, hearing sirens screeching towards the house. "Where is he? Did you catch him?" she demanded.

"No, no—he's gone," he murmured into her hair. "The police are on their way. What the hell happened? Are you all right?"

"What do you mean *gone*?" she said, pushing him away.

He gently turned her around to check her skull. "He disappeared. I don't know where the hell he went. The police are on their way, I said. Stay still for a moment." He tried to steady her in his arms.

But she struggled to her feet. "They'll never get to him in time! I've been such an idiot!"

24

The draft was coming up the stairs from the studio. And to think the whole time she believed that the roof was her domain alone. She'd been dead wrong on that score, too.

"Jenna, come back," Nicholas called out behind. "You can't bloody well go after him alone!"

But who else could? Hoisting herself up through the skylight, all she could think of was how blind she'd been. How could eyeprints help when she still refused to see?

He'd been inside their house the whole time; he'd come and gone, probably using the same routes she'd taken. He'd been up there with her when she believed she was safe!

The studio was empty but she flicked on the light by the door and stumbled out to the roof, calling to the shadowy landscape. "You won't get away with this, Jake, do you hear me? Nicholas knows who you are and the police are coming!"

Stumbling over to the chimney wall, she hoisted herself up, scanning the dark peaks for movement. There he was, heading back towards the Marlytree end. But why not go towards Nicholas's unit and exit to the ground from there? So much shorter. She drove down the peak after him.

She heard Nicholas shouting from somewhere but that didn't matter, nothing mattered but getting that bastard. This was personal—her uncle, her friend, now her dog. This was between him and her.

She scrambled down to the next roof after him, struggling to keep upright against an assault of dizziness. Balancing along the roof spine was challenging enough with vertigo, and to make things worse, it had begun to drizzle.

Twice she fell to her knees to steady herself and twice she hoisted herself up and plowed on. He could not be allowed to get away this time. There were sirens blaring, someone shouting behind her, plus lights flashing on the street below. Nothing but distractions when she needed every brain cell fixed on tracking the moving target. They couldn't catch him up here, anyway. They'd need ladders and fire trucks, and he'd be back on the ground slithering into the night before they figured out what the hell was going on.

Maybe he planned on reaching the ground into Mrs. Chester's yard? No, she thought: they'd catch him the moment his feet hit the ground and he knew it. He must be heading for an interior access, but where? She knew these roofs better than anybody. Surely she'd know if there was another way inside a house from the roof besides Dunn's studio and Nicholas's now-ruined skylight? So, where the hell was he headed? The hatches were all bolted shut. Wait—of course: the vacant house! She had to get there before he did.

Somewhere over Mr. Rambolt's roof, she lost sight of him. Balancing on trembling legs, she strained for a glimpse of movement. No shifting shadows, nothing but the brooding sky and the ruckus on the streets below. Somebody still shouting from far away. "I know you're up here somewhere, Jake. Why not come out and face me? You're such a damn coward! Try having some guts for once!"

And then an eyeprint of the three chimney pots silhouetted ahead slipped into her mind like an overlay on top of current reality —one, two, three fat cylinders topped by a broad-brimmed hat. The middle pot bulged slightly on the right. She crept forward, pretending to be unaware. When she was at the foot of Mr. Rambolt's peak with the chimneys looming down from overhead, she sprang upwards, planning an ambush, but only managing to get halfway up before a shadow dislodged from the chimney and struck her hard.

She fell on her back, his weight walloping the wind from her lungs as he landed on her from above. Immobilized, all she could do was stare up into that ski-masked face, waiting for the final blow.

But then another shadow dropped down from nowhere. She couldn't grasp what was happening as the struggling shapes glommed together and tipped towards the edge of the peak, rolling to a stop onto one of the dormers below.

Jenna turned to look. Dazed, she couldn't figure out what the hell was going on, until she realized that somebody wrestled her attacker. She pushed her way up. Impossible to tell who was besting who, but somebody was going to be thrown over the edge. "Nicholas?" she gasped. Could that fool man really have followed her up here?

The men were well-matched in size and build but one was considerably younger and more agile. Jenna watched, stunned, as Nicholas sent a fierce left hook into her attacker's jaw before the younger man bucked him off long enough to grab him by the throat.

In response, Nicholas gripped Jake by the shoulders and butted his skull with his own, sending the young man reeling back against the window before he twisted around and sprung for the peak. Jenna readied herself to trip him somehow but he leaped past her. Now Nicholas's head and shoulders hung over the edge.

Jenna looked down. "Shit! Hold on, I'm coming." In minutes she had coaxed him away from the drop and helped him up to the peak. "Straddle the roof like you're riding a horse, do you hear me?"

The head-butt had left him stunned.

"Stay here!" she yelled at him. "Don't move. I'm going after him!"

"It's not Jake, damn it!" Nicholas said with a moan. He was stretched on down over the roof spine, one hand grasping hers. "Will you listen?"

Jenna took a deep breath. "Not Jake?"

"I ... read Alex's message on your phone. He found ... a copy of your aunt's will leaving everything to *Harry*."

"Harry ..." Jenna stared into his shadowed face, confused. "My aunt's will?"

"Your aunt ... has a will leaving everything to Harry ... upon her demise, get it?" He squeezed her hand.

It took a few seconds to sink in. "Oh, shit! That's where he's heading!" She flung off his hand and jumped to her feet. "Don't follow me!"

⚭

NO TIME TO THINK. SHE HAD TO CATCH HIM BEFORE HE REACHED Aunt Clair. She arrived at the double unit numbers 46/47 and crouched over the open hatch while turning on her phone light. Descending into the bowels of that house may as well be an excursion through hell, but nothing would stop her. She'd get him if it were the last thing she did.

She stumbled down a narrow, cranky set of stairs, her phone light trained on the path ahead. Multiple footprints in the dust. Down to the third floor, the second, the first, trailing through the yawning house, the scent of dust in her nostrils, her vertigo lessening but still intense.

On the main floor she hesitated. Did he bolt out the back door or the front? Neither. That would send him straight to the police. She heard a noise from below. Of course—he was heading for the basement, the basement! She hated basements. Basements are where the demons lived, and right now every story her aunt ever told her rang true.

Down, down, down she went, half expecting to be ambushed, but everything was far too still.

The basement was a mass of stored wood, sheets of drywall, and tools, and yet her phone light easily picked out the dust path threading through the piles. It was heading straight for the wall adjoining the neighboring house, which made no sense until she found a little door no more than three feet tall.

In seconds she was ducking under and into the adjoining house, following the footprints through another storage maze, through to the next wall and on to the next. Unknown to her before this, every house in the row had one of these little doors, which must be original to the structures. Most had been sealed off but recently opened—kicked, knifed— into a world of shelves and trunks, boxes and boxes. Most remained hidden behind something or other, but all those barriers now lay pushed aside as if the demon didn't care if anyone discovered his secret paths.

Oh, God, had she only gone down instead of up in the first place, she might have discovered his route long ago. She had never, ever descended her aunt's basement in her life, even as a child. Basements were where the bogeymen lurked and how true that was!

Forgetting to count the basements, when she reached her aunt's it took a moment to register. If her uncle hadn't kept her old childhood bike propped beside the stairs, she'd never have recognized that she'd arrived at her aunt's. She bolted for the stairs.

The house was dark and still. She flicked on the hall light in passing while calling out for Aunt Clair. Something creaked overhead. He was going to harm her aunt, she knew that, and yet she had no defense, no offense. And she didn't care. She'd think on her feet; she'd think of something.

But nothing prepared her for what she found when she reached the bottom of the stairs. "Oh, shit," she cried, looking up. "Don't do this, Harry, please!"

Harry stood at the top of the first-floor landing holding a wheelchair in which Aunt Clair lolled seemingly unconscious.

"What have you done to her?" Jenna cried, taking the first step up.

Harry lurched the chair forward, holding the wheelchair just at the tipping point over the top stair. "If you make one move, she falls. She's drugged but the fall's sure to kill her, right?"

"You poisoned her on that food!"

"No, I used the bismuth. Old bag always takes it after Thai."

Jenna froze. "But why are you doing this? Why all that pointless killing? Was it all for the money?"

"All you rich bitches don't know what it's like to claw for everything you want, and I mean everything. You're so fucking entitled, the whole lot of you. It wouldn't even occur to you to give some of your filthy wealth away to the needy like me. No, we have to be your dogs and follow you around day after day to get even so much as a morsel tossed in our direction. Makes me sick."

"And you think that stealing and killing makes you better than us?

Are you delusional? I don't care what the hell your motives were, it's too late. We're on to you now, everyone's on to you. It's over, why hurt her?"

"No fucking way! If I'm going down, she's going with me."

She had to keep him talking. "You killed Uncle Dan, didn't you?"

"Yeah, all part of the plan. With him out of the way, old batty Clair here and I had more time together. She craved attention and I bloody gave it to her in spades. I promised to be there for her when you wouldn't; I said I'd be her son, and stay with her forevermore. Yeah, I knew the will would seal the deal. She offered. I didn't even have to ask. She wanted a son and I made myself available."

"And Suzanna died because she was ... what? At the wrong place at the wrong time."

"She was always hanging around. She saw my face, but you weren't part of the plan until you decided to go crawling over that roof during that rainstorm—stupid-ass bitch. I didn't even realize that your aunt inherited your fortune if you died before her as well as the old man's until a few days ago. How could I resist? One little push and then I could finish you off, too. I'd make it look like an accident, only things got messy. Suzanna Lake was there staring down at you and Hewitt. I had to finish her off."

"What about Jake?" She took another step up. Now the doorbell was ringing and someone was pounding on the door.

"Jake's too lily-livered to do anything. He knew what was going on all along," Harry shouted down. "I said I'd kill him if he said anything. Still will when I get my hands on him."

Police sirens blasted around the house. They knew they were in there. They were coming!

But not soon enough.

Harry cocked his head, listening. "Say goodbye to Auntie, Jen, because she's going down," and he bent down to release the chair brake at the same instant that Aunt Clair suddenly jerked forward and shoved him hard. "Like hell I am, sonny boy!" she called.

Jenna flashed an eyeprint of Harry tumbling towards her while Aunt Clair clutched desperately at the banister to keep the wheelchair from toppling, everything registering in a flash of teetering bodies and glinting metal.

Jenna pressed herself against the banister while levelling a fierce kick at Harry just seconds before reaching up to catch Aunt Clair's fall as she let go of the handrail, her body toppling forward still seated in her chair. Both Jenna, Aunt Clair, and the wheelchair hurled downwards, landing on top of Harry, who was struggling to rise.

What happened next, Jenna barely remembered. An eyeprint of her shoving away the wheelchair and Harry rolling onto his knees, her reaching up to whip one of the metal picture frames from the wall and smashing it down on his head. And then Aunt Clair's crow of triumph while she held a shard of glass to his throat. "Shall I finish him off, Jenna?"

Jenna snatched the shard from her hand just seconds before the police broke through the door.

25

"The police said they'd be by again later today," Aunt Clair said as she lay back in her bed. "Really, the second time in as many days must put this close to harassment, especially for two women suffering from multiple injuries incurred during an encounter with a ..." Her aunt paused.

"A serial killer," Jenna said. Fingers of light and shadow played across the room as the sun dipped lower in the sky. She imagined herself perched on a rooftop, bathed in golden light, alone and in peace. But it wasn't to be. Maybe never again. She'd been grounded.

"Surely not. Harry was a conniving bastard—oh, I do like to swear. Your uncle wouldn't permit it, you know. Maybe now, I shall just let it rip—but really, wasn't he just a poor twisted lad, when all's said and done, mentally ill, perhaps?"

"That poor twisted lad is still a serial killer, mental illness or not. He's responsible for four deaths, and earns the term fair and square," Jenna said. "Besides, being a greedy little shit doesn't make his motive any purer. Nicholas was right, money rules. Harry lured you into signing that will with him as sole beneficiary."

"It was the wrong thing to do, no matter how you look at it. What was I thinking? I guess I was angry at you for leaving me, but that's still no excuse. You remain my sole heir, as it should be."

"You know the money was never the issue with me."

"It doesn't matter. You are my only living relative and I love you. Anyway, I paid those two boys enough as it was. And that Jake— nothing but a pathetic weakling. That's what hurts me most. To think that young man was willing to do nothing while Harry continued to kill. I just can't fathom it. If it hadn't been for you, Jenna, if you hadn't kept searching and risking everything to bring those two to heel ... well, it just doesn't bear thinking about. You are a true hero."

Jenna snorted. Sitting back in the chair with one hand bandaged and a sprained ankle, she felt the opposite of heroic—all the mistakes she made, all the errors of judgment. And now look at her—all banged up ... and she had been blind in a way that provoked this shit-storm from the beginning. "Nicholas turned out to be a little more heroic than he expected but Mac's the real hero here, albeit pint-sized."

She gazed down at the little dog, his leg in a doggy cast, and kitted up in his own makeshift sling/carryall so she could take him up and down the stairs. Actually, she didn't carry him so much as send him down with the chairlift, the key being that everybody in the house still got around. "All he's ever tried to do is protect us."

"Yes, dear little Mac," Aunt Clair said, smiling down at the terrier, who wagged his tail at the sound of his name and tried to heft himself up from the doggy bed. "You did try to warn me about those two, didn't you? But I didn't listen, foolish old woman that I am. Just stay down, dear. You're in no condition to dash around at the moment, any more than the two of us are. We'll all heal soon enough."

Jenna bent down to scratch Mac's ears. "We're just lucky that the police aren't pressing charges for something or other, Auntie. So if they come a-calling, we'll let them in, and tell our story again and again for as long as it takes. The truth, I mean," she added.

"Chief Inspector McKinnon's lecturing is punishment enough, surely? And they have no idea how close I came to offing that serial killer of ours. To think he killed my dear Dan. He killed everyone, and would have murdered you and me, too!"

Jenna could hear her hysteria rising. The doctor had warned that keeping her aunt's mind on other things was paramount. There was the high blood pressure and the guilt, all contributing to this whirl of nerves. "But he didn't kill us, did he? We caught him, Auntie, both of us. Just take a deep breath."

"You caught him. I was merely entangled in his web of deceit, like the foolish old woman everyone believes I am—I was so taken in—but I could have finished him off, oh, yes, I could have. I wanted to. I had that shard in my hand and was just about to plunge it into his jugular—"

"But I stopped you." Though it took everything she had. Jenna pressed her eyes closed. Why hadn't she let it happen? It probably would have been cited as self-defense, and she almost threw the kid off the roof herself just minutes before, anyway.

She couldn't let her aunt do it, that's why. The older woman's current self-recriminations were bad enough, let alone bloodying the waters with a killing. "Anyway, the two of them are in jail now, though I'm sure Jake will only get a year or two. He just stood around and let it happen, after all."

"You understand why I was so foolish, don't you, Jenna?" Aunt Clair said, sitting up in the bed as her cast stuck out straight in front of her under the covers.

"You've told me countless times, Auntie. I get it."

"I'm not always such a complete fool, you know, and consider myself to be a reasonably intelligent woman. But your uncle's death threw me in more ways than I knew, and I became so needy. I do so hate being needy, but there you have it: I thought I could buy loyalty and love, but I couldn't. Writing that will was idiotic, I know, but I thought it the only way I could prove my commitment to my 'new son.' You understand that, don't you?"

Jenna sat forward and held up her hands. "I get it, Auntie. And he manipulated you, remember? Besides, you haven't had that much experience with people. Books and movies aren't enough. You need more real-life friends, as we discussed." As if she was one to talk, she who'd spent her life avoiding the muck of human inter-action. The irony was killing her. "Anyway, I hold myself respon-sible for not staying with you, but now I'm going to move back to

London and live nearby. Let's work at putting this behind us," she finished.

But Aunt Clair wasn't listening. "He promised to stay with me, never leave me, and always be around to be my companion. Oh, I even imagined grandchildren—not that I've had much experience with young people, you understand. They'd probably drive me right around the bend, but it would be something new." Her voice had risen shrill and she was literally wringing her hands. "I was paying for his university, too, you know—not that the monies were ever really going to his studies. How could I know I was padding his bank account, or his sock drawer, or whatever, and that he wasn't attending any university? How could I know he was a lying sonofabitch?" she wailed.

And now the police had all of her aunt's journals, which presumably would further prove that, despite her active imagination and endlessly inventive thinking, Aunt Clair was blameless in the plot that entangled her. Jenna hadn't read every entry, but gleaned enough to know that despite her intelligence and her amazing insight in some things, her aunt was still surprisingly naive. People were often seen as one-dimensional, paper characters that walked in and out of her narrow world. Sara, for instance.

"To think that he thought that killing Dan paved the way for him to worm into my good graces. And for it to be true. My poor Dan!" Aunt Clair continued, her voice wavering. "If I had seen through Harry's machinations earlier, he might still be alive. Oh, Jenna, I didn't know about the engagement. Why wouldn't Dan tell me?"

"He would have eventually, Aunt Clair," Jenna said softly. "That was obviously the plan had he lived long enough."

"Jenna dear, I am so grateful that you are returning to London but I wish you'd consider living with me in this house. I can renovate it to your specifications. Regardless, how will we go on, knowing as we do that I am responsible for my brother's death by virtue of my appalling foolishness?" Aunt Clair waved her bandaged hand in the air as if trying to grasp at something long gone.

Jenna leaned forward and, in an act of pure desperation, offered a diversion she hoped would keep her aunt from spinning into another hysteria loop. "I have an idea: Why don't you work on that concept you had for the two of us going into business together?"

Aunt Clair paused, her hand midair. "You mean the roofing espionage business?"

"Not espionage exactly—that's a government spy enterprise—I mean the rooftop detective work, or whatever it was you were dreaming up." It was a desperate act of diversion on Jenna's part, and she prayed it would keep her aunt occupied, at least until life settled down.

"But you're going to keep on writing."

"The two aren't mutually exclusive. Just think about it, work up a plan or something."

"Oh, my, Jenna, would you really go into business with me? I would so love that. I could seek out our clients and keep the books and you could keep flying upwards, as you were always meant to do."

Always meant to do. Oh, hell, maybe this diversion exercise wasn't such a good idea, especially since she had no intention of following through. Jenna swallowed. "Let's just consider the possibility for a bit, that's all. You work out the specifics and we'll go from there." And then she had a sudden thought. "How exactly were you thinking you could locate our clients, anyway?"

"On the dark web, Jenna," Aunt Clair said, her face alight. "Harry told me all about it, and I quite know my way around now. We wouldn't deal with criminals exactly, just with those desperately in need of acquiring information in untraditional ways. They do exist, you know. One just needs to contact them, on the sly so to speak, maybe incognito. Isn't this thrilling?"

Jenna hoisted herself to her feet. What had she done? "Thrilling, right. Well, you work on that while I go downstairs and check on our tea. Sara's busy baking down there, by the smell of it."

"Oh, that Sara. Jenna, I really must say—"

"Don't. She's part of our agreement, and you did promise me. I will live with you as long as we share the decision-making. She's part of my terms. Now play nice."

Aunt Clair sighed and sank back against the pillows while picking up her tablet. "Very well, dear."

And then Mac started barking. "Hush!" Jenna told him, as if that made a difference. "Stay here, Fuzz-face." She hobbled to the top of the stairs and gazed down, straight into Sara's upturned face.

"Nicholas Hewitt and that lady are here, Jenna. Is she the one?" she whispered.

"I think so. Keep them in the kitchen. I'll be right down." Jenna hopped back to Aunt Clair's bedroom and poked her head through the door. "Aunt Clair, she's here."

Her aunt dropped her iPad on the bed and looked up. "So soon? I daresay I'm not ready. I know I said I would like to meet her, but must it be today? Might we not delay the meeting for just a few more weeks?"

Jenna smiled. "No way. You promised, and I think you'll like her. Besides, you agreed that it's best that you interact with lots of different people, and we may as well begin with her, your first trial run. Uncle Dan loved her and hoped that you would come to, as well—as sisters, maybe. Do it for him. Remember, she just lost her brother, too. You have lots in common. Maybe you need each other."

"Very well."

"I'll ask her to come up, then."

Turning, Jenna hobbled back to the stairs and began the laborious descent. Better than crash-landing, she told herself en route.

Fran and Nicholas were sitting at the kitchen table drinking tea when she hobbled in.

"Oh, there you are!" Fran said, jumping up. "You do look quite the wounded soldier," she said, dashing over to give Jenna a quick hug as Nicholas stood watching her quietly.

God, Nicholas. What was she going to do about him?

"Would you like tea?" Sara asked as she delivered a plate of fresh biscuits to the table.

"I would, thanks." Jenna lowered herself into the chair Nicholas offered, careful not to meet his eyes, to even look at him. It was the total hijacking of her senses that hit her hardest. That was supposed to be done with by now. Once she slammed into the real man, she fully expected this uncontrollable yearning to be done. If anything, it had made it worse and far more complicated.

"Shall I go up and see her now?" Fran was asking. "I could bring a tray of tea and scones for the two of us."

"An excellent idea," Sara offered. "I find that warm buttery scones usually put her in a more receptive mood for almost anything. Well, that may not be quite true."

"It's a good theory, anyway," Jenna said.

"Perhaps we should add a shot of whiskey, then?" Nicholas suggested in that damned melty baritone.

"I think not," Sara said, shooting him a quick, appreciative glance. "What I mean to say is, ah, I think that a very poor idea, even though I'm sure a tipple may be in order at some point." So, even Sara was not immune to the man's substantial charms.

"It was a joke, Sara," Nicholas told her, gazing up with a grin.

"Yes, well, I shall just prepare a tray, then, shall I?" she said, turning away, her face flushed.

Minutes later, Fran was on her way upstairs carrying tea and scones for her inaugural visit to Aunt Clair, while Sara descended to the basement to discuss blocking off the interconnecting crawl space with a contractor.

That left Jenna sitting across from Nicholas, at a total loss.

"Fran's having a difficult time with Brian's death and I'm just hoping your aunt won't make it worse," he began.

"Aunt Clair isn't unkind by nature, and she's promised to make an effort in this as well as other things," she said, gazing down at her bandaged hand. "This is a good idea. It was hard letting go of the idea of being boss of a big magazine enterprise but I needed to face the fact that it was all wrong for me from the very start. Now I do."

"Fine. I'm glad. What does your hand agree about that, too?"

She flexed her fingers. "Pardon?"

Nicholas reached out and picked up her hand, stroking one long finger gently over the bandage. "I said, how does your hand feel about you staying, seeing as you were talking to it a moment ago?"

"Um, my hand as well as the rest of me thinks it's what needs to be done, that I have to rejoin the living, take care of my aunt while still living my own life in my own way." Her eyes lifted to his at last. "And reengage with people by stop running away. Grow up, in other words."

"So, you really are staying," he said softly. "I thought for certain that your aunt would break your last nerve and force your own personal Brexit."

Jenna smiled, all defenses gone. She was in such big trouble. "No, I'm not running away this time. Instead, I'll find strategies to make this work." Be an adult, take responsibility, the ultimate price of love. "I'll adapt, in other words," she told him.

"I'm sure you will." Nicholas released her hand and sat back in his chair, crossing one ankle over his knee, gazing at her with a little smile on his lips.

"So, next weekend," she hurried on, "I'm flying home to begin the business of packing and shipping my things over to London. I'll get a flat nearby. Fran's suggested I rent her townhouse across the park. My magazine's new editor has agreed to let me work from here, maybe start a London office, or something."

"And will you stop roofing?"

There was the question she'd asked herself a thousand times but had yet to form an answer. She gazed across at him.

"And what if I don't?"

BOOKS BY THE AUTHOR

Did you enjoy *Downside Up*? **If so, please leave a review. They are so important for an author's success. I would love your support!**

There are more books coming in this trilogy, including shorter episodes between full novels, and some off them will be free to newsletter members only. To stay tuned for new releases and to join the newsletter list, check out my webpage here: **http://www.janethornley.com**. The first free episode, *Acting Up: Jenna's Story,* which is a the prelude to the series, will only be available for newsletter subscribers.

Other suspense books by Jane Thornley include:

Frozen Angel **(paranormal suspense)**

The Crime by Design **humorous thriller series which includes:**

- *Rogue Wave*
- *Warp in the Weave*
- *Beautiful Survivor*
- *The Greater of Two Evils*
- **Books 1-3 available in a boxed set**

Books are available through all online vendors and in two formats.

Printed in Great Britain
by Amazon